What readers are saying about THE HOUSE

'READ THIS BOOK!!' Lea, Netgalley Reviewer

'Totally lived up to hype . . . five stars, easy!'
Robert, Netgalley Reviewer

'Gosh what a book . . . you'll want to finish it in one go!'
Michelle, Netgalley Reviewer

'Damn, this book was GOOD!' Bentley, Netgalley Reviewer

'I enjoyed every page . . . wonderfully crafted, clever and
heart-wrenching' Heather, Netgalley Reviewer

'The perfect psychological thriller!' Paige, Netgalley Reviewer

'Exciting, entertaining, and thoroughly gripping to
the end' Pauly, Netgalley Reviewer

'O.M.G. I just devoured this gem' Brandi, Netgalley Reviewer

'Wow . . . definitely one for you to put on your reading list!'
Jacob, Netgalley Reviewer

'An utterly amazing read that will have you glued to the
pages' Ana, Netgalley Reviewer

'Had me hooked from the very first page' Nicki, Netgalley
Reviewer

'Kept me on the edge of my seat right till the end!'
Sarah, Netgalley Reviewer

The House

SIMON LELIC

PENGUIN BOOKS

PENGUIN BOOKS

UK | USA | Canada | Ireland | Australia
India | New Zealand | South Africa

Penguin Books is part of the Penguin Random House group of companies
whose addresses can be found at global.penguinrandomhouse.com

First published 2017
001

Copyright © Simon Lelic, 2017

The moral right of the author has been asserted

Set in 12.75/15 pt Garamond MT Std
Typeset by Jouve (UK), Milton Keynes
Printed in Great Britain by Clays Ltd, St Ives plc

A CIP catalogue record for this book is available from the British Library

ISBN: 978–0–241–29654–7

www.greenpenguin.co.uk

For Anja.
And for her grandpa.

When my hand slips from the knife, my first thought is that using it wasn't as difficult as I assumed it would be. I feel elated, initially, until I notice the blood. It flows quickly, determinedly. It stains my sweatshirt, my trousers, even the floor, and that's when my elation turns to fear. It's gone wrong, I realize. This thing I've planned for so carefully: it has all gone drastically, horribly wrong.

I

Jack

The police were outside again last night. I watched them in the alleyway from the spare-bedroom window. They couldn't have seen me. I'm fairly sure they couldn't have seen me. And anyway, so what if they had? It's not like I was doing anything wrong. It's perfectly natural, isn't it? Like the way motorists slow down to get a view of an accident. Probably the police would have assumed it odd if I hadn't been watching. I mean, I couldn't tell from where I was standing, but I bet the rest of our neighbours were all watching, too. All with their lights off. All cloaked discreetly by their curtains. What I didn't like was the impression I had that everyone out there was also looking discreetly at me. That the police being out there, at that time of night, was all just a show. A reminder.

God, this is hard. Harder than I thought it would be. It's knowing where to begin as much as anything. I'm not Syd. I know what she thinks, what conclusions she's drawn already, but I don't process things the way she does. If she had gone first, I don't know where we would have ended up, and I'm pretty sure I wouldn't have had a clue about where to go next.

I guess for me the only logical place to start is the

day we first saw the house. This was back in April. It's September now. The fourteenth. At 3.17 in the morning, to be precise. Syd's in bed, but I couldn't sleep even if I wanted to. I doubt she's sleeping either, to be honest. I don't think she's slept properly in weeks. Me, I drop off easily enough. Every night I don't think I'm going to, but it's exhaustion, I suppose, the weight of worry. Tonight, though, our decision made, I just wanted to get on with it.

There's a lot to get through and not a lot of time.

The open day, then. I suppose it has to be, though there's very little about the day itself that was unusual. I recall how busy it was; how many people, when the time came, narrow-shouldered their way through the front door. Because there was a queue, you see. Not a line, but one of those messy, I-was-here-first scrums you see at bus stops. We'd arrived forty minutes early and already there were half a dozen couples ahead of us.

But that wasn't uncommon. Not for a house viewing in London. The strange thing was that it wasn't just the house that was up for sale. Whoever bought it would also be buying everything the house contained. And once Syd and I had got inside, we saw that the entire place was stuffed with junk. Actual dragged-home-from-the-skip junk. Books, too, and clothes, coats, pictures on every square inch of wall, boxes stacked heedless of shape or size, plus furniture big and small in every crevice. It was like a live-in, life-and-death version of Jenga.

Oh, and birds. Clearly the current owner was into dead stuff. Taxidermy: doing it, hoarding it, I couldn't tell. There was a hawk, a seagull, even a pigeon amid the scattered flock. Syd must have noticed them, too. I remember being surprised she didn't turn around the moment she did and walk straight out.

The story the estate agent gave us was that the owner had met a woman on the Internet. She lived in Australia, apparently, and he'd dropped everything to run off and be with her. Just like that. He'd been approaching retirement age anyway, but even so he chucked in his job, abandoned his friends and signed over his house – dead pets and all – to the estate agent to sell as one bumper package. Which made a good sales pitch, I suppose, and accounted for the state of the place – but personally, right from the off, I just couldn't see it. I mean, what sort of person would do that? And – setting the storybook explanation aside for a moment – why?

So yes, that was odd, and for me more than a bit off-putting. Maybe it wouldn't have bothered me so much if I'd fallen for the house itself. I mean, the lay-out wasn't a problem and there was more than enough space (lounge, kitchen, separate dining room, plus one, two, three bedrooms – not including the uncon-verted attic). The building, though – it was creepy. There's no other word to describe it. The garden was overgrown and the paintwork about as attractive as a skin complaint. The house stood alone ('detached', marvelled the brochure) as though it had been shunned. There was a row of terraced houses on one side, huddled together as though for safety, and a block of flats with its back turned on the other. It looked – and felt – somehow ostracized.

So I suppose all I'm saying is I didn't like the place. All that junk, the building itself: it just felt wrong. The problem I had was that Syd was clearly smitten. I knew she would be. She knew she would be: it was Syd who'd found the house on the Internet and who'd insisted we arrive at least half an hour early.

'So-oo,' I remember her saying to me, once we'd finally finished looking around. 'What do you think?'

We were in the lounge, beside the fireplace. I remember this older guy kept staring at me from across the room. I was conspicuous in trainers and a T-shirt, whereas all the other blokes my age wore a collar, pressed jeans and polished brogues. They were City types, basically, or – like the man who kept staring – fathers of spoiled little rich kids. And probably that was the other thing that was stopping me sharing Syd's enthusiasm. It had taken Syd and me more than two years to scrimp enough for a deposit, whereas most of the couples we were up against had likely earned theirs from a single bonus. So on that playing field, with London rules – how could the two of us be expected to compete?

'I think it's like *The Hunger Games*,' I answered uncomfortably. What I meant was that bit in the film before the action starts, where the contestants are drifting around, pretending to be friends – to be allies of whatever – when really they're just itching to kill the crap out of one another.

Syd looked at me blankly. I knew for a fact she'd seen the movie at the cinema, but her memory about stuff like that isn't the greatest. She smoked a lot when she was younger and I'm not talking Marlboro Lights. She did a lot of drugs, actually. I'm not saying I've never dabbled myself, but there're certain people they affect more than others. Syd had a difficult upbringing. Horrendous, actually – so bad that she's still never told me the whole story. And when, later on, she had her troubles, the drugs I reckon played a part. She says they didn't. She says all the damage had already been done. But weed, coke, pills, what have you: that stuff definitely leaves a mark.

'Just . . . all these people,' I explained. 'I mean, I knew there'd be other interest, but nothing like this.'

Syd slipped her hands around my waist. 'Forget about everyone else for a moment. What do you think about the *house*?'

I paused for half a second too long. 'I like it,' I said at last. 'I do.'

'But?'

'But . . . nothing. It's just . . . it's kind of dark, that's all.'

I think Syd assumed I was merely playing my role, in house-hunting as well as in life. Syd dishes out her affection as though she's sharing wine gums, whereas I trail stoically beside her, kicking tyres and knuckle-tapping walls. It's rare that I know what I'm wary about exactly (what's actually supposed to happen when you kick a tyre, other than the reverberation in your toes?), but it's a part I've somehow settled into. It's what men do, I've learned from somewhere. My father, probably, who could suck the joy out of riding on a rollercoaster. Plus, as I say, Syd definitely needs a counterweight. It's why we're so good together. She stops me gazing at my feet so much; I stop her floating off into the sky.

'That's just the weather,' Syd countered. 'All these people. Plus, I mean, have you seen all of this stuff?'

I was half expecting her then to mention those birds. She didn't.

'There's an attic, too,' I said. 'If the rest of the place is like this, what must it be like up there?'

Syd glanced towards the ceiling. I joined her, worrying in that moment whether the whole building was liable to suddenly cave in.

'Well,' said Syd, 'we'll just have to hire a van or something. A man. Assuming we can still afford it.'

She smiled then and tucked a stray strand of hair behind a perfectly formed ear. In the house in which I grew up there was this blossom tree outside my bedroom window. Cherry, apple, I've no idea. It flowered pink, but never actually bore any fruit. The leaves, though, were this deep, rosewood brown, which came aglow when caught by the light. Syd's hair, which she never dyes, is exactly the same colour.

'Jack? I'm not going to make you live somewhere you don't want to. If you really don't like it, then let's just leave.'

It wasn't a guilt trip. Syd genuinely meant what she'd said. So maybe I should have said something. Maybe I could have put an end to it all then and there.

We did leave . . . but in the end we put in an offer as well. Just for the hell of it. And, I'll admit, because Syd was clearly head over heels and I wanted her to be happy. Besides, what harm could it do? I didn't love the place, but I didn't hate it exactly – and anyway we couldn't afford it. The mortgage we had agreed wouldn't even get us to the asking price and the details stipulated offers over. So there was no way we'd get it, not given the level of interest. All those people, with all their money . . .

I felt safe because we shouldn't have had a chance.

Sydney

Jesus Christ. I knew this would be a bad idea. I fucking *knew* it.

First off: this isn't a ghost story. OK? Let's make that very fucking clear. *The house stood alone as though shunned.* Who do you think you are, Jack – Stephen King? Creepy house, creepy furnishings, a happy(*ish*) couple moving in all dumb and cheerful. All the elements are there. If this really were a Stephen King novel there'd be cats turning into zombies by chapter three.

But I say again: this isn't a ghost story. It's ... I don't know what this is. That's why I'm writing it. That's why *we* are. Right, Jack? Isn't that what we agreed?

I know what he's trying to do. He wants you to think that we're just spooked, that we've imagined the whole entire thing. Or that *I* have. (The drugs, Jack? *Really??*) But the clues. The *reminders* or whatever you want to call them. I have them right here in my desk drawer. And this *thing* on the surface in front of me. Looking at me. Staring at me. I don't want to but if I chose to I could reach out and touch it. It's *real.* Like the blood: that was real too. Remember the blood, Jack?? How I wished we'd both of us imagined that!

He's in denial, that's what it is. He's trying to act like none of this is happening. Part of Jack's problem is he can't stand the idea of people thinking badly of him. He gets all hot and sweaty if someone tells him off for putting his feet up on the train. So this . . . what this looks like . . . he can't handle it. Not that I'm handling it exactly but at least I'm acknowledging it's happening. Because it's *like* a horror story, I'll admit. I've seen things in the corner of my eye and imagined things I know weren't really there. But that . . . it's just . . . it's *part* of it. You see that, Jack, don't you? Surely you must fucking see that!

I'm so angry right now I don't know if there's any point in my going on. I mean, if buying the house was my idea then writing this was most definitely Jack's. I let him talk me into it but only because it was better than doing nothing. That's what I thought, anyway. Now? Now I'm not so sure.

Oh, and just for your information, Jack: of course I dye my fucking hair.

And wine gums. *Wine gums.*

I need a cigarette. I need a cigarette and I don't even smoke!

So I've been for a walk.

Around the common, I was about to type, but in reality to the newsagent's for a ten pack of Marlboro.

Reds. I smoked two in a row standing on the corner: a shooter of nicotine and traffic fumes. There's nothing like a breath of fresh air to calm the nerves, don't you find?

I don't usually swear like that, I promise. I swear, more than most people my age (more than most paratroopers, probably), but not, what? Let me count. Four f-bombs in just the first few paragraphs. It's just . . . I'm nervous. I'm freaking out, in fact. Soon enough you'll understand why.

But what I've decided is, maybe I'm overreacting. To what Jack wrote, I mean, not to what's been happening to us. In *those* circumstances, I think I've been pretty fucking calm. (OK, that's it, I promise. No more swear words for the rest of this entry. Breathe, Sydney. Think yoga.)

My first reaction was: this isn't a confessional. How *dare* you talk so glibly about my past? How dare you be so bloody judgemental? (Is bloody a swear word? My rule's going to be, if I've heard it on *EastEnders* it doesn't count.) Like the drugs: *there're certain people they affect more than others.* What Jack means is, how could you have been so stupid, Syd? After everything that happened to you, how could you have allowed yourself to fall into that trap? What Jack doesn't understand – what I'm not sure he's ever understood – is how desperate I was to feel something other than what I felt. For a way out. *Any* way out. When you're caught inside a dungeon, even the faintest flicker in the dark is like a promise of daylight. And if it turns out not to be, if it turns out instead to be a burning staircase . . . Well, you take your chances anyway.

Do you understand *now*, Jack? That feeling of any out will do? I would have thought that, given recent events, you'd at last be getting a taste of it. That after this you'd –

I'm getting worked up again.

Breathe, Sydney – remember? *Observe your breath.*

And anyway, what am I talking about, 'after this'? Like it's over already. Like what's happened is anything but the sodding beginning.

What I *started* to say was, maybe my initial reaction was wrong. Maybe a confessional is exactly what this is. A chance to say all those things we've been thinking but were always too polite or too repressed or whatever to voice. Halfway through that second cigarette I started thinking, this could be like one of those spaces. You know, like a psychiatrist's office or something, where *everything stays in this room*. Somewhere you get to be honest but also feel totally safe.

A safe place. A *haven*: the very thing your home's supposed to be. I must admit I like the sound of that.

I've also been thinking about what we agreed. What we said was, we wouldn't just write down what's happened but also what we thought and what we felt. For authenticity: that was the word Jack used. (So there's a chance whoever ends up reading this will actually believe us, is what he didn't say.) So maybe that's all

Jack was doing: precisely what we agreed to. Plus, it's not like what he wrote came as a surprise. I know he thinks I'm being hysterical and I know he sometimes thinks I'm not all there. It's just, when you see those things written down like that . . . it's like . . . like . . . like just because you know your boyfriend takes a shit every morning, doesn't mean you want to see him on the toilet.

Oh my *God*. Where did *that* come from??

All I'm really trying to say is, I'm not so angry any more. Or, that I am, but that probably all the things I'm angry about, I was angry about them already. And not just them. I've had enough therapy in my life to recognize my mind's all fuc– all *frigging* over the place. The way I reacted was just a release. And you know what? I *do* feel better. I've never been much of a writer. I've never even kept a diary (if *only*. I could have made a fortune cashing in during that misery-lit boom) but I'm beginning to see the attraction. One of my counsellors actually suggested it once (don't ask me which one. I've seen so many different therapists over the years they've morphed into one cardigan-shaped blob): keeping a journal. Recording my thoughts. It might help, she/he suggested. I pooh-poohed her, told her I'd try it and then didn't. Huh. Maybe I should have taken the advice after all.

God, my hand hurts.

I'm going to stop now. I'm rambling, for one thing. And it's not just my hand that's getting tired. Jack won't be happy with what I've written. We're no further on than when I started. But at least we haven't gone backwards. Right, Jack? And I'm convinced now. This *does* help.

Just not in the way you'd imagined.

Jack

I said. Didn't I? Right at the start. I don't process things the way you do. And the whole point of writing this, I thought, was the two of us trying to understand. I mean, I know you're scared, Syd, and I know you're upset, but it's just possible none of this is what you think it is.

And *ish*. What you said about us being happy*ish*. We were happy. We are. OK, maybe not happy right now exactly, but I know we can be again. We just need to . . . we need to get past this. OK? Which is what writing this is all about. Not snapping at each other. Not sniping. The way we've both been acting towards each other recently – I thought we'd agreed to put all that behind us. To do this jointly, you and me. *Together.*

Sydney

Wow. Short and sweet. I feel like I've been sent home with a note from the headmaster. *Sydney hasn't been taking her school assignments seriously. Her attitude is impacting on the work of others.* In fact I think I may have that note somewhere. Or my mother does, probably. She kept them all. In a little (not so little) green shoebox, together with my equally unglowing school reports. Going through them was a way of chastising herself. After the other marks I'd borne had finally faded, they were a reminder that the scars she'd let me suffer were all still there.

But I deserved it. Then, now. Because Jack's right. With everything that's been happening I've lost sight of the fact that none of this is his fault. Even the house, for example. It's true what Jack said: he never wanted it. Not to the extent I did. I fell in love with the place right from the start. In spite of the junk and irrespective of the decor and never mind that we couldn't actually afford it. I just thought . . . I don't know. Or maybe I do but I realize that it sounds cheesy. But honesty, right? *The truth, the whole truth and nothing but.* Honestly then, what I thought when I walked into the house was that it was somewhere Jack and I could be together until we were old. A *forever house*, that's what they call it on the property shows, which when I hear it always makes me want to puke. But that didn't stop me thinking it even so.

Which I suppose more than anything makes it *my* fault. The house, everything that followed: it's down to me. So that's something else I should be apologizing for: that I dragged us both into this in the first place.

But the story. Stop feeling sorry for yourself, Syd, and get on with the story.

The smell, then. Should I start with the smell? Or is that me jumping too far forward?

Maybe it is, because I honestly can't recall when we first noticed it. I remember precisely the moment we first *discussed* it but I can't be sure if it was there right from the start. There was so much, you see, that was strange about the house. That was part of the reason I so adored it. There was a *richness* to it, a *complexity*, in terms of its history and its atmosphere and, yes, its odours. There were smoke smells on top of drain smells on top of book smells on top of something coming from somewhere that was vaguely floral. The jasmine, possibly, from the overgrown garden. And remember, it wasn't as though we'd moved into an empty box. You know that smell when you walk into a library? Or a museum full of curios but empty of people? An *old* place, not one of those Millennium-branded buildings. It was like that, like a thriving marketplace of memories, where all the good smells mingle with the bad. The sweetness with the sweat, the sewage with the sage. Everything seemed . . . *interconnected*. The way an ecosystem is. So the point is, I honestly can't tell you when I picked that one smell out from all the others. When I first noticed that coming from somewhere in the house was the scent of . . .

Wait.

Do you know what? I've been thinking about the other thing Jack said, about us being happy. And I think actually I'm going to use *that* as a starting point. Because it's important that whoever reads this understands that when all this began we really were.

We'd got what we wanted, after all. Against all odds. Evan, the estate agent, he said the owner of the house wanted it to go to a couple. A potential family. (Just as an aside here: a mother? *Me?* HAHAHAHAHA!) So that's how/why it came to us. 'Just lucky, I guess,' is the way Evan put it, like he didn't quite believe it himself (and, quite possibly, like he was rueing his lost commission). The owner – one Patrick Barnard Winters – had requested to see the full roll of bids and, reaching the bottom of the list, had decided just from our names that he liked the sound of us. Mr Jack Walsh and Ms Sydney Baker. Personally, I couldn't think of a name much *less* inspiring than Sydney Baker – that was part of the reason I'd chosen it.

But maybe the seller had a favourite uncle called

Jack. Maybe his mother's maiden name was Baker. Who knows? Whatever it was, it must have been something fairly compelling to convince him to forsake twenty grand. *Minimum*, Jack reckoned. Some of those City types, he said, they'd probably opened their wallets even wider than that.

And I guess that's why Jack went along with it, because he realized we were getting a bargain. And I know Jack wouldn't mind me saying this but it's a fact he's always liked a bargain. It's his dad in him. Roy Walsh, who'd hoarded dishwasher tablets even before he'd coughed up to buy a dishwasher, just because he'd found them two-thirds off one day at the Co-op. And who'd once – in my presence – haggled for ice cream.

So yes, we were elated. House-hunting in London: it's like you're bleeding. Slowly at first, almost unnoticed, but every disappointment is another paper cut. The excitement, you eventually realize, is really just giddiness and after a while all you feel is cold and numb. I'd lost count of the number of places we'd viewed but we'd made offers on – and been outbid on – twelve.

Yup. *Twelve.*

And half of *those* weren't even that great. When we'd started looking we had a list of requirements a sheet of A4 long. A wish list, they call it on *Location*. Nothing outlandish. Nothing, we thought, unreasonable. A bit of character, some outside space. Just the usual. After three months of looking we'd cut the list in half. After six we were down to a single word.

London.

Though probably we'd have settled for Croydon too.

I stayed positive. I got excited whenever we went to see somewhere new, still imagining that this next place could be *the one*. Partly that's just me. My 'training'. (Conditioning? Whatever the hell you call a decade and a half of therapy. *Psychological warfare*, maybe.) Partly – mostly – it was because I knew that if I showed Jack how disconsolate I was becoming, he would have suggested we re-evaluate. Consider waiting. *Give up*, in other words. And that's something I never do. Not because of my training. That part's just me.

You see, having a place together is something we'd always dreamed of.

Actually, scratch that. You *dream* of flying. Of winning the lottery. Owning somewhere to live, a home that's yours and no one else's – that's not a dream. It's a *right*. Not just ours but God knows we'd earned it as much as anyone. Jack reckons I had a tough childhood but his wasn't exactly an episode of *Happy Days*. And we'd saved, scrimped, begged, borrowed: done all the things you're supposed to do and then some. So for us to then struggle the way we did just to find somewhere worth offering on . . . and then to be gazumped *every time* . . . it was torture. Which is perhaps a bit melodramatic but all I'm really trying to say is, when we got this place, it was a relief.

Imagine . . . imagine you're a smoker. Maybe you don't have to imagine. But imagine being a smoker and boarding a twelve-hour flight. Which is delayed. Which, when it finally reaches its destination, is made to circle for another three hours. And then there's taxiing and passport control and baggage reclaim and customs and then, when finally you find a place where you won't get arrested for lighting up, your Bic doesn't work. And then someone walking past offers you a match.

It was *that*.

We had sex in the hallway. Jack and I, almost the instant we walked in. This sodding *owl* staring at me the entire time. 'Bloody owls,' Jack said when I pointed it out. 'Bloody perverts, the lot of them.' Which was exactly the right thing to say because instead of freaking out I just started laughing. Jack had to *drag* me to the bedroom in the end. I was laughing so much I couldn't even stand.

So, yeah. We *were* happy. No more sleeping together in a single bed. No more flatmates (or, in my case, housemates. Three of them. All as damaged and as fucked up in their own way as I am). No more wasting Saturdays studying cracks and checking for mould. We could (and *would*, we'd promised each other) have friends over any time we felt like it. We'd leave the washing-up for as long as we pleased and deliberately waste the hot water. We'd sing, dance, watch TV, cook breakfast together, all naked. Just because we could. We'd *live* our life rather than sit around for another year waiting for it to start.

So I take it back. That *ish*, Jack? I'm sorry, I do: I take it back.

Jack

It's the waiting. That's what's getting to me, way more than I thought it would. It's like the time I went for blood tests, after this trip to Kavos I went on with my mates and ended up on the beach with this girl. Which happened way before I ever met Syd, by the way, and which is something I never, ever did again.

And conveyancing. Waiting for the house to go through. That was incredibly stressful, too, even though there was basically nothing for us to do. Because of that, probably.

It wasn't like this, though. Neither one of those things was like this. This is worse – much worse – mainly I guess because I still don't know what exactly I'm waiting for.

Syd's right. The house: it was a bargain. OK, so it wasn't exactly my dream home or anything (for the record that's a cottage on the north coast of Devon, overlooking the sea, near some woods and an hour minimum from the closest Starbucks), but the price we got it for in my mind made up for a lot. We didn't need three bedrooms, but it's like most things, I suppose. No one needs an iPhone. Or a convertible. Or a

Dualit toaster. But some things, they're nice to have even if you'd struggle to justify them if you were hauled up before, let's say, Jeremy Corbyn.

Three bedrooms. I could have a study. Or a den? Half a one anyway, and Syd could set up her yoga mat on the other side. As for the spare room . . . neither one of us had any family that was likely to come and stay (apart from my parents, maybe, at some point – if they could bring themselves to set aside for a night their feelings about Syd) but it would be useful for putting up friends and, who knew, maybe one day, if Syd ever came round to the idea . . . Well. It was nice to have options, that's all I'm saying, particularly after living the way we had. I'd met Syd at a conference her firm was running on mental health care. I'd been sent there by Lambeth Council as a delegate and she noticed my job title and commented on my age (this was four years ago, so at the time I would've been twenty-four, the same age as Syd), on how demanding being a social worker must be, and I'd acted like no, really, it's not such a big deal, while also trying to convey that actually, yeah, it was, but managing events, that must be pretty tough too, and . . .

I'll spare you the details.

The point is, since we'd known each other we'd lived a minimum of eleven Tube stops apart. We'd discussed moving in together before, but we knew that if we did it would take us longer to save up for our own place, so instead we decided to tough it out. For a year, we thought, tops. It turned out to be the better part of three. So getting the house, getting the keys . . . it was all exactly the way Syd said it was. The anticipation. The relief. That bloody barn owl. Maybe I never loved the house the way Syd did, but I definitely loved the fact that it was ours.

So anyway, we're in. Still not entirely understanding how we'd swung it, but once the contracts had been exchanged what did we care? And, for a short while at least, I changed my mind. The house seemed less creepy than it had before and more characterful. Less gloomy, more atmospheric. It *was* odd, though. The stuff, I mean; all the junk the former owner had left behind. Because before the smell, before what it led to, it already felt to me like . . . I don't know. Or actually I do know, I'm just wondering how much of what I'm putting down is accurate. Whether things have got twisted. Tinted, in the light of all the stuff that's happened since.

But yes, I think I felt it even then. This new life of ours that Syd and I were both so pleased about – I definitely had a sense that it was something we'd stolen.

The smell.

We'd run out of money so we couldn't pay for house clearance and anyway we thought it would be fun. You know, going through all the previous owner's old stuff. It was Syd's suggestion really. Me, I would have dumped the whole lot in bin bags and taken it all either to charity shops or the tip, but Syd convinced me by talking about all the things we might find. There might be furniture we could use, or books we wanted to read, or inspiration in a stack of correspondence for my elusive, long-gestating novel. Treasure of one kind or another, anyway.

(I know, I know: ironic, right? Considering what we did find, I mean.)

We'd got rid of those birds. Or I had, before Syd would even contemplate moving in. (It won't take a minute, I'd told her. All I need to do is open a window. But Syd had been too resolute on the matter even to groan.) We'd cleared the kitchen too, and the master bedroom. The rest, though – we were in no hurry. It's not like we were struggling for space. Between us the only furniture we owned was my old sofa, plus the mattress we'd had delivered the morning we picked up the keys. So day five maybe, day six, we were sitting on the carpet in the second bedroom going through a mountain of old vinyl we'd discovered. There was a record player in there too (an actual record player, completely unironic), and as we came across LPs we liked the look of we were sticking them on the turn-table. The previous owner, he'd built this seriously formidable collection of movie soundtracks. Nothing more recent than *The Godfather*, and nothing with lyrics, but as well as the obvious composers (Maurice Jarre, Ennio Morricone, Bernard Herrmann), there were some real, hard-to-come-by classics. An original Max Steiner, for example. Another by Miklos Rozsa. As I said: treasure.

Syd, she was pulling out all the show tunes. *My Fair Lady*, *Oklahoma!*, *Grease*. *The Sound of* bloody *Music*. We were taking turns to educate each other. Neither one of us prepared to learn a thing, but each of us having a grand old time nonetheless.

Until Syd started sniffing at one of the record sleeves.

'Syd?'

She was looking at the soundtrack of *To Kill a Mockingbird* as though it was something distasteful.

'Do you smell that?' She sniffed the cover again, then the air.

I did. I'd smelled it for a while. It was just damp or something. A mouldy pair of trainers we'd yet to discover at the bottom of one of the wardrobes.

'It's not the record sleeve, Syd. Gregory Peck's far too much of a gentleman to make that kind of smell in front of a lady.'

Syd smiled and rolled her eyes, bumping my shoulder with the record sleeve.

'It's like . . .' She sniffed again. 'What is it? Is it coming from in here?' She uncrossed her ankles and got to her feet. Syd never wears skirts, only trouser suits or jeans. She doesn't like showing her skin, particularly on her arms. The way she feels obliged to dress makes her feel self-conscious – 'mannish' in her words – but the truth is she's got no reason to worry. Whatever she's wearing, whatever the situation, she moves with the grace of Audrey Hepburn.

I joined her in chasing the smell around the bedroom, only slightly annoyed because it was my record we were being distracted from on the turntable.

We ended up on the landing, inhaling and exhaling like a pair of overexcited police dogs. All I can think, looking back, is that the smell had worsened that day because of the weather. It had been cool and wet for most of the month – for most of the year – and finally, on that bright day in May, we were getting a taste for the first time of the impending summer.

'It's definitely stronger out here,' Syd declared, a shard of light from the landing window cutting right across her furrowed forehead.

The smell did seem to be at its worst where we were standing. The trouble was, there didn't appear to be anywhere it could have been coming from. There was no space on the narrow landing for anything but the pictures on the walls (black-and-white family photographs mainly, interspersed with the occasional, obligatory, bird). The nearest door was the one to our pop-up music room, the door through which we'd just come.

'Is it the drains maybe?' Syd asked me. 'The soil pipe or something?'

I was only seventy-five per cent certain at that point what a soil pipe actually was, but if I was right it didn't seem that type of smell. It was more like . . . rotting fruit. Or the bins at the back of a restaurant.

I looked up.

Syd joined me.

'The attic?'

I shrugged. The hatch was directly above our heads. We hadn't been up there yet. It would be crammed with junk, we'd supposed, and there were other parts of the house we wanted to clear first. Plus, personally? I'm not overly friendly with spiders.

'Shall I get the stepladder?' I asked. It wasn't really a question. More a delaying tactic.

'I'll go up,' Syd said, sensing my fear. She makes clucking sounds whenever she sees a spider, then carries them to the nearest window *in her hand*.

'No,' I countered. 'Don't be silly.' My father again, channelling through me when he wasn't even dead. Because drainage issues? Involving ladders? That was man's work.

I was glad I said it, though. I was glad in the end that I did go up that stepladder first. Because once I figured out how to turn on the torch and I realized what it was that was up there . . . Well. I had a chance to warn Syd, if nothing else.

'Don't come up here,' I called out. 'Syd? I mean it. Don't come up.'

Sydney

I'm not going to talk about the attic. I'm going to talk about Elsie Payne.

I remember thinking she would blow away. It was her hair whipping behind her like a kite string, the wind-splash ripples in her raincoat. The fine weather that was to last for most of the summer had taken a few days off and for a short time that month it felt like we'd tripped straight into autumn. Elsie was like a leaf dislodged prematurely from the tree, green in her mac and with that splayed stalk of blonde, struggling through the weather for a safe place to land.

I followed her to the shop on the corner. I liked that, that there was a shop on the corner, and that it wasn't a Londis or a Tesco. Mr Hirani, who ran it, didn't worry overly about the paintwork, and whatever signage had once existed was evident now only as shadow. But inside there was everything you could need. Cornflakes, cumin, cat food – even, at an extortionate mark-up admittedly, champagne. *The shop* it was known as in the neighbourhood. As opposed to *the shops*, which referenced the more uniform parade of south London outlets a fifteen-minute walk away on the local high street.

I'd never noticed Elsie before. Not that I would have expected to necessarily: we'd only been living in the house for a few weeks. But when we'd moved in I'd taken a fortnight's holiday (as much time as I'd taken off work in the preceding two-and-a-bit years) and, either by sitting on the window seat on our new landing or by dawdling through the surrounding streets myself, I'd become familiar – at least by sight – with many of the local faces. There was Mr Hirani, of course, who was so reliably behind the counter in his shop I half suspected he must have invested in a catheter. There was Pink Woman (her clothes, not the woman herself. Her skin was actually this deep toffee brown) and Russian-Mob Man (who turned out to be Kevin from Essex, but who looked exactly like a Russian gangster right up until the moment he opened his mouth), as well as the Guitar Cowboy (guitar case, cowboy hat) and Telly Savalas (just a lookalike, more's the pity). Oh, and the JAMIE! family, who seemed to communicate exclusively by yelling – you guessed it – JAMIE! Unloading the car, preparing for school: there wasn't a task the family carried out in public that didn't seem to hinge on the deployment, like cannon fire, of that single word.

There were others, too, whose habits and routines I'd come to recognize. But not Elsie, not until that morning.

I guessed from the size of her that she was ten or eleven, though it turned out she was really thirteen.

And though she never tripped or even stumbled, her gaze seemed permanently angled towards the clouds, as though she were using them to navigate or were imagining herself part of their world. I spent several moments that first time I saw her searching for the thing she was staring at – an aeroplane, I thought, or a wheeling bird – until I realized there was nothing so specific up there. Nothing I could make out, anyway.

I'd almost caught up with her by the time we approached Mr Hirani's shop. The little bell rang when she pushed open the shop door, then again as I followed her inside. A twitch in her shoulders betrayed her surprise that I'd entered so close behind her but she didn't turn. She simply moved a little faster towards the counter.

'Elsie,' said Mr Hirani. He was not a man given to smiling, I'd learned, or in fact offering any expression at all – but there was a smile for Elsie in his smoker's voice. (That was another thing about Mr Hirani. From the sound of him he smoked sixty a day but I'd never seen him outside with a cigarette. I'd never witnessed him leaving his stool. Maybe everything he needed to accomplish he accomplished after shutting up shop. Bite to eat, chain-smoke some Bensons, then a massive, long-anticipated wee.)

And talking of cigarettes, it was two packs of B&H that Mr Hirani slid unasked for by Elsie across the counter. She opened her hand above his and let fall into his palm a crumpled banknote. Before he'd even uncreased it to see what denomination it was, he was already handing over Elsie's change. She counted it carefully – twice – in a manner that, if an adult had been doing it, any self-respecting shopkeeper would have considered insulting. Mr Hirani didn't blink. If anything he appeared to be counting – double-checking – with her.

I caught his eye. I suppose my reservations about what I'd witnessed must have showed. I mean, I'm not exactly a stickler for regulations. The right to die, the right to get high: I'd march for both. And personally I was smoking when I was nine and my first line of coke was a present from a so-called friend on my fifteenth birthday. That doesn't mean I'd condone it, though. When it comes to kids (who I would define, desperately optimistically I realize, as anyone under sixteen), nanny statism, I feel, does more than simply serve a purpose. It's vital, *inviolable*. To the same degree that a child's innocence is corruptible. Anything that makes kids' lives safer: I'd do more than march for it. I'd die for it.

So, yeah – that must have showed. Mr Hirani knew me well enough by that point to know I had a serious sugar habit and that I had a weakness for sour-flavoured Skittles. Still, I was new to the neighbourhood and he didn't know if he could trust me. Hence the look he was giving me, which initially I mistook for concern – presumably for his self-preservation. His face, though, was hard to read at the best of times and I realized that actually it was a warning. Not to say anything. Not to *interfere*. Perhaps in any other context I would have mounted that high horse I tend to drag around with me – if, say, we *had* been in a Londis or a Tesco, and on the high street and not at the core of a neighbourhood I'd only recently begun to think of as my home. But that day, for once, I was quick on the uptake. I understood that what I'd witnessed was none of my business. Also, that it was almost certainly only a very minor scene in a drama that was playing beyond my sight.

I made up for it, of course: the lack of damage I did then. I made up for it and more. But that was later. For the time being I remained an observer, obedient to Mr Hirani's silent counsel and relieved, actually, that I'd been absolved of my duty to make a fuss.

Elsie pocketed her cigarettes and slid from the counter towards the door. As she passed me I caught my first proper glimpse of her face. Only in profile, and just for an instant before she sank tortoise-like beneath her coat collar, but I noticed the stormy shading of her eyes and the high-boned fragility of her cheeks. I saw her fringe cut so low it tickled her eyelids and I saw the bruise, old and fading, that was nevertheless still visible above her lip.

I'd come in for sugar. Something about what had transpired made me pretend that, instead of Skittles, I wanted milk. I paid hastily, then walked out of the shop without looking like I was rushing. This time

Elsie wasn't dawdling. She didn't gaze up towards the sky and she barely checked before she stepped out to cross the street. I followed steadily behind her, trying not to *look* like I was following her, but if she'd turned she wouldn't have been in any doubt.

We passed the church and the Evening Star (I liked that about the neighbourhood too: that the pub and the church were directly across from one another, so that if you were to walk down the middle of the road they'd be like a devil and an angel calling out to you across opposite shoulders) and then rounded into one of the residential streets. It was the turning before ours but I took it anyway. The houses were identical to those in the terrace next to us: red brick, two storeys, with crenulated stonework around the windows and the doors that roughly one in three owners had painted white.

Gradually, like a ship slowing, Elsie came to a stop. I continued as close as I dared, then paused unhidden by a lamp post. She'd got out her change again and as before appeared to be checking it. This time, rather than putting it back in her pocket, she wrapped it in a fist and approached the nearest front door. The house she was aiming for was one of those directly behind ours. I counted from the corner. Five in, which meant it would be visible from the spare-bedroom window.

There was movement in one of the windows – on the first floor, on what I presumed was either the landing or in a box room – and I looked up. All I saw, though, was a retreating shadow. Elsie's father? The form had been too broad to belong to a woman. I stared a little longer and that's when I saw movement again. Whoever it was hadn't gone away. They'd merely withdrawn enough so that I could only just see them.

When I looked down again Elsie had her key in the lock. She paused and I wondered whether she'd sensed movement above her too. But then she turned, and looked directly at me, and I realized she'd known I was following her all along. She smiled. Was it a smile? Even now I'm not entirely sure. It was *something* anyway, an acknowledgement of one kind or another. It was shy, almost wistful. It was the same expression I saw her give me two months later, when we spotted each other on the platform of our local train station and I stood watching as she threw herself off.

Jack

'*Arse*hole.'

I raised my head from my paperwork in time to see Bartol hammer down the phone. He saw me looking and broke into a grin.

'Relax, *amigo*. He couldn't have heard me. The fascist prick had already hung up.'

Bart had been in trouble before for speaking his mind. In fact it was a daily occurrence, but what I mean is he'd almost lost his job. He was a housing officer, the same as me. But whereas I was like a holding midfielder – dogged, reliable, with consistent if unspectacular performances – Bartol was our glamorous foreign signing, singularly programmed to attack. He scored plenty, turned no-hopers now and then into valuable points, but he pissed off a lot of people on the way. The opposition, yes, but also members of his own team. Even me, every so often, but never to the extent that I wanted him to get fired. At the risk of sounding like an eight-year-old, Bartol Novak was my best friend.

'Who were you talking to?' I asked him. 'No, wait, let me guess. Your bank manager. Or Tony Blair.'

Bart grinned still wider. 'That fucking landlord,' he

replied, and his expression darkened. 'Do you know what I'd like to do? I'd like to tell him about Susmita's situation. Maybe if he understood what she's been through, he wouldn't insist on being such a cold-hearted prick.'

Susmita was a rape victim. Her attacker had left her with a broken wrist, a shattered jaw and twin boys she'd refused to have terminated because abortion ran counter to her beliefs. She loved them dearly, in spite of their provenance, and after losing her job and her place at a shelter, she'd been desperately trying to rebuild her life. Bart, though, was about the only friend in London she had. He was trying to find a home for her, somewhere permanent, in the private sector because social housing was full. It was one of those cases that for Bart had become deeply personal – in part, I suspect, because Susmita was so astonishingly beautiful and my friend had fallen in love. To be fair, crush or no crush, with some cases you just can't help yourself. You know there's a system, that there's a limit to what you can and cannot do, but sometimes . . . Well. You wouldn't be human if you didn't stretch the rules.

'Seriously, what an arsehole,' said Bartol again. He shook his head, stared for a while, and I could tell he was about to mention the VSO. 'It's people like him I'll be glad to see the back of when I finally join the VSO.'

Joining the Voluntary Service Overseas was Bart's

long-term escape plan, a bit like my dream of writing a bestseller. You have to have one, working in social services. On the toughest days it's your escape plan you cling to in order to keep yourself afloat. The difference between my plan and Bart's was that his was more or less in sight. In fact I didn't doubt that one day he'd do it: just walk out on his life in London in exactly the way he always said he would. Bart was a romantic. He pictured himself building community halls in Eritrea, uncorking water supplies in South Sudan. His only reward would be the thanks of the locals and a cameo on *Comic Relief.*

'Yeah, well,' I said. 'Better a pissy landlord once in a while than a long-term relationship with dysentery.'

'I'm sick of pissy landlords. When did you last meet a landlord who *wasn't* pissy? All the property owners in this city, they act like they're fucking anointed. Which I suppose they are, but that doesn't give them the right to empty their bowels over the rest of us.'

'Hey. That's me and Syd you're talking about, remember?'

'Oh. Right. I'd forgotten,' said Bart, with a grin that told me he'd done no such thing. 'So how is it out there among the middle classes? Joined any book clubs lately? Hosted any dinner parties?'

Bart had a flat-share in Elephant & Castle. He liked to make out he was keeping it real, but the true reasons he lived where he did were, a, he couldn't afford a place of his own and, b, it was vital to his mental well-being that he was able to walk to and from work. He didn't like buses and he was out-and-out terrified of the Tube. The confined space, the press of people: just the thought of the Northern Line made him shudder. He claimed it was because of the war. The Croatian war of independence, that is, back in the early nineties, even though Bartol had been a toddler when his family had moved to England to escape the violence, and the only memories he could possibly have been repressing were those from a childhood spent in Royal Tunbridge Wells.

'Loads,' I answered. 'We would have invited you, but you know how it is. All of our other friends know how to use a knife and fork.'

'Show-offs,' said Bart. 'Hey, you were telling me about your attic. About how brave you were, overcoming your perfectly rational terror of those teeny tiny little spiders.'

I had been, until the landlord Bart had been chasing had finally deigned to return one of his calls. To be honest I'd been glad of the interruption. I'd started the story about the attic without knowing whether I really planned to finish it. Not because I didn't trust my friend or value his opinion. I just . . . I guess I was still struggling to work out what exactly I'd seen up there — and how to put it into words.

'It was just . . . a cat,' I said. 'A dead cat.'

'That was making the smell?'

I shrugged, nodded.

When I'd swung the torch beam from my spot by the hatch, the attic had shown itself to be surprisingly empty. Not empty empty. There were boxes, a roll of carpet, an old water tank: all your typical loft-level artefacts. Mostly, though, it was cobwebs and dusty space. It explained why the rest of the house was so chock-full. The things most people would consign to the garret, the previous owner had been either too lazy or too infirm to carry up a ladder. I didn't know which. At that point we still knew next to nothing about him, other than the story about him emigrating. And it was that as much as anything that had been bothering me. The cat was one thing: the smell of it, the sight of it, the difficulty I had getting it past Syd. But it wasn't just the cat that I'd discovered.

'It was in the corner,' I said to Bart. 'I couldn't tell what killed it. Maybe, I don't know . . . I figured maybe it got trapped up there.'

'How? I mean, was there a window or something?'

'I didn't see one. But you know what cats are like. They can get in anywhere there's air.'

'Maybe it got injured in a fight or something, then crawled away somewhere to die.'

'Right,' I said. 'I guess.' Although the cat had looked as though it had got involved in something more serious than a fight. Two of its legs were bent at odd angles and its fur in places appeared almost to be singed. 'But the point is there was something else as well,' I went on. 'The cat, it was right at the back. The attic was only boarded around the hatch, so I had to walk over the rafters to get to it.' And through like a million of those cobwebs, I didn't add. 'But once I was there I could see into this little alcove. Like, this space tucked away behind the water tank? And there was a shoe-box. A big one, all by itself. Sort of . . . hidden there.'

Bart was watching me with a curious little frown. He was dark-haired, dark-skinned and, much as I hate to admit it, hideously handsome. Even when he frowned — especially when he frowned — he could have passed for a model. One of those earnest types advertising something life-changing — like chewing gum, say, or underwear.

'What was in it?'

I could tell from Bart's tone that he was genuinely curious, and I was sure as well that I was about to disappoint him.

'Kids' stuff,' I said.

'Kids' stuff? What do you mean, kids' stuff?'

I twitched a shoulder. 'Like, a box full of stuff a kid would keep. A little girl, I'm guessing. You know, like a treasure box. But treasure that's not really treasure.'

'I don't follow.'

'Like . . . there were some shells in there. Like ones collected from a beach. And a bookmark, the head of some doll, some dried flowers. A Care Bear. Lots of postcards, all blank, but like a collection. Just, you know: treasure.'

Bart was looking at me like I was talking in tongues.

45

'You never had a treasure box?' I asked him. 'When you were a kid?'

'No, Jack,' Bart said. 'I never had a treasure box. I had a money box, but it was always empty. My parents, they –'

'I know, I know. Your parents fled their homeland with nothing. You've told me before, Bart. A thousand times, probably.'

I was pissed off at him all of a sudden and I wasn't sure why. I'd been expecting more of a reaction, I suppose. Or, a reaction more like mine.

'OK, Jack, so you found a treasure box. What happened next?'

And that just irritated me even more. 'What do you mean, what happened next? Nothing happened next. That's it. That's the end of the story. It just ... it freaked me out, that's all. Finding a little girl's stuff hidden away like that.' Although that wasn't quite true. There had been something else: one final detail I hadn't mentioned yet.

'What was it that freaked you out exactly? I mean, the doll's head I can probably get on board with. The Care Bear, too. They're creepy little fuckers, the lot of them.'

Ordinarily I might have smiled at that. Probably Bart was expecting me to.

'Did you show Syd?' he asked when I didn't, pretending too late that he was taking me seriously. 'What did she say?'

I didn't like that either: that Bart should mention Syd. In part, frankly, because I'd always been a little suspicious of how well the two of them got on whenever we were all together. Not jealous exactly, just suspicious. Don't get me wrong. Me and Syd: it's the most secure in a relationship I've ever felt. But that in itself tends to make me worry, even if most of the time it might seem like there's nothing to worry about.

Plus, the other thing was, I hadn't told her. Syd, I mean. I hadn't even told her about the cat. I'd told her it was a pigeon. I don't know why, but I thought a pigeon would upset her less than a cat would. Syd's got this aversion to mortality. Which, to be fair, I suppose we all do, but what I mean is it's her own personal take on my fear of spiders. Those stuffed birds she'd just about coped with, but a rotting cat, on the other side of the ceiling of the room in which she sleeps? It would have set her back months.

'I didn't want to worry her,' I said to Bart. 'And I didn't want her taking the piss.' I glared at him meaningfully.

'I'm not taking the piss! Christ, Jack, when did you get so sensitive? I'm just . . . I'm trying to work out what the big deal is. So you found a box of stuff. So what?'

'Not just stuff. A little girl's stuff, in a house where there's no other sign of any children and hidden in a spot where no one would ever find it. Plus, the bloke who lived there before us, he'd owned the place for

47

thirty-odd years. There's no way the things in the box were that old.'

'But it doesn't *mean* anything. Does it? Unless I'm missing something.'

'How do you know? There's hardly going to be an innocent explanation for it, is there?'

Bart was watching me, and I expected him to roll his eyes and turn away. Instead, all of a sudden, he started laughing. A big, booming, Eddie Murphy-style laugh that for an instant made me want to punch him.

'I'll tell you what it means,' he said. 'It means you've obviously got that novel in you after all. Maybe I'd work on some of the details, maybe put some human bones in that box instead of a bunch of dried flowers. But that imagination of yours is clearly working overtime.'

I tried to stay angry. It was hard, though, in the face of Bart's grin. And actually I felt a measure of relief. Because I'd never wanted my friend to agree with me, I realized. I'd wanted him to laugh, to mock me in exactly the way he was doing now.

I didn't smile exactly, but I came as close as I could manage. I even allowed myself to believe that Bart was probably right. Probably I'd only been irritated in the first place because I recognized I was spooked over nothing. Even the bit I hadn't mentioned yet: probably I was overreacting to that part, too. There was a name, you see, handwritten on the inside of the box. On the underside of the lid, to be precise, in felt-tip that had long ago faded.

But it was just a name. A fairly common name at that. There'd been nothing in the contents of the box to suggest its presence was anything but a coincidence. I mean, even if Syd had seen it . . . if I'd let Syd see it . . . there was every chance she would have said the same thing.

Sydney

I grew up thinking love was just a lie. Not just a lie. A *deception*. Like Father Christmas or the Easter Bunny or God. Fibs that change how we feel, that trick us into believing the world is a better place than it really is. That distract us, in fact. Blind us, purposefully, to cold reality, so that we don't fight the way we should and instead *submit*.

It was Jack who changed that for me. Who showed me that love was really real.

That time we met? At the conference? I'd woken up that morning and inhaled three lines of coke. In fact, once registration was over, I had it in mind to make another visit to the Ladies. Jack was the last delegate to arrive and I was sitting in the hotel lobby, tapping his unclaimed badge against the table, when finally he blustered in through the double set of doors.

'Bloody trains,' were his first words to me. 'Has it started already? I'm so sorry I'm late.' He looked like he'd set out that morning all neatly packaged but, like a parcel that gets waylaid en route to its destination, had somehow come unravelled on the journey. His suit was wet and his tie was crooked and his hair was a hybrid of contrasting styles – neither one of which, I later discovered, was the one he spent ten minutes every morning trying to summon from the bathroom mirror.

'Mr Walsh?'

Mr Jack Walsh, I'd imagined, was older, tireder and pastier. He wasn't my age, like the man before me (the boy, rather, because I still hadn't learned to think of myself as anything more evolved than a girl), and certainly he wasn't as good-looking. I'm not talking jutting-chin and gleaming-smile good-looking: Jack was a little rougher around the edges. His ears were slightly too big, his nose a fraction too small. His eyes, though, were this deep tobacco-coloured brown. They were kind eyes. Curious too. They didn't look cruel, or dulled, the way mine did.

'Ow. Bugger.'

He'd pricked himself on the pin on the back of his name badge. Then, when he noticed me trying not to smile, he flushed.

'Sorry,' he said again. 'This is seriously not my morning. Should I . . .' He pendulummed his finger between the two closed doors on the wall behind me.

'Actually,' I said, 'they're kind of halfway through the first session. Maybe you want to hang on and get a coffee?'

We weren't supposed to admit latecomers. I always did, but today – on a whim – I enforced the rules. He looked so crestfallen I immediately wished I'd smuggled him inside.

I checked my watch. 'They'll be breaking up in fifteen minutes,' I said. 'And you're not missing anything, I promise. The opening session, it's really just an introduction.'

I smiled and he smiled back. He went to get that coffee and even fetched one for me. A cappuccino, he'd guessed, with three packs of sugar balanced on the lid. I accepted it gratefully. I didn't have the heart to tell him I drank my coffee black.

I watched him after that through the morning sessions. Most people at these events we run, they're only there to scam a day out of the office. Jack was actually paying attention. It's stupid, I know, but even then – even before I really knew him – he made me feel that I was doing something worthwhile. I'd never felt that way before. I'd only taken the job because it paid well, and I'd only been offered it in the first place because the man who'd hired me had clearly valued my cleavage over what was missing from my CV. But seeing Mr Jack Walsh, social worker, sitting there scribbling earnestly in his notebook, I felt . . . valued, I suppose the word is. *Validated*. For the first time, basically, in my whole life.

I'd never had a boyfriend before.

If you'd asked me, I would have claimed I'd had *relationships*, but none had lasted more than four dates. Four dates, I've found, is about as much time as you can spend with a bloke before he expects you to part company with your knickers. And it's not that I have a problem with sex. I mean, I do. Clearly I have a problem with sex, but not in the sense that I don't like doing it. I've *fucked* plenty of men. Thirteen, in fact, not counting Jack. But fucking isn't the same as having sex (OK, OK: *making luuurve*). It's when sex becomes meaningful that I pull up the drawbridge: that moment you really let someone close. So once we've moved from coffee to the cinema to drinks and then maybe dinner, that's when I invariably shut down. I become a bitch, is usually the easiest way. I'll snipe, snigger, turn up late or, once or twice, not turn up at all. I'll ingest a mound of coke and start babbling, not bothering to disguise the signs of my cistern-top habit – my not-so-little white lie – or I won't take anything, not even a drink, and I'll sit there saying nothing at all. It takes surprisingly little to scare men off, I've found. Sometimes all that's required is a well-placed burp.

I tried to play the same game with Jack. I'd allowed our run of dates to stretch to five, mainly because he managed to make me laugh so much and also because for our fifth date he'd suggested we visit London Zoo. Which is basically my favourite thing to do in the whole city. It feels *innocent* somehow and I craved innocence. Some people, I know, would take objection to that. There's nothing innocent, they'd say, about keeping animals locked up in cages. But even if they're in cages, at least they're cared for. And what's so fucking fabulous about the big wide world anyway? Out there it's all about survival. *Freedom*: it's just another term for living in fear.

Plus the thing with zoos is, I like monkeys.

And that's where it started, as it happened. Beside the monkey cages. That's where I almost let Jack slip away.

'You know, there's a Monkey World near where my parents live,' Jack said. 'We should go there some time. Take a trip.'

'To Monkey World?' I answered, already starting to feel light-headed. 'Or to your parents' place?'

'Either,' Jack said. 'Both. And maybe afterwards you can tell me if you noticed any difference.'

He was looking at the gibbons, tapping a finger against the enclosure, so he couldn't have noticed the expression on my face.

I turned away.

'Syd?'

We'd been sharing a stick of candy floss and I dropped the whole lot in the nearest bin.

'Syd? Where are you –'

I'd started walking. Jack hurried to catch up.

'My parents aren't that bad,' he said, buzzing around me like a wasp with a wounded wing. 'I mean, they are, but what I mean is you don't have to meet them. Ever, if you like.'

Ever. As in *for* ever.

I stopped.

'I've given you the wrong impression and I'm sorry,' I said, which to be fair was about the most upfront in that type of situation I'd ever been.

Jack frowned as he tried to process what was happening. For a second I thought he was going to react the same way all the others had. Stage one was confusion. After that, sometimes, was denial, but all roads eventually led to anger.

'It's fine,' Jack said.

I thought it was a tactic. A prelude to an onslaught of abuse. 'What?'

'I said, it's fine. I mean, I don't want to meet your parents either.'

I just stared then. He wasn't following his lines.

'I'd like to hear about them,' he went on. 'At some point. But I'm fairly sure I wouldn't ever want to meet them.'

I narrowed my eyes at him. 'You think you know me? Is that it?'

Jack was already shaking his head. 'I barely know myself,' he answered. 'But I know I like you. And I know I'm not in any hurry.'

I laughed then, I think. I may even have put my hand on my hip. 'Well, that's a relief. I'd hate to think I've been holding you up.'

Jack shrugged, shook his head. 'Just the opposite,' he said. 'I feel like I've achieved more in the three weeks since I met you than I have in the past twenty-four years.'

Which left me speechless. And – trust me – rarely am I ever speechless.

'But as I say,' Jack went on, 'I'm not in any hurry. You know how to reach me if you change your mind.'

He turned then and started back towards the gibbons.

'Hey. Hey!'

Jack moved to face me. 'That was quick,' he said, daring to grin.

'Fuck you,' I replied. Not exactly original, I realize. 'What do you think? That time is like some magic eraser? That all you need to do is sit back and wait for a couple of weeks? You *don't* know me, Jack. Even the bits you think you've guessed. I guarantee you haven't got a clue.'

He seemed to recognize that grinning at me had been the wrong thing to do. 'Look, I . . . I didn't mean to imply that I *did* know you. But maybe you don't know me the way you think you do either. That's all I'm saying.'

I didn't answer that. Mainly because I suspected he had a point.

'I'm not after anything, Syd. I just . . . I like spending time with you, that's all. Genuinely: that's *it.*'

It was like I'd attempted to slam the door but Jack had surreptitiously stuck out a foot.

'Look, Jack. I'm sorry. I really am. But this is as far as I can go. I'm a mess. OK? My life: it's a fucking mess, and I should never have implied you might become part of it.'

'I'm used to mess,' Jack answered brightly. 'I am. I mean, come round to the flat one day and take a look at my bedroom.'

It took him half a second or so to register what he'd said.

'Shit, Syd. I didn't mean . . . I just meant . . .'

'I know what you meant, dummy.' I kept frowning but the corners of my mouth twitched involuntarily upwards.

'Look, how about we go and get a coffee or something?' Jack tested. 'A cappuccino, right? Three sugars?'

It had become our first private joke. Even today if Jack's going up somewhere to order and I tell him that's what I want, he knows to bring me black with none.

'And then what?' I answered. I wasn't smiling yet but I wasn't frowning any more either.

Again Jack shrugged. 'And then we drink,' he said. 'That's all. Today, right now, that's all.'

We had sex together nine months later. No: we *made love*. It was my first time. And for those nine months and thirty-six seconds (hey, I'm not judging. Nine months is a long time to hold it in for any man) Jack behaved like the perfect gentleman. He taught me to trust him. He taught me to trust, full stop. And I guess that's where all of this is leading, the point I set out to make. I wished you'd trusted me, Jack. The things you found? The things you kept from me?

I just wish you'd believed in me the way I've always believed in you.

Jack

I did keep secrets, I admit – though in my defence not as many as Syd thought I did at the time. And for the most part I only kept them because I was trying to protect her. That box is a perfect example. I knew she'd get upset over it, so what was the point in opening old wounds? And the night I thought I heard someone in the house. Even if I'd told Syd about that when it happened, there's no way she could have known what it really meant, not with the degree of certainty she has now. Probably she would have said I was imagining things; that I was just on edge because of the way I felt about the house. Which, to be fair, is exactly what I put it down to myself.

So we're in bed. Me and Syd. I'd been having trouble sleeping, which wasn't like me at all. Normally I sleep for seven hours solid. No dreams, no wee breaks, nothing. Lately, though, I'd started waking up in the middle of the night. I kept imagining I was hearing things. Like . . . noises. Not house noises. Noises like something moving about. But it was like I said. We'd only been in the house for four or five weeks and I still hadn't fully settled. I didn't dislike the place as much as I had the first time I saw it, but that elation I'd experienced after we'd moved in was definitely in the process of wearing off.

Finding that box hadn't helped. That cat as well, which the more I thought about it, the more confused I was about how it had got up into the attic in the first place. (I'd double-checked after my conversation with Bart and there definitely wasn't a Velux or anything, nor even a loose tile as far as I could see. Plus the cat's legs, I was sure, had been broken.) And don't forget too that we were still surrounded by all the former owner's old stuff. I was beginning to wish we'd thrown everything into bin bags on the day we'd moved in, because now that Syd and I were both back at work I didn't know when we'd next get a chance and even without the stuffed birds it was like living in a scene out of *Psycho*. Like in that big old house up on the hill? Or in the office. You know, when Anthony Perkins makes Janet Leigh a plate of sandwiches? And all his stuff is scattered all around them: on the walls, on the surfaces – all this weird, creepy-looking stuff, which when you see it you just know things aren't going to end well.

But whatever. I woke up again, is the point. At one fifty-nine in the morning, according to the display on my phone, and this time, even if I can't swear it was true all the other times, I definitely had the feeling I'd heard something out of the ordinary. And I'll be honest, it wasn't burglars at first that I was afraid of. All I could think about initially was Norman Bates's mother. And that cat. Our mystery visitor. Syd mentioned Stephen King earlier and *Pet Sematary*'s always been one of my personal favourites. Not the film, the film's pants, but the novel . . . It's like that bit in *Friends*, where Joey is so terrified of *The Shining* he keeps the book in the freezer? I'm like that with *Pet Sematary*. And I don't know if you've ever read it, but there's a cat that comes back from the dead. Church, its name is, short for Winston Churchill, and it's kind of alive except not, not really, and lying there in the middle of the night I was imagining that cat I found sort of clawing its way up from where I'd buried it in the garden, then getting into the house somehow (I guess however it got in last time), coming up the stairs, along the landing, towards our bedroom, and then . . . and then . . . and then who knows, quite frankly. I mean, even the cat in the Stephen King book doesn't really *do* anything. But I wasn't thinking logically. It was two o'clock in the morning and my imagination was basically working overtime.

For a moment I lay there just listening. It wasn't Syd who'd woken me. She was face down on her pillow, so still I could barely hear her breathing. In normal circumstances she would have been the one lying awake looking at me. Syd's had trouble sleeping all the time I've known her. She'll have two, maybe three hours a night when she's underwater, and all the rest of the time she'll be paddling in the shallows.

'Syd?'

No response. I tried poking her, just gently, and that's when I heard it again. The sound that had woken me. It was a shuffling, skidding sort of sound: more the slip of a sole than the clunk of a central-heating pipe.

I sat up in bed. I checked to see whether the noise had registered with Syd, but she still hadn't moved. I fought the urge to shake her awake, to force her to sit up and listen with me. But at that moment there was nothing to hear. Whatever sound I thought I'd detected, it didn't repeat.

Now, I've seen enough horror films in my time to know never to go wandering about alone when there's a suspected zombie in the vicinity, feline or otherwise. But there was no way I was going back to sleep, not until I'd at least had a quick look around. Plus, countering whatever fear I felt, I heard my dad's voice telling me to stop behaving like a six-year-old. My old man would never have been afraid of spiders, for instance. He would never have worried about things that went bump in the night, not unless it was his good-for-nothing son coming home tipsy after a night out with his mates. That would have roused him, I guarantee it. But other than that? About the only thing my father was afraid of was the prospect of maybe one day being called upon to express some emotion that wasn't indignation.

I eased myself silently from beneath the bed sheets.

Given how muggy the previous evening had been, the chill that greeted my bare feet took me by surprise. Oddly, though, it also gave me some encouragement. The floorboards were solid, real. The cold of the night air was real, too.

There was nothing on the landing. I mean, there was, but I didn't see it then. As far as I was aware it was empty except for the pictures the previous owner had left hanging on the wall. The attic hatch was sealed (I'd taken to looking up virtually every time I passed beneath it) and there was nothing except shadows on the top section of the stairs. I glanced into the bathroom as I passed it, and then into the spare room – still stuffed with junk – to check the window. When the weather was warm we'd taken to leaving it open. The windows in the main bedroom were painted shut and opening the one in here was the only way we'd discovered of enticing in some fresh air. But it was closed. I moved on to the box room, which for the time being Syd was using as her yoga studio, and then made my way back along the landing to the top of the staircase.

Here I paused. Checking upstairs was easy. But at night-time, to me, downstairs always felt like a different world. And although I was no longer worried about being accosted by Anthony Perkins dressed in drag, burglars remained a distinct possibility. The house was hardly the most secure. The windows were single glazed, the door locks old and insubstantial.

Bart, he sleeps with a tennis racket under his bed. It's a London thing, I think. I was surprised, when the topic came up, how many other people in the office admitted to sleeping close by to something they could swing. One bloke has a baseball bat wedged down the side of his mattress. Miriam from HR has the sword her great-grandfather wore in World War I propped handily against her bedside table. Personally I'd never even considered what I might use, in the case of intruders, as a weapon. Syd, I'd joked when the others had asked me. But I would have been grateful for something hefty in my hand now.

I started down.

'Hello?'

There was no sign as far as I could tell of anything untoward. There was no light, no noise, no movement in the air. But it was chilly down here, too, as though a window, if not at the top of the house, had been left open somewhere.

I checked the front door as I passed it and saw the chain was firmly in place. The living-room windows were painted closed in the same way as the ones in our bedroom were, but I looked in anyway. I passed the dining room – what would have been the dining room, had it not currently been a staging post for the tip – and gradually worked my way through the darkness towards the rear of the house. I'd been aware all along that if someone had actually broken in, it would most likely have been through either the back door or the window in the kitchen. It was here that the house was least secure, and most accessible from the network of alleyways that separated our row of houses from those in the next street over.

I would have switched on a light had I not been worried about waking Syd. I almost called out again too, but resisted for the same reason, and anyway I was still feeling silly for having done so the first time. I'm not very good at sounding threatening, and that 'hello?' had come out like an impression of a bad Lionel Ritchie song. Besides, who did I think was going to answer? It was like that question you get on US immigration forms. *Are you, or have you ever been, a terrorist?* Well, shit – you got me. And here was I hoping you wouldn't ask.

The door into the kitchen was pulled to just far enough to block my view. We didn't usually close it, but that didn't mean we hadn't last night. I tried to see into the sliver of gloom between the edge of the door and the frame, but it was as impenetrable as a darkened window. I held my breath, listened, then started to edge closer. I reached out a hand, pushed open the door . . .

And found nothing. The room was empty, the window closed and the back door secure. The kitchen was coldest of all, but it was also the most exposed part of the house, and I could only assume the warm front had broken sooner than the weathermen had expected it to. As for the noise I thought I'd heard . . . the boiler, the pipes, the ancient floorboards – any of a hundred things might have made it, assuming I hadn't imagined it in the first place.

Feeling like an idiot, and to the soundtrack of my father's scornful laughter in my head, I made my way back upstairs. I stopped in the bathroom, used the toilet, swallowed some water. When I got back into our bedroom, Syd was still fast asleep. She was lying on her side, cocooned in the duvet, and I felt impatient all of a sudden to curl up next to her. As I lowered myself on to the mattress, however, she shifted slightly, then spoke.

'Your hands are cold,' she muttered.

When I looked at her she hadn't opened her eyes.

'What?' I replied, turning more fully to face her.

She snuggled deeper. 'Your hands,' she mumbled again. 'When you touched my cheek. They're freezing.'

She rolled on to her front then, and all I could see of her after that was the messy protrusion of her hair. I sat there, staring, my lips parted, and felt a drumbeat building in my ribcage. From feeling exhausted I was suddenly once again wide awake. You see, the thing was, I hadn't touched her. Not when I'd got up, not when I'd come back into the room. Whoever's hand she thought she'd felt – it wasn't mine.

Sydney

I've had some vino. A bit too much, probably, although in another sense just the right amount. Enough, I hope, to talk some more about Elsie.

I like to run. I'm not a fitness freak or anything. My body's more messy bedsit than hallowed temple. And I don't run to offset my love of Skittles. I've got this weird metabolism, where I can eat as much sugar as I want but I balloon if I so much as make eye contact with a loaf of bread. So Christmases and holidays aside, generally I'm a completely muscle-less nine-and-a-half stone. Whether I run or not makes very little difference. But I make time for it whenever I can. I enjoy it, in an odd, God-make-it-stop kind of way. Basically, even though it often feels like I'm about to die, running reminds me that I'm alive.

I was still tweaking my route – gauging distances, trying to work out which direction felt most like going downhill – which is how on that weekday morning in June I found myself trotting past a kids' play area I hadn't even realized was there. It was on the edge of the nearby common, through a short but shadowy railway tunnel I'd been building up my courage to venture through. The playground was empty, save for a single figure rocking gently on a swing.

I didn't recognize her right away. She had her back to me and anyway I was focused more on whether I'd inadvertently hit a dead end. I hadn't – there was a path that looped around the railings – but even so I was already slowing and when I realized it was Elsie I came to a stop.

She hadn't noticed me, despite my raucous breath and pounding heart. I felt like a hunter who'd stumbled downwind on a deer. No less unwelcome. No less deadly.

The swing was meant for toddlers, the type with safety bars around the seat. Even Elsie – slight, skin-and-bones Elsie – couldn't fit inside it, so instead she'd balanced herself on top, her knees pulled level with her chest and her bum wedged so low it seemed stuck. She was looking at the clouds again. Not swinging: swaying. Dreaming, it looked like.

'Hi,' I said, a sound that reverberated like a gunshot.

Elsie slipped so quickly on to her feet she might have been oiled. She faced me and the swing, reacting raggedly, hit her thighs. Elsie didn't flinch. She was looking at me and then beyond me, checking presumably that I was alone. I couldn't tell whether she recognized me until she spoke.

'It's you,' she said. 'You're new.'

I puffed a breath, de-sweated my brow. 'I don't feel

new,' I said, smiling. I took a step and Elsie mirrored it, re-establishing the distance between us. I took another step, towards the railings, and this time she held her ground. I pulled my ankle up behind me to stretch my thigh, my free hand resting lightly on the unpainted metal.

'I had no idea this place was even round here,' I said, nodding towards the rather cursory-looking slide. There were climbing bars too, as well as a scattering of farmyard animals impaled on springs. The equipment didn't look old exactly. It looked ravaged, like a set of toys unwrapped on Christmas morning that by nightfall already needs replacing.

Elsie seemed uncertain at first whether to answer. 'It gets busy here as soon as the mums come out. This is about the only time of day it's ever empty.'

There was graffiti scrawled on the coloured panelling of the climbing frame. Bored graffiti: names, dates, tits, dicks. I pictured the older kids descending on the playground after school was out. Not to play. To *drape*. It was come here, I imagined, or get moaned at for loitering in the street.

'Do you come here often?' I asked Elsie, wondering if she was old enough to register the cliché.

'Why do you ask?' Elsie wrapped her arms around her midriff. She was wearing her school uniform, I noticed, and there was a rucksack lying on the concrete beside the swings. I didn't have my watch with me but I'd left the house at a quarter to seven. Clearly

Elsie had got up even earlier than I had and, from the way she was dressed, it seemed she intended to stay out until it was time for her to go to school.

'Sorry,' I said. 'It's none of my business. It's just . . . I wasn't expecting to see you here, that's all. I wasn't expecting to see anyone.'

I swapped legs, wondering how long I could keep standing there like an out-of-shape flamingo before Elsie would decide I should probably be moving on.

'Not often,' she finally said, in answer to my earlier question. 'I mean, all the time, sometimes. Sometimes hardly at all.'

I smiled at that.

'Well,' I said. I wobbled and set both feet on the floor. 'I should probably . . .' I pointed ahead. Awkwardly, the path I'd been tracking ran in a loop around the playground, meaning if I continued to follow it Elsie would be forced to watch me until I made it back into the tunnel. I moved instead to head back the way I'd come.

'I've got hot chocolate,' Elsie's voice called out behind me. 'And . . .'

I looked around.

'And cigarettes,' she added. 'Although . . .' She wiggled a finger at what I was wearing, at what I was in the middle of doing. 'I'm guessing you probably don't.'

I faced her fully. Before that day I hadn't had a cigarette in eight months.

'Are you kidding?' I said. 'Cigarettes and hot

chocolate. The only thing you're missing is a bag of marshmallows.'

Elsie dived into her rucksack. She surfaced, brandishing a packet of Fruit Pastilles. 'Will these do?' she said, smiling, and she waggled them invitingly in the air.

We sat side by side on separate swings. I was too big to wedge myself the way Elsie had – or, were I to try, I had my doubts I'd be able to get back out – but it was surprisingly comfortable being balanced across the struts. I felt a slight chill sitting there in only my sweaty running top but as the heat of the day began to build it wasn't an entirely unpleasant sensation. The quiet was nice too. The stillness. It isn't quite as hard to find peace living in London as most non-Londoners tend to assume – the trick is being willing to get up early – but even so it feels precious whenever you *do* discover it. It's like being let in on a secret.

'I like it here at sunrise,' Elsie said to me. 'The sun, it comes up over that little patch of trees.'

She was looking ahead, out across the wildest section of the common. I was imagining the scene – the contours, the colours – but I was also thinking again about how long Elsie must have been sitting here. First light that morning had been at five. I remembered because I'd been woken by the glow from behind the curtains.

'I don't usually get up so early,' she said, as though she'd eavesdropped on my thoughts. 'It's just ... I don't always sleep that well.'

I'd guessed enough about her life by that point that I didn't need to ask why.

'We shouldn't be smoking these, you know,' I said, peering at the lit end of my cigarette. I took another puff and exhaled towards the sky: the only cloud in what was so far an unblemished sea of blue.

'I know,' Elsie said. 'I don't do it very often. Only when I can get hold of them.'

I did my best to keep my frown sisterly. 'You didn't seem to have much trouble the last time I saw you,' I said. I'd already noted, though, that Elsie and I were smoking Silk Cuts. At Mr Hirani's she'd bought Benson & Hedges.

'Those weren't for me,' Elsie answered.

'They were for ... your mum?' I tested. 'Your dad?'

'My mother died when I was two,' Elsie stated matter-of-factly. 'The cigarettes were for my father.'

I waited but she didn't add anything more.

'So your own supply ...' I prompted. 'I mean, no offence, Elsie, but you don't exactly look eighteen.'

She did take offence, I think, briefly. But then she gave a guilty little shrug.

'I get other people to buy them for me.'

'Friends, you mean?'

She shook her head, at the concept it seemed to me

as much as at my suggestion. 'Strangers, mostly. Older kids. Some just laugh, some say they'll do it if I give them half. Others . . . I guess they take pity. I don't like that they do, but at least then I get a full pack of twenty.'

She inhaled with her lips in a pout, then exhaled before the smoke could have reached her lungs. Good for her, I remember thinking, as I sucked my own smoke practically to my stomach.

'I saw you,' Elsie said, from out of nowhere and in a tone that suggested she was attempting a confession. 'I wasn't prying,' she added hastily. 'It's just . . . our houses, they're right across from one another. Out back, I mean. Ours is the one with the dirty windows.'

I'd already identified the house Elsie lived in – I'd picked it out from our spare-bedroom window the day I'd followed her home from Mr Hirani's – but even if I hadn't I would have known which house she was referring to. It wasn't just the windows that were dirty. The back garden, which was mainly concrete, was more junkyard than usable outside space.

'You were dancing,' Elsie said. 'You and . . . your boyfriend?'

I smiled, nodded. 'Jack,' I said. 'His name's Jack.' As for the dancing, she must have been watching us the day we'd played those records. The day Jack found what he found up in the attic.

'You looked happy,' Elsie said. 'It was nice.'

73

Again I smiled. 'I'm not sure I'd call what we were doing dancing.' I remembered twirling Maria-like to *The Sound of Music*, mock waltzing with Jack to *2001*.

Elsie smiled then, like secretly she agreed but didn't want to be rude.

'You should come over,' I told her, turning abruptly on my swing. 'The previous owner, he left this huge stack of records. You're too young to remember half the movies probably but there's a record player and space on the rug and Jack . . . Jack's brilliant. If nothing else I guarantee he'll make you laugh.'

Elsie was already shaking her head. 'I can't,' she said. 'He won't let me.'

There was the same finality to her tone I'd noticed the only other time she'd alluded to her father. What might I have said to her right then, I wonder? How would things have turned out differently if I'd been braver?

I had an idea.

'Have you got a torch?' I said to Elsie.

'What?'

'A torch. You know.' I mimed clicking on a button.

Elsie shrugged. 'I don't know. I guess. Why?'

'Do you know Morse code?'

'Who?'

'Morse code. It's like a language. Like . . . dots and dashes.'

Elsie tucked her chin against her neck. 'I don't think so. Should I?'

74

'Probably not,' I said. 'But it doesn't matter. I don't actually know Morse code either.'

Jack found me that night sitting in the dark beside the spare-bedroom window. I had my dressing gown across my knees and a cup of cold coffee on the floor beside me. My torch was in my lap, temporarily idle.

'Syd? Are you in here?'

The flashes from across the way seemed to have ceased, so I picked up my torch again and echoed Elsie's pattern. She'd drawn a flower, from what I could tell. I made mine taller, with four large petals, and then made a jagged, flighty motion that was supposed to represent a bumblebee.

'Syd? What are you doing?' Jack moved hesitantly towards me. He looked at me and then out of the window, where Elsie was responding with a great big tick. As big as she could manage, anyway. I was using the whole expanse of glass. Elsie's communication was more confined, as though she were beaming out her messages hidden beneath her duvet.

'Just chatting,' I said to Jack. I smiled up at him and he half-smiled back.

'Well . . . will you be long? It's almost midnight.'

'God, really?' I checked my watch. 'OK, OK, just one more. Last one, I promise.'

Fortunately it was my turn to draw first. I turned on my torch and swept the light from one corner of the window to the other. I covered the beam, then made the same motion across the glass starting this time from the opposite side – so that the light, as Elsie would have seen it, formed a cross. A moment passed and then Elsie signalled back with the same pattern.

'An "X"?' said Jack. 'What does that mean?'

I looked at him but he really didn't know.

'Just saying goodnight,' I told him. And then I rose and kissed him on the cheek.

Jack

I'd never been to Evan's office before. Whenever we'd met previously, we'd arranged to get together at the house, so I was surprised first off by how shabby it was. I'd become accustomed to gleaming glass; to fridges stacked with bottles of sparkling water and arrays of HD television screens. Evan Cohen's premises looked more like the estate agencies I remembered passing on the scruffy side streets of my home town. There was a window displaying the various properties up for sale, but the details had been stuck on with Blu-Tack in loose, misaligned rows. Most had yellowed. Only very few had been labelled as 'sold'. The display more than anything suggested the building was no longer in use. If my eye hadn't caught on the peeling gold lettering still clinging to the glass-panelled door, I would almost certainly have walked straight past.

The entrance was locked, but I noticed movement in the shadows through the window so I tapped a knuckle timidly against the glass.

'Hello? Is anyone in there?' I saw movement again, and then an outline, and then the door was opening wide.

Evan was fat in the way rugby players are fat: like

you could tell he was overweight, but there probably wasn't much of him that would wobble. He wore a suit, which like mine had seen better days. It was hard to judge how old he was. Whenever I'd met him previously he'd acted my age, but to me he'd always looked much older. Early forties at least. There was grey spreading from his temples and a smoker's crimp to his pale-green eyes.

'Yes?'

'Er . . . hi,' I said, and I waited for him to recognize me. He didn't, clearly, but he'd twigged by now that I was expecting him to.

'Evan? It's Jack. Jack Walsh? You sold us the house on –'

'Jack!' One of his arms had been barricading the open door. I wasn't sure if it was my imagination, but I thought I noticed him hesitate slightly before letting it fall. 'Come in, come in,' he said, suddenly effusive, and he grinned at me as he gestured me inside. It was a salesman's grin, though: one that died before it reached his eyes.

'I hope I'm not interrupting anything.'

'Not at all, not at all. What can I do for you? I must say I'm surprised to see you. I thought you'd be busy spending all that money you must have earned on eBay.'

He'd cracked some version of this joke every time we'd spoken since the morning we made the offer on the house. *No need to worry about that mortgage, Jack. You'll be covering the repayments purely from the money you'll be raking in on eBay.* Or, *I've got two words for you, Jacky-boy: eBay. Stick all this rubbish online and before you know it you'll be better off than when you started.*

I trailed him into his dimly lit offices, stepping over junk mail and free sheets on the way. It was late morning on a weekday. I'd only stopped by myself on the journey between appointments for work. Business hours then, and yet Evan Cohen Estate Agents Ltd had decidedly shut up shop.

'Are you moving premises or something?' I asked.

Evan hesitated for half a second before answering. 'Exactly,' he said, 'that's it exactly. Moving premises,' he echoed, as though it was a phrase he'd decided he liked the sound of. From the look of things he'd been seated at one of the desks when I'd disturbed him. His jacket was slung carelessly over the chair back and there was a copy of the *Racing Post* splayed on the surface, annotated here and there in blue biro. 'So. Jack.' He settled on the desk's corner. 'You're not thinking of selling up already, I hope?'

'No, no plans on selling,' I told him. 'To be honest we've barely moved in. I was just . . . I was hoping you could give me some information.'

'Information?' Evan repeated, looking slightly wary. Because information was something he couldn't charge for, I assumed, and what estate agent do you know who willingly gives anything away for free? 'What kind of information?'

'Just, you know – about the house.'

In truth I wasn't sure what exactly I'd come for. Since finding that box, and since that night I'd chased my shadow around the house, all I knew was that something about our new home didn't feel right. I'd even started wondering again about the story we'd been told about the previous owner. A man in his sixties meets a woman over the Internet and, through the power of Skype, they fall in love. Maybe, at a stretch, I could believe that part. But that he would then give up everything to run off and be with her? Without the two of them ever having met? Call me a cynic (Syd has), but personally I just couldn't see it. I mean, who does that? It was like *Cocoon* meets *You've Got Mail*, and about as plausible to my mind as either one.

'Like . . . about the man who owned the house before us,' I said. 'Patrick Winters? I was hoping you could tell me something about him.'

Evan smiled then, as though it wasn't the query he was expecting. 'What is it about Winters you want to know?'

'Well, just for starters . . . that story you told us about him leaving. Was it true?'

Evan's smile slipped halfway to a frown. 'Hey. I didn't lie to you, buddy.'

'No, I know, that's not what I meant. What I meant was, did you *believe* it was true? I mean, it's kind of weird, don't you think? Especially . . . you know. Considering his age and everything.'

Those photos on the landing were mainly of Winters, I'd worked out. He'd had dark hair in his younger years, but at some point around his early forties it had fairly swiftly bleached itself white. In the most recent images Winters looked decidedly older than his sixty-something years. He was still tall, but hunched, and had at some point acquired a walking cane. Not your typical inhabitant of the world of online dating, is all I'm saying.

Evan allowed himself another grin, his indignation for the time being set aside. 'Haven't you heard, Jacky-boy? Sixty's the new forty. And most of these pensioners know their way around the Internet better than your average ten-year-old.' His grin became a conspiratorial leer. 'Twenty quid says Winters could get his hands on the good stuff before you or I could finish googling "hard core".'

He winked then and I thought of Syd. She hates it when blokes wink. She thinks it makes us look slimy, and in Evan's case I could hardly have disagreed. The previous times I'd met Evan I'd actually quite liked him. Syd had never much cared for him, and it was beginning to dawn on me that she'd been a far better judge of his character than I'd proved.

'All I'm saying is we can't begrudge the guy,' he went on. 'He's all alone. He's sitting on a pile of bricks worth more money than he's earned in his entire life-time. Why *not* take a chance with a bit of stuff he takes a fancy to in some chat room?' He laughed then, an invitation for me to laugh with him. 'No disrespect or anything, but blokes like Winters have to take it where they can get it. It's either that or pay for it. Right? And why pay when you can get it for free?'

I knew exactly how Syd would have answered that. She would have called Evan an oily, misogynistic creep, and perhaps also pointed out that it was attitudes to women like his that had kept our society rooted in the dark ages and political power in the hands of the privileged, penis-wielding few. Me, however: I just smiled.

'Hey,' Evan said, 'if you're worried the deal you got was too good to be true – don't be. You got a break, that's all. And it's not as though Winters didn't come out of it all right.'

This time I shifted uncomfortably. I'd known all along that Syd and I had got the house for less than we should have, and though I'd been elated about that initially, lately I'd mainly felt guilt. Partly that was to do with work. I spent my days fighting a system that was skewed, and it didn't seem right that I should be celebrating just because it happened to have skewed itself for once in my favour. But that wasn't all. There was something else that was nagging at me – something which at that stage was just a feeling, but was underpinning my unease even so.

I changed the subject. 'What about family? Did Winters have any, do you know? Like, children for example?'

I was thinking about that box again. There were signs among those photos on the landing that Winters had had relatives with kids, but no indications he'd had any himself. There was nothing to suggest he'd even been married.

'Not that I know of,' Evan said, shrugging. 'But don't take that as gospel. I only ever actually met the bloke twice.'

But what he told me tallied with what some of our neighbours had said, too. I'd asked around, you see. Just casually, and couched in more general queries about how well they'd known Winters, but nobody remembered seeing Winters other than on his own. He kept himself to himself, was the prevailing response. Which is what neighbours always say, right? *He seemed harmless enough, always kept himself to himself.* Even – perhaps especially – if the person in question has just murdered his entire family with an axe.

'What about the house itself?' I asked Evan. 'When you were there, did anything ever strike you as . . . Well. As odd, I suppose. Like . . .' spooky, creepy, scary '. . . unusual,' is what I settled on.

Evan appeared bemused at first, then slowly it seemed to dawn on him what I meant. 'What's the matter, Jacky-boy? All those stuffed animals keeping you awake at night?'

I didn't bother explaining that Winters's birds, if nothing else of his, had been disposed of. Besides,

Evan was more on the money than he realized, and I couldn't help but flush.

'No, it's just . . . never mind,' I said, shying from Evan's grin. 'Look, I . . . I don't suppose Winters left a forwarding address or anything, did he? A mobile number or something you could let me have?'

Evan sucked air through his teeth. 'Sorry, buddy. I couldn't give you that type of information without the vendor's permission. Even us estate agents have got a code of practice.' He said this as though with another wink.

'Right,' I said. 'Well. Thanks anyway.' I didn't know what more I could ask.

'Hey, no problemo.' Evan rocked on to his feet. 'If there's anything else that starts bugging you, just give me a shout. You know where to find me.' He was smiling broadly now and offering his hand. I had no choice other than to take it.

'Thanks,' I said again, 'I will,' even though I had no intention at that point of ever bothering Evan Cohen again. I did go back, of course. Later. But when I did the offices were boarded up and Evan was already long gone.

I found him anyway. Patrick Winters. Through a database of council-tax records we had access to at work. The landline on file was one that had been disconnected, but there was an email address, and when I wrote to him explaining who I was, he replied within a couple of days. He even agreed to speak to me. He was living in Perth, it turned out, on the western coast of Australia, so when I called the number he'd given me at 9 a.m. my time it would have been early evening his. He didn't sound sixty. He sounded like he had more energy than me. Which I suppose should have been my first clue, because the dating thing, the story I'd been told about him leaving – it checked out. Every bit of it.

I was on a work phone so I couldn't speak to him for very long. But Winters was utterly convincing. The new-found love of his life was a woman called Sheila, he told me, which Winters thought was hilarious (an Australian woman called Sheila. Geddit? He was contemplating changing his name to Bruce). The only regret he had about leaving England, he said, was that he hadn't done it sooner. No, he didn't need or want any of his stuff. He was just sorry to have inflicted it all on me. A cat? No, he'd never owned a cat. What kind of box? He didn't have a clue what I was talking about. Bin it, he suggested; bin it all. I had no idea, he told me, how liberating it felt to escape that feeling of 'stuffocation'. Everything he owned now he could have fitted in a single suitcase, he said, and out there he got by with even less. A toothbrush, some flip-flops, a pair of Speedos: that was all he really needed these days. Which, setting aside the mental image his pronouncement gave rise to, I actually found somewhat inspiring. For half a dozen wistful seconds, I was almost tempted to follow his lead.

It was only as we were wrapping things up that Winters said something that brought me forward in my chair. I thanked him for his time, and then again – almost as an afterthought – for having picked me and Syd as buyers. But he turned that around, insisted he was the one who should have been thanking us. Who'd have thought, he said, that selling a house during a property boom would have proved so problematic? He was just grateful we'd come along and made an offer, because if we hadn't there was no telling how long the process might have taken.

He hung up the phone then, and I was left staring at the receiver. Because there it was: the source of the unease I'd been struggling with before. Just lucky, I guess, Evan had told us, when Syd and I had expressed our surprise that the bid we'd made for the house had been accepted. But it wasn't simply down to luck. It couldn't have been, not given what Winters had just told me, and when I knew for a fact that at the open day there'd been people falling over one another to submit their offers. It was as I'd suspected: there was some other reason the house had come to us. And if that was the case, I had to wonder about something else as well. The debt we owed. Me and Syd. Because if my father had taught me anything, it was that real bargains are few and far between. Everything worth having has a price attached. It's just a question of how and when you're made to pay.

Jack

I almost said something. To Syd, I mean. I wanted to. The problem was, nothing I'd discovered amounted to anything tangible, and I couldn't think of a way of telling Syd that wouldn't make it sound like I was jumping at shadows.

The closest I came was one evening when we were curled up together in the living room. It was the home-liest room in the house, mostly due to all the books Winters had left behind on the bookshelves, which themselves covered almost an entire wall. The heavy curtains were drawn and the sidelights were on, and the TV was babbling in the corner. I can't recall exactly what we were watching. Some BBC2 comedy, I think, like a quiz programme or something, which normally would have had me chuckling at the very least. Not that night, though. That night Syd could have flipped over to one of those trashy American makeover shows she loves so much and I probably wouldn't even have noticed.

'Syd . . .' I started to say.

She was nestled against me, her shoulders enfolded by my arm, and her left hand linked loosely to my right. She didn't answer and I angled my head so I could see her.

'Syd?'

She blinked and moved her eyes from the television screen towards mine. 'Huh?'

It was only at that point that I realized Syd hadn't been laughing at the comedy programme either. 'Hey. Are you OK?'

'Sorry,' she said. 'I was just . . . I'd zoned out, that's all.' She smiled at me weakly.

'Is something on your mind?' I asked her, my own preoccupations temporarily forgotten.

I felt her shoulder rise briefly into my armpit. 'Just thinking about a friend of mine, that's all. She's . . . having a bit of trouble.'

I lifted our joined hands towards my lips and kissed Syd's knuckles. 'Want to talk about it?'

She considered for a moment, then shook her head. 'That's OK. To be honest I'm not sure what exactly there is to say.'

A corner of my mouth, at that, gave a little twitch. For a few long seconds we both stared vacantly across the living room, our minds adrift amid our thoughts.

I shuffled upright.

'We should look at paint charts,' I declared.

Syd responded with a flummoxed laugh. 'Paint charts?'

I extricated myself from Syd's warmth and leaned to gather up the stack of brochures that had made their way on to the shelf beneath Patrick Winters's old coffee table. Crown, Dulux, Farrow & Ball – the last of which Syd had picked up from one of the aisles in the DIY store in spite of my outraged protestations. ('Fifty shades of sludge,' I judged. 'And fifty quid a can, too. Whoever pays that for a tin of paint is going straight to hell.')

'Here.' I tossed two of the brochures into Syd's lap, opened one of the others in mine. 'I reckon it's about time we did something to make this place feel more like home. I mean, so far all we've done is shift stuff in and out of boxes.'

Once again Syd laughed, surprised by my sudden enthusiasm. The last time either one of us had so much as mentioned DIY was the week before we'd moved in. We'd been raring to go at that stage, before the move itself had sapped our energies. And in the end we'd been put off as well by the enormity of the task we'd suddenly been faced with. Possibly if the house had been empty we would at some point have made a start, but with so much still to clear we'd willingly allowed ourselves to become distracted. And it occurred to me that maybe that accounted for the unease I'd been feeling lately as well. Maybe all I was doing was subconsciously manufacturing a reason to avoid committing emotionally to the house, in order that I could put off picking up a paintbrush for as long as possible.

'So which room are we going to tackle first?' Syd asked, fanning the pages of one of her brochures.

'Let's do it the other way around,' I said. 'Let's pick colours we like, then decide after that where we're going to put them.'

'Got one,' Syd announced, virtually the instant I'd finished speaking. 'Raspberry Bellini.'

I looked where she was pointing. 'Purple?'

'I'd say it was closer to red. And anyway I wasn't looking at the colour. It's the alcoholic content that interests me.'

'Here, then: Appletini. Or this one: Tequila Sunrise.'

Syd made a face, shuddered. 'Tequila. Yuck.'

I'd forgotten about Syd's relationship with tequila. They'd been close, once, until one night at a mutual friend's twenty-fifth birthday party they'd abruptly – and rather messily – fallen out.

For a moment or two we sat in silence, flicking pages.

'Do people get paid to think up these names, do you think?' Syd asked.

'I think you'll find it's a highly specialized role,' I replied. 'Six years' training, another three in an apprenticeship writing greetings cards . . . and anyway you're supposed to be looking at the colours. Here, what about this for our bedroom?' I was pointing to a shade of red that in a bedroom would have been practically indecent.

'Classy. Maybe we could put a mirror on the ceiling while we're at it.'

I raised my eyebrows like that wasn't such a bad idea and earned a jab from Syd's elbow into my stomach.

'Seriously, Jack, this is making me hungry. Lemon Meringue Pie,' Syd quoted. 'Apple Cobbler. Millionaire's Fudge Delight. Which is brown to you and me, in case you're wondering.'

I gave a snort – half at what Syd was saying, half at one of the names on the page in front of me. 'Forget hungry. It's making me horny. Subtle Touch,' I read aloud. 'Velvet Glove. And, ha, Golden Spray.' The adolescent in me sniggered. The adult, too.

Syd, beside me, couldn't stop herself smiling. 'I've got one,' she said. 'Salty Whip.'

I giggled again and bobbed my head appreciatively, then after a second held up a hand. 'Ladies and gentlemen, we have a winner.' I pointed and angled the brochure so Syd could see.

'Electric Banana,' she read, smiling.

I grinned and moved the brochure so I could look again. 'I think my mum has one of those hidden in her sock drawer.'

'Jack Walsh!' Syd declared, in mock outrage, and this time her elbow was sharp enough to puncture me of air. I feigned being winded, which only encouraged Syd to tickle me, and we started scuffling until somehow we ended up horizontal. Syd was still giggling as I kissed her.

'You weren't kidding about feeling horny,' she said.

I grinned down at her. 'Who'd have thought?' I answered. 'Paint-chart porn.' And this time Syd was the one to kiss me.

Afterwards we were lying there on the sofa. I'd tugged my hoodie across us as a makeshift blanket, though the evening was warm enough that we didn't really need it.

'Jack?' Syd ventured, sleepily.

'Mm?'

'You started to say something. Didn't you? Earlier. Before you got . . . distracted.'

I looked and saw she'd parted one eye. There was a gleam clearly visible through the gap.

'Before you distracted me, you mean,' I corrected her, and traced my fingertips along her bare spine.

Her eye shuttered again and I watched her smile.

'Well?' she whispered.

'Well what?' I mumbled back.

'What was it you were going to say?'

The hand I was stroking her with paused . . . but only for an instant.

'It doesn't matter,' I said, and I shuffled a little lower on the sofa. Because at that moment, it didn't. Just lying there like that, holding Syd and being held by her . . . I could almost have forgotten what it was I'd been so worried about.

Sydney

It lasted a week. Me and Elsie. Our night-time chats.

I can't remember how exactly but we'd progressed from drawing pictures to playing games. We'd tried hangman, which worked so long as we kept the words short. The problem was, most of the three- and four-letter words I knew weren't suitable for a thirteen-year-old's consumption. I didn't doubt Elsie knew just as many swear words as I did but I didn't want to be responsible for her developing a vocabulary as degenerate as mine, and when she guessed 'tit' before I'd even confirmed any individual letters I had to draw a line. (Literally, even though I was laughing as I did it.)

After hangman we tried a contest where one person would blink their torch in a particular pattern (short flash, long, short short, long, looooong: you get the idea) and the other person would have to remember it and copy it. I flashed the beats from my favourite songs when it was my turn ('Rid of Me' by PJ Harvey, 'The Fear' by Lily Allen, 'Imagine' by do I really have to tell you?) and though there was no way I could be certain, I was fairly sure Elsie was doing the same. I tried not to think about the fact that Elsie would almost certainly never have heard of any of the tunes I'd chosen, just as I would no doubt never have recognized hers.

Eventually we settled mainly on playing noughts and crosses, which sounds dull I expect but was actually hilarious. Normally with noughts and crosses no one ever wins, which somehow seems to be the entire point. In our version it was a challenge just to fill the board. Not only did you have to remember where you'd placed your marks, you also had to remember where the blanks were, and which spaces the other person had already taken. Usually the games we played would end with one or other of us making a mistake and the other person winking out their laughter. Whenever anyone did win it was usually Elsie – at first, I thought, because I was letting her, although it turned out she was the one going easy on me.

So that's what we were doing when it happened. We were halfway through another game and it was Elsie's turn to place her mark. (I was occupying the top two corners. On Elsie's only go so far she'd put her blob right in the centre.) All of a sudden her torch beam started dancing. I thought at first she was scrubbing away the game and I pictured her laughing in frustration. But the dancing went on for far too long. Six, seven seconds maybe? And then abruptly the light went off. In its place I saw a shadow – an outline darker in the middle of the windowpane than the blackness all around it. Too big to have been Elsie.

About the right size for her father. He was looking out, I realized. Searching. And although I'd meant to turn it off, my own torch was glowing guiltily in my lap.

I fumbled for the switch to kill the beam but I knew I was already too late. The shadow withdrew from Elsie's window and the only thing in the darkness left watching me was a thin and fragile-looking moon.

Jack

I keep thinking this is like trying to do a jigsaw, one where the pieces are all jumbled up and you don't even know if they're all part of the same puzzle. Or a dot to dot. One of the hard ones. Where everything seems to follow in sequence, but no matter how many times you add a line you still can't guess the final picture. And actually that's the most frightening thing about it: not knowing how what's been happening connects to what.

Take Elsie. My instinct is to talk about the house, about what we found there – about all the things that have happened to us since. But maybe I'm getting it all back to front. Maybe Syd's clearer on this than I am. I mean, maybe she's only writing about Elsie because she feels she has to, but that doesn't mean she hasn't got the right idea.

I was minding my own business. It was, what? Nine thirty or so on a Sunday morning? I was up early because I'd stayed out late, and I can never sleep after I've been drinking. Partly it's the alcohol. Mainly it's the worry that at some point over the course of the evening I've made a fool of myself. Which I'm pretty sure I hardly ever do, but it's why me and alcohol have a lukewarm relationship at best. This isn't a criticism, but there's no way I could drink as much as Syd does, for example. I just wouldn't feel confident I'd be able to stay in control.

But anyway, Syd and I had been out with Bart and four or five others. Nothing extravagant. Just to a bar in Borough Market. It had been my idea – another attempt, like with the paint charts, to put the unease I'd been feeling behind us. A sort of house-warming without the house, if you like. We'd been meaning to have a proper party, and this was our way of celebrating until we'd made enough progress with the decorating to be able to invite people over.

When I'd woken up that morning I'd left Syd face down between our pillows. My plan was to be back before she woke up, the coffee brewed and the bacon frying, and the newspaper laid out on the kitchen table. I like the reviews section. Syd likes the sport. She doesn't follow any team in particular, but she enjoys the psychology of it all. The mind games. Plus, if you ask me, she's not averse to a picture or two of Roger Federer wearing shorts.

I was just coming out of the shop when I saw him. Not Roger Federer. This bloke, he reminded me a bit of John Malkovich, in that film where he's trying to kill the president. He was shorter than John Malkovich though, and broader. He was bald the way people used to be, before they discovered they'd look better with a grade one. He didn't have a comb-over or anything, but his hair was thick around his ears, in contrast to what was missing on top. I thought at first that he was smiling, which is why I didn't stop when I saw him coming towards me. I assumed he'd mistaken me for someone he knew. Then, when he didn't look away, I got paranoid, and my first thought was that I'd left the house wearing my slippers. The lack of sleep had made me groggy and quite honestly I wouldn't have put it past me. So I looked down, just in case. I had my trainers on, which was a relief, so I looked up again – and that's when he grabbed me by the throat.

I dropped the newspaper, the thin blue carrier bag I was holding too, and all I could think about initially were the eggs I'd bought to go with the bacon; that probably if we were going to eat them still, we were going to have to eat them scrambled.

'Morning, neighbour,' said John Malkovich, and he drove me against the wall of Mr Hirani's shop.

I couldn't respond because he had his hand around my windpipe. Also because, quite honestly, I had no idea what to say.

'Stay away from her,' my assailant hissed. 'You, your bitch girlfriend: you stay away from my daughter. Do you understand me?'

I didn't. I didn't have a clue who or what he was talking about.

'I said, *do you understand*?' he said again, and this time he loosened his grip enough for me to answer.

'Who . . . who are you?' I gasped.

His knee came up into my groin. 'Ask your missus,' I heard him say, just before I collapsed on to the pavement.

Syd was already up when I got home. She was hunched over a cup of tea at the kitchen table.

'I just got bloody assaulted,' I told her as I limped into the room.

She must have assumed I was talking in metaphors. 'I know how you feel,' she said, squeezing her forehead into a frown. 'The wine they serve at that place comes in buckets. Remind me next time to stick to halves of lager.'

I dropped the carrier bag into the sink and tossed the newspaper straight into the recycling. 'I mean it, Syd. I just got assaulted. Some . . . nutter . . . he just . . . he grabbed my throat and then kneed me in the bollocks. Right outside Mr Hirani's shop.'

Syd's brain was stuck in sleep mode. I'd got her attention, but she was clearly struggling to process what she'd just heard.

'I'm calling the police,' I announced.

'What? Jack, wait.'

I carried on looking for my mobile.

'Jack! Stop a minute. Are you OK? What . . . I mean, who . . .' I sensed rather than saw her shake her head. 'Jack, please. Stand still and tell me what happened.'

'I told you what happened!'

'But . . . are you OK?'

'Yes, I'm OK. OK? I'm fan-bloody-tastic. *Where the hell is my phone?*'

It wasn't on the side where it usually lived and it wasn't plugged into the charger. I better not have lost it, I was thinking. Please don't tell me I've lost it. On top of everything else, that would be just bloody –

'It's here. Jack? Your phone's here.' Syd was wiggling my iPhone in the air. 'It was on the floor by your jeans so I brought it in for you.'

'Thanks,' I growled, and held out my palm.

Syd withdrew the phone just a fraction.

'Jack, please. Just explain, will you?'

I pressed my lips together and exhaled through my nose. I explained, one more time. It didn't take much longer than it had the first time.

'But why would anyone do that to you?' Syd said. 'Did they take anything? Your wallet or . . .'

'No, he didn't take anything. He didn't even look. He just . . . he said something about his daughter, that was all. Syd, please, I –'

'His daughter? What about his daughter?'

I had my phone in my hand now. There was a text from Bart, which I noticed with a flash of irritation he'd also sent to Syd (*hola amigos! how r the heads?*), and a missed call I knew I would have to deal with later, but I was concentrating for the time being on bringing up the keypad.

'Jack? What about his daughter?'

Syd lay her fingers across mine, stopping me from seeing the screen on my phone, and I raised my head to protest. But then it came back to me. The things the psycho who'd attacked me had said. I'd been focused before on what he'd done. 'He told me to stay away from her. And he said to speak to you. To my *missus.*' I let the hand that was holding my phone drop to my side. 'What's going on, Syd?'

Syd turned to look out of the window. She got up and closed the venetian blind.

'Syd?' I repeated. 'Is this something to do with that girl you've been hanging around with? Elsie, is it? The one who lives across the way?'

'I'm guessing,' Syd said. 'This bloke, what did he look like?'

I told her and this time Syd nodded.

'I've only seen him from a distance but I'd say that sounds like Elsie's father.'

'But why would he . . . I mean, I thought Elsie was just . . . that you and she were only . . .'

What had I thought exactly? I'd known Syd had smoked cigarettes with this girl while she'd been out running – although in retrospect, when Syd had told me, I'd perhaps focused more on the fact Syd had smoked again than on what she'd been doing talking to Elsie in the first place. I'd known as well that every night that past week Syd had been sitting at the spare-bedroom window messing about with some made-up version of Morse code. But I'd thought she was just . . . I don't know. Keeping a lonely girl company. Pretending like she was thirteen again and enacting lost scenes from her childhood. It hadn't crossed my mind that Syd might have been doing anything that would get anyone in trouble.

'Did anyone see?' Syd asked me, interrupting my train of thought.

'See what?'

'When he grabbed you. Elsie's father. Did anyone see?'

'No. I don't know. I mean, it's Sunday. Nobody else is even up yet.'

'What about Mr Hirani?'

'I don't know,' I said again. 'I don't think so. He would have come out. Wouldn't he? But what difference does it make whether anyone saw? It doesn't change what happened.'

'You can't call the police, Jack.'

'What?'

'Jack, please. You can't call the police.'

'Of course I'm going to call the bloody police! Did you hear what I just told you? He grabbed me by the throat. I thought I was going to pass out.'

'If there weren't any witnesses, he'll just deny it. The police won't be able to do a thing. And Elsie, she . . . he'll take it out on her, Jack. She'll be the one who pays.'

'Who *pays*?' I echoed. 'What do you mean?'

Syd took a breath. She looked again at the closed

slats of the kitchen blind, then back at me. 'He's hurting her, Jack.'

My mouth opened then closed again. 'Hurting her?' I finally said. 'Like . . .'

'Like beating her. Hitting her. *Hurting* her.'

'But . . . are you sure? Why didn't you tell me?'

Syd shook her head. 'Because I wasn't sure, for one thing. I mean I was but I didn't have any proof. And just lately you've seemed . . . distracted. Worried. I didn't want to have to get you involved until I'd worked out what to do.'

My irritation with myself manifested in a sigh. These past few weeks I'd got worked up over things that for all I knew had been solely in my imagination, and all the time Syd had been struggling with *this*. Not just Syd. Poor Elsie, too.

'The friend you mentioned the other night,' I said. 'The one you told me was in trouble. You meant Elsie. Right?'

Reluctantly it seemed, as though she knew I would be blaming myself, Syd nodded.

'I'm sorry, Syd. I should have asked. I just . . . I've been preoccupied, I guess, like you say, and –'

Syd interrupted me by taking my hands. 'You did ask, Jack. Remember?'

'I know but –'

This time she silenced me with a kiss. 'All that matters now is what we do from here. And as much as I try I just can't come up with an answer.'

I frowned at that, pulled slightly away. 'Surely we've got no other choice. We call the police. We have to.'

Syd left her hands resting on mine, as though she was worried I was about to bring my phone back up to my ear.

'Please, Jack. Don't. There's a reason no one was there to witness it when he attacked you. And it's the same thing at home. If he's careful enough to hurt you without anyone seeing, he'll be careful enough to cover his tracks with Elsie too.'

I sighed again and slid my phone on to the table.

'So . . . what? He gets away with it? He attacks me in the middle of the street and I'm supposed to let him walk away?'

I knew the answer already, of course, even if I wasn't ready to accept it. Syd was just staring at me, as though she didn't like it any more than I did.

'What about . . . social services?' I said. 'I mean, forget about what just happened. I'm talking about your friend now. About Elsie. They can help her, Syd. I know exactly who to call.'

Syd was already shaking her head. 'They won't help.'

'They might, Syd.'

'They won't. They never do!'

Which was massively unfair, on the one hand, and I felt a certain sense of wounded professional pride. But on the other hand it was Syd talking and Syd had earned the right to be as critical of social services as she damn well pleased.

'Things are different now, Syd. Better. I've seen it for myself. I promise you.'

'But it's the same thing. Don't you see? Like with the police. Social services are going to want to see evidence. Any bruises Elsie's got, her father will explain away. And Elsie's not going to say anything. Trust me.'

'She might. Mightn't she? Given the opportunity.'

Once again Syd was shaking her head, in frustration now more than anything. 'I just . . . I don't know, Jack. I mean I barely know the first thing about her. About him. I know she needs help but I can't . . . I mean . . . it's not that simple. It's never that simple. I just don't want to make things worse for her.'

'But how would you have reacted? If, when you were Elsie's age, someone had come along and . . .'

'And what? People did come along, Jack. Plenty of fucking people *came along*.'

All at once Syd was glaring at me. I wanted to say something, but I didn't know what.

'Look, I'll talk to her,' Syd told me before I could apologize. 'OK? Before we do anything else, let me just talk to her first.'

It was a compromise and I wanted to accept it, but it wasn't like talking to Elsie didn't have its dangers, too.

'I'll be careful,' Syd assured me. 'Really, Jack. I know a place and . . . I'll be careful.' She smiled at me. 'I promise.'

Sydney

It was my eighth day waiting and as cold a morning in July as I could remember.

'Elsie?'

I'd been rotating glacially on the roundabout. I stood when I saw her, caught unawares by an onrush of relief. I'd been desperately trying not to think about what Elsie's father might have been putting her through as punishment for the friendship, unsanctioned, that she'd struck up with me. There were no obvious signs that she'd been hurt but when she saw me she turned the way she'd come.

'Elsie, wait!'

When I caught up with her it was back inside the tunnel. I reached out to try and grab her by the arm.

'Elsie, please. Just wait a moment.'

She shook her head, shook me off.

'I can't speak to you.' She was cradling her forearm where I'd grabbed for her, even though I'd barely made contact with her sleeve.

'Elsie, please. Of course you can. Or if you can't speak to me you can listen. Can't you? Just for a moment.'

She was terrified, I could see it. That prick, I remember thinking. That balding, bullying *prick*.

'What happened to your arm, Elsie?'

She let her hands drop to her sides. 'Nothing. Nothing happened. Just leave me alone.'

It was damp underfoot even though it hadn't been raining and the tunnel stank of beer cans and piss. I hardly noticed, though. I'm not sure how I'd expected Elsie to greet me but I know I hadn't prepared myself for this.

She tried walking away again. This time I moved around to block her exit.

'I want to help you, Elsie. Please let me help you. Everything you're going through: I've been through it too. I've been through it and . . .' *Worse*, I almost said. And I worry now that I actually believed it. I mean, how sodding arrogant is that?

I'd stopped myself from saying the word but Elsie caught the sense of what I was implying nonetheless.

'Screw you,' she said and even though I'd heard her swear before, I recoiled as though she'd reached out and slapped me. She brushed past me, openly clutching her arm now, and I was too stunned in that instant to try to stop her.

'Elsie, wait, I . . .'

She was only a pace or so from the tunnel's entrance. Almost in daylight . . . but then I called out and hauled her back into the dark.

'Don't let him win, Elsie. Don't let him turn you into a coward.'

My words echoed around the archway of the

tunnel. Elsie stopped and for a second, ten, twenty she stood perfectly still. I opened my mouth to say something more but a part of me I rarely ever listen to – a part of me I mostly never fucking hear – warned me I'd already said enough.

When Elsie turned she was crying. She looked so small all of a sudden. So lost and tired and defeated that for a moment I almost cried too.

'It's too late,' she said, shaking her head. 'I'm just so worried it's already too late.'

We found a bench overlooking the common not far from the play area. It wasn't raining, but it looked about to and the bench was under the cover of a sycamore tree. We were out of the wind as well, in a spot almost as secluded as in the tunnel.

'You should put some ice on it.'

Elsie considered me doubtfully. I was looking at her forearm. It was blotched with bruises – on the underside mainly, as though her arm had been raised when it had been damaged to cover her face.

'Ice for bruises,' I instructed, 'pressure for cuts. The odd painkiller can help sometimes too. Although . . . maybe stay off the pills if you can avoid them.'

'Cuts?' Elsie echoed. 'Your father used to cut you?'

'God, no.' I rolled up my own sleeve and showed her my scars. Other than Jack, I'd never willingly shown them to anyone. 'Cuts would have been too difficult for him to explain. These were entirely my own creation.'

I turned my arm to inspect it. I tried not to look at the scars at all and I always dressed in a way that covered them. In Elsie's presence I found myself considering them more objectively. Mostly my memory of how I'd suffered them was as messy as the marks themselves but a few – the most pronounced – I remembered vividly. When I'd got them, what I'd used. *Why.*

'They're on my legs too. Naked I look like a chopping board.'

It was a joke – not a very good one – but Elsie didn't find it funny. 'I bet that's not true. You're . . .' She looked at the ground. 'You're beautiful.'

Which in any other context would have been the funniest thing I'd ever heard. One thing I could never be accused of being is *beautiful.*

'See these?' I pointed to some dots amid the dashes: hard little nodules of shiny flesh, most still pink around the edges even after all these years. Fresh they'd looked like mini solar eclipses. Now they looked like the calloused remnants of some medieval pox. Even though I tended to conceal them, the scars from where I'd cut myself I didn't much mind. It seemed futile wasting energy resenting them when I'd inflicted them entirely on myself. Those other marks, though, I hated. If I could have I would have gouged them out. Once – one evening when I'd been particularly off my trolley on a cocktail of vodka and magic mushrooms – I'd even tried. 'These are cigarette burns,' I explained to Elsie. 'When he found out I was cutting myself he thought he'd join in the fun. Because at least these *look* like I could have done them to myself.'

Elsie was staring at the marks intensely. As I'd been talking I hadn't noticed how closely she was looking, but when I did I felt suddenly ashamed. I pulled down my sleeves, hooking the ends as I habitually did around my palms.

Elsie turned away from me. She was trying to lift up the back of her coat. I watched her, until I realized she was waiting for me to help.

'Do you see it?' she said.

'What am I looking for?' I answered as I gathered up the fabric. 'All I can see is . . . Jesus Christ, Elsie.'

And I'd thought my arms were a mess. The skin around Elsie's left shoulder blade was a silvery moonscape of scar tissue. There were lumps of knotted flesh around thin, shimmering valleys, so that the entire area formed a patchwork of crevices. It started at the midpoint of her spine and stretched to the base of her neck.

'He did that with a beer bottle.'

'Jesus Christ,' I said again. 'How did he manage to explain that?'

Elsie shrugged. The damaged skin didn't shift as it was supposed to. It held its shape, like something viscous trapped under cling film. 'He didn't have to.'

'He didn't take you to the hospital?'

'He treated it himself. Cleaned it, bandaged it, all

that. It was weird because even though it was him who'd done it, he acted afterwards like he really cared if I got better. Like he was sorry.' Elsie turned to try and get a view of the faded injury herself. 'I remember thinking that maybe what he'd done wasn't that bad. If it meant it was the last of it. You know? If it meant it wouldn't ever happen again.'

I did know, all too well. Not once did my father ever tell me he was sorry. But occasionally, after something bad had happened, I managed to convince myself that he *looked* sorry – and that maybe, deep down, he genuinely was. But that was all part of his game. Because that's what it was for my father: one big, hilarious fucking game.

'He was drunk when he did it,' Elsie was saying, as she wriggled her coat down so it covered her waist again. 'All the worst things happen when he's drunk. Except when he's *so* drunk he can't even stand up. You've probably seen him,' she went on. 'In the alley-way? Or heard him even. That's the way he walks home from the pub. I say walks. If he falls over on the way, knocks over someone's bin, that's when I know it's safe to go to sleep.'

I had indeed heard a clatter from the rear of the house once or twice and, now that I thought about it, always sometime around midnight. I'd assumed it was cats.

'What about your dad?' Elsie asked me, hesitantly.

I blinked. 'My dad?'

'You said . . . before. You said you'd been through it too.'

It was odd. I was trying to be the grown-up, to be open with Elsie so she'd open up to me, but every time the attention turned my way I had an urge to crawl back into that tunnel.

'My dad . . .' I began. 'He . . . he never drank, nothing like that. He didn't even have that as an excuse. And I don't think he ever *enjoyed* the things he did. The violence, I mean. Hurting me. I mean, he did but . . . it wasn't the point. He wanted to *control* me, that's all. That's the part he liked best.' My eyes met Elsie's and rebounded. 'It took me a while to realize that, mind you. At the time all I could think was that it was my fault. That he was only hurting me because of something I'd done.'

I watched Elsie from the corner of my eye and saw her gaze drop towards her knees.

'Mine enjoys it,' she said after a moment – and that was all.

We watched the clouds for a time. Rather than bringing rain the morning had brightened and sunlight filtered weakly through the branches of our sycamore. It didn't cheer me as it might have. It only reminded me how rapidly our time here was already starting to wane.

'So what happens now?' Elsie said into the silence, as though she'd been having similar thoughts herself.

'Now . . .' I echoed. I took a breath and exhaled it

slowly. 'Now, if you'll let me, I'll talk to Jack. He'll talk to some people he knows – some good people, Elsie – and then . . .' And then what? Quite honestly I had no idea. 'And then . . . they'll help you. They'll help put an end to it.'

'Is that how it happened with you?'

'I . . . in a manner of speaking,' I lied.

Elsie nodded, reassured. 'Was he punished? Your father. I hope he was punished.'

'He was,' I agreed, tentatively. 'Just for . . . other things.'

Elsie squinted at me through the sunlight. 'Other things?'

I adjusted the way I was sitting. That tunnel was beckoning again. 'It's complicated. But my father was bad in other ways too. He stole people's money. Slyly. Subtly. They found out what he was doing and he went to prison.'

'Like Al Capone,' Elsie declared.

'What?'

'Like Al Capone. I saw a documentary. He was like this massive gangster and in the end they couldn't get him for all the bad stuff he was doing so they arrested him for not paying his taxes.'

I had to smile, at the thought of Elsie watching documentaries as much as anything.

'So that's when you left?' she said. 'When he went to prison?'

I wiggled my head. 'More or less.'

'Do you think my father will go to prison?'

'Do you want him to?'

Elsie didn't answer right away. She turned and looked out across the common. 'Sometimes I hope he rots in there,' she said, with a steeliness to her tone that frightened me. But then it softened. 'Other times,' she went on, 'I just wish it could be like it was after he hurt me. That time all he was doing was looking after me.'

I wanted to hold her then, to wrap my arm around her narrow shoulders. It would have made me feel better . . . but it wouldn't have helped Elsie.

'You know why he was doing that, don't you?' I said to her, my voice even firmer than I'd meant it to be. 'Why he was so desperate for you to heal?'

She looked at me then almost pleadingly, the way she would have had she dared to show me her favourite toy but instead of admiring it I'd snatched it away. It took all of my self-control just to wait for her to answer.

'Because he didn't want to get in trouble,' said Elsie at last.

'Right,' I said. 'Because he was worried about himself. Not you, Elsie. He doesn't give a damn about you.'

Elsie dragged the heel of a palm across each of her eyes. 'I'm scared,' she said, so softly I almost didn't hear her.

This time I reached for her hand. I almost flinched, it was that cold.

'Do you know what?' I said. 'You remind me of the bravest person I ever knew.'

She looked across.

'My sister,' I told her. 'She was about your age the last time I saw her. She even looked like you, a little bit.'

My sister: two words I'd avoided uttering virtually since the day I'd left home. I'd told Jack about her, again when I was loaded and because I'd recognized that if I wanted to be with him I would have to. But Jack had been perceptive enough afterwards to know never to mention her unless I did, and I hadn't ever spoken about her again. To anyone. I only brought her up now, talking to Elsie, because I thought it would help. I genuinely thought it might help.

'Now my sister was beautiful,' I said. 'She was slight like you and had these cheekbones, and big brown eyes you couldn't look away from. They were just . . . they were bottomless.'

'What was her name?' Elsie asked me and I replied before the syllables could stick.

'Jessica.'

'Did you call her Jess?'

I laughed at that, unexpectedly. The laughter also brought a tear. 'Only if I was trying to annoy her. She hated it when anyone called her Jess. She said it made her sound like a cartoon cat.'

Elsie frowned.

'*Postman Pat*,' I explained. 'It . . . never mind. It was just a stupid TV show.'

I wiped my eyes the way Elsie had, hating myself for having fallen to pieces. For going back on a promise as well. I'd spent the best part of a decade crying about my sister. It was weak, and self-indulgent, and one day I simply decided it had to stop. It was the same with the drugs. I didn't *need* them, not chemically, not to the extent some people do. I'd just wanted them because, for a short while after I took them, they made things easier. I'd given up both – the crying, the coke – at exactly the same time: the same time as well that I'd got serious about my relationship with Jack.

Elsie seemed as surprised as I was that I was crying. 'What happened to her?' she asked me, once again in a voice that was barely a whisper.

It was obvious to us both that I didn't have to answer. Elsie wouldn't have been offended and Christ knows I'd already said enough. But somehow I didn't feel like I had any other option. That door I'd unbolted was open wide now, all the dark things inside tumbling out. And it was like I said before: it was something I felt Elsie needed to know. Like a parable. A lesson that would help her make her own choice.

And so I told her.

I told her and almost killed Elsie too.

Jack

Karen, she said her name was. Detective Inspector Karen Leigh. She was here today. This morning. It's Wednesday, and normally on a Wednesday I'd be at work. On any weekday, actually, but that's not the point. The point is Detective Inspector Karen Leigh called by 'just on the off chance' she'd find me in, when under normal circumstances there was no way she would have. Which means she knew exactly where to find me. Which means she would have had to ask around. Which means . . .

Shit.

I don't know what it means.

Maybe it means I'm just being paranoid. But there's that line, isn't there, that thing people say, about how just because you're paranoid it doesn't mean no one's out to get you. Something like that. The first part, the *just because you're paranoid*, it's been running round and round my head today like a song that's snagged. It's tuneless, though, more like a taunt. And for some reason – a reason, actually, I can guess – the voice taunting me belongs to a little girl.

Just because you're paranoid . . .

But the police.

They asked about everything. Literally: everything. It's as though they've been thinking along the same lines Syd has, except somehow they've reached a different conclusion. Or the same conclusion, actually, if you think about it. Which is nuts. It's just . . . I mean . . . it's totally nuts.

But I don't think I helped myself. I opened the door and right away I was on the back foot. This probably sounds stupid, but part of the problem I think was that I wasn't doing what I was supposed to be doing when they knocked. I was supposed to be finishing up some paperwork, but instead what I was doing was watching *Murder, She Wrote*. Just, you know, to take my mind off things (probably not the best choice, I realize), and only for the past five or ten minutes, but even so it felt like I'd been collared in the act.

'Mr Walsh? Jack Walsh? I'm Karen. Detective Inspector Karen Leigh, but Karen's fine. This here is my colleague, DC Granger. Don't mind him. He looks like a thug, but really he's a pussy cat. Normally I don't bring him along when I'm interviewing witnesses, mostly I save him for the suspects, but the problem at the moment is we're struggling to find any.' A smile then, half a breath's worth, before: 'May we come in?'

It was like being assailed by a Jehovah's Witness. I mean, I'd barely opened the door and already I felt like I'd been beaten into submission. So what could I do? I couldn't say no. Who says no to the police when they haven't done anything wrong? Or maybe that's the only time anyone says no. Maybe by letting them inside without even double-checking why they were here (like I really had to ask) all I was doing was confirming their suspicions. Assuming they even had any suspicions at that point, and that it wasn't only after I'd spoken to them that –

Jesus, Jack. Get a grip.

What was it Syd said? *Think yoga.* Which doesn't actually help me at all, because when I think yoga the only thing that comes to mind is middle-aged women in leotards.

Sorry. Sorry. Now I'm rambling. I tend to do that when I'm nervous. Which is part of the reason I came off so badly after talking to the police.

So I asked them in.

I didn't ask them in. I let them in.

And then, when I'd let them in, I offered them tea. Just, I don't know. Just because that's what my mother would have done. And the guy – the detective constable or whatever – he declined, but call-me-Karen, she asked for milk – just a splash – and two-and-a-half level teaspoons of sugar. Three, she told me, would make her jumpy and two just didn't taste right. So again, just making the tea, I felt under pressure. I didn't make a cup for myself, because frankly I was worried about spilling it. But the problem then was I didn't know what to do with my hands. Plus, when I was back in the lounge, I sat down. Which was another mistake, because the police, they didn't. The woman – Karen; she said to call her Karen so I will – Karen stood by the fireplace holding her tea, and the man, DC Granger – who even if I was related to him I'd probably still call DC Granger – he kept his hands in his pockets and sort of wandered nonchalantly around the room.

'Nice place,' he said.

I couldn't tell from his tone whether he was mocking me. Us, rather: me and Syd. Because, sure, it's a nice room, but right now it's also basically an empty cube. There's the sofa, a couple of chairs, the television, but all the pictures on the walls, all the books, the birds, the stuff Winters left behind – obviously that's all long gone, right down to the last LP.

'Thanks,' I said. 'It will be. We just need to . . . you know. Paint. Redecorate. What have you.'

What have you. Who these days says *what have you* who isn't eighty? I was: I was turning into my mother. People in authority always made her nervous too, even though the worst offence she'd ever committed was putting the bin out early before we went away on holiday.

I wanted to sip my tea, but I didn't have any. Karen . . .

I can't call her Karen.

Inspector Leigh, she was watching me with this curious little smile, as though she was enjoying me acting like an idiot. She was about half the height of her colleague, and half the width, but – and maybe this is just the authority-figure thing in me again – somehow she seemed to dominate the room. She was in her early forties, I guess, with hair so red it was almost orange, and this intense, inquisitive look in her eyes. That smile I'd noticed lingered, so that by the end of our interview I'd come to wonder if it wasn't actually her default expression – or at least her default expression when regarding me.

'The tea's perfect,' she announced, toasting me. 'Thank you. I wouldn't have asked for one if I'd realized you weren't having one yourself.'

'It's fine, honestly,' I answered. 'No trouble.' I reclined, felt like Hugh Hefner, sat forward. I'd never realized until that point that the cushions on our sofa sank so low.

'Mind if I take a look around?' said DC Granger, a voice from a different conversation. He hitched a massive thumb towards the door and was already starting for the hallway before I could answer.

'Er . . . sure.'

Inspector Leigh watched me as I watched him go. Once her colleague was out of the room she carefully set her cup down on the mantelpiece. 'Well,' she said, 'I suppose I should explain why we're here. You've already spoken to some of my colleagues, I believe. And you're familiar with everything that's happened.'

It wasn't a question, but I nodded anyway.

'Well, Jack – can I call you Jack? Well, Jack . . . DC Granger and I, we're just following up. Just putting some flesh on the bones, as it were. Would it be OK if I asked you a few more questions?'

'Sure,' I answered. 'Of course.' And then I laughed and said: 'Do I need a lawyer?'

It was a joke! Just a bloody joke! But for an instant Inspector Leigh let that smirk of hers sink into a frown.

'Do you think you need one?'

'What? No. I mean, I was just, you know. Just kidding,' I finished lamely.

There was half a beat before the inspector answered. 'I see.' She looked around, smiled again. 'May I sit down?'

'Please,' I said, half getting up from my own seat. The inspector carried over one of the dining chairs and positioned herself so that our knees, once we were both sitting, were almost touching. I would have edged backwards, but there was nowhere on the sofa for me to go.

'So,' said Inspector Leigh, pulling out her notepad. 'Some of these questions you will have answered before, I realize, so I apologize in advance for . . . Jack?'

I'd been looking beyond her to try and locate her colleague. I'd thought I'd heard him in the kitchen, but from the glimpse of the room I had from where I was sitting I couldn't see him.

'Don't worry,' said the inspector, her smile extending slightly. 'He won't steal anything.'

I laughed dutifully. 'No. Of course not. Sorry.'

'No need to be sorry.'

The phrases she chose, her body language, her sense of personal space – they were close enough to what most people would consider normal that at first I thought it was just her. You know, that it was all just a part of who she was. I mean, some people – some police officers in particular, I would imagine – they're just a bit socially awkward. That's not a criticism. For one thing I count myself among them. But it was an act. I realized that about a second after she'd gone. She must have read me the moment I'd opened the front door, seen exactly how best to set me on edge. Needy, eager to please, afraid of authority: probably it was all written on my face. Unless she'd also been briefed by one of her colleagues – one of the ones I'd spoken to before. If so, that meant she *had* been looking into me, and her finding me at home, alone, there was no on-the-off-chance about it.

Just because you're paranoid . . .

We must have sat there like that for almost an hour. She was right, most of the questions I'd answered before – where I was, what I'd been doing, what I'd seen, heard, witnessed – and I stuck to the same story I'd set out the first time. I even settled into something like a rhythm and gradually, particularly with DC Granger out of the room, I was beginning to feel slightly less uncomfortable. Until Inspector Leigh abruptly changed tack.

'Tell me about your work,' she said, setting her notepad face down on her lap.

'My work? What about my work?'

'You've been having some trouble at work, from what I understand.'

My smile was a tic. 'How do you . . .'

Maybe because I didn't finish my question Inspector Leigh didn't feel obliged to answer, and anyway it hardly mattered how she knew. She'd found out somehow.

'That's not . . . I mean, it's got nothing to do with this,' I said, and at the back of my mind I thought of Syd, saw the incredulity – the irritation – in her eyes.

'I didn't mean to imply that it did,' said Inspector Leigh. 'I'm just curious. But of course if you'd rather not talk about it . . .'

'No, it's not that. It's just . . . there's nothing much to tell, that's all.'

'I heard that you've been fired. That there's the possibility of criminal proceedings.'

'Criminal . . . no. What? Criminal proceedings? Who told you that?'

This time when she didn't answer, she did it openly.

'No,' I said again, as much to myself this time. 'I've just . . . I'm on suspension. That's all. It's all just a . . . a misunderstanding.' *Criminal proceedings.* All at once I had a new taunt echoing in my head, the voice still that delighted little girl's.

Inspector Leigh watched me for a moment, then shifted angles once again.

'Tell me, Jack. How long have you known Elsie?'

'Elsie? Elsie Payne?'

'Mmm. How long have you known her?'

'I . . . I don't know her. Not really.'

'You know what happened to her?'

'She's in hospital.'

'She's in a coma.'

'Right. That's what I mean. My girlfriend, Syd, she –'

'Sydney Baker. Your partner. Co-owner of this property.'

'Right. Sydney, she and Elsie, they –'

'I know all about Ms Baker's relationship with Elsie, Jack. We spoke to her outside the ICU.'

'You did?' Syd hadn't mentioned that. Unless Inspector Leigh meant today, that very morning. I thought Syd had gone straight to the office, but she's been spending so much time at the hospital lately that it was certainly possible she'd stopped off again on the way in to work. That's where she's been writing most of her entries: sitting in an orange plastic chair in a hospital waiting room. She's there so often in fact that I'm beginning to wonder whether I should be worried about her. Which I realize sounds ridiculous given the circumstances because there isn't a moment currently I don't worry about us both.

'I was asking you about *your* relationship with Elsie, Jack. How long *you* had known her.'

'That's kind of what I was saying. I don't know her. Only through Syd.'

'But you were upset? About what happened to her?'

'Well . . . yes. Naturally.'

'And you're the one who raised Elsie's case with social services. Is that right?'

'Yes, I suppose so. I mean, we both did. Me and Syd.'

Inspector Leigh nodded as though in sympathy. 'It's been a difficult time for you, clearly. With how things turned out with Elsie, with Ms Baker being so upset. With your problems at work, too, and this big new house of yours . . .' She swept her eyes across the living-room ceiling, which all at once had never felt higher.

I was waiting for the question. Inspector Leigh seemed to be waiting for me to answer.

'Right,' I agreed. 'Difficult, I'd say, is putting it mildly.' I tested a smile, hoping for another dose of sympathy. I couldn't tell from the inspector's reaction whether I'd won any.

'I imagine you've been feeling quite frustrated,' she said. 'Angry, too, no doubt.'

I waggled my head. 'I guess so, yeah, I mean . . . wait. Angry?' All at once I saw where this was going – where it had been heading all along. 'Not angry,' I said, categorically. Angrily, even, you might have said. 'I don't get angry.'

'You're sure about that?'

'Absolutely. I just . . . I don't. Ask Syd. Ask anyone.'

Inspector Leigh's smile, this time, told me she already had.

'What about after a drink or two, Jack? Say, during a session at the local pub. Might you get angry then?'

I swallowed, but somewhere in my throat there was a blockage. The pub. She knew about what had happened at the pub. I suppose I shouldn't have been surprised. If anything I should have been more prepared.

'That was different,' I said.

'What was?'

'The . . . thing you're referring to.'

A frown like she really didn't know. And yet somehow, even though she was frowning, she was still managing to maintain that little smirk.

I stood up, awkwardly to avoid a clash of knees. I moved into the middle of the room, and was about to ask for a break, when I spotted DC Granger leaning against the door frame. I hadn't noticed him returning and I had no idea how long he'd been standing there.

'There's a knife missing from your knife block,' he said, as though he'd been part of the conversation the whole way through.

'What?'

'In your kitchen. There's a knife missing from your knife block.'

I looked at Inspector Leigh, immobile and impassive, and then back at Dwayne Johnson over there filling up my doorway.

'It's probably in the dishwasher.'

DC Granger shook his head, slowly. 'I checked. It's not in the dishwasher.'

'You checked in our dishwasher?'

A shrug like a rolling boulder. 'It happened to be open. I happened to look.'

Which was basically a DC Granger-sized lie. There's no way the dishwasher was open. When it's open you can't even get to the sink. But it wasn't the dishwasher at that point that was worrying me. It was the knife. The missing knife. I'd been aware it was gone. I'd just never before thought to wonder why.

'I think ... I think I'd like you to leave now,' I said. I'd meant to sound bold. Affronted. The way an innocent taxpayer in situations like this is supposed to sound. Even to my ear, though, I didn't come close.

To my surprise Inspector Leigh didn't argue. She stood up as though she'd merely been waiting for me to ask.

'Well,' she said. 'Thank you for your time, Jack. And for the delicious cup of tea.'

That smile. She'd asked me before about whether I

got angry, and if ever I had a right to it would have been then. At her demeanour, her insinuations. But as soon as I was alone once again in the hallway, all I felt was a swelling sense of dread. Because this was real, I realized. Whatever it was – whatever it is – there's no denying any more that it's real.

Jack

It's getting late and Syd's still not home. I want to call her, to tell her about today, but also I don't want to panic her. On the other hand, if she was going to panic she probably would have done so already. She saw this coming, after all. It won't be any consolation to her, I realize, but there's very little that would console her just now.

I don't know what to write. Or I do, but I'm struggling to make a start. That's what I hate most about when I worry, the fact it stops me from doing anything else. But I don't suppose I really have a choice. We're barely halfway through – halfway to the point we're at now – and time is clearly running out. If we don't figure this out before the police come back, who knows if we'll get another chance?

The stuff at work, then. I told the police it wasn't connected. It's what I said to Syd, too; what I've been repeating, like a mantra, to myself. But it's not as though I can just ignore it. And apart from anything it's beginning to dawn on me that I've been wrong so far more than I've been right.

I mentioned a missed call, if you remember. After

my run-in with Elsie's dad. The call was from a friend of mine. He . . .

Wait. This won't make sense unless I go back further. Maybe I can't tell you how this part ends yet, but I can at least be clear on how it began.

There was something else I said earlier, too. When I was talking about Bart, about how he'd been trying to help Susmita? What I said was, once in a while, in a job like ours, you wouldn't be human if you didn't bend the rules. Which I suppose was a prelude to a confession. This confession. Syd spoke before about the stuff I kept from her and this is one example of something I should definitely have told her about right at the start.

There was this family.

Wait, no.

There was this woman. Which already makes it sound like I fell into the same trap Bart did, but it's nothing like that, I promise. This woman, she came to our offices looking for help. She was being evicted, she told me. She was hazy on the reasons why, which perhaps should have set off some alarm bells, but most people in her situation when they come to us, part of the problem is a lack of information. They often don't know exactly what's happening to them, or – even more commonly – what they're supposed to do about it. And Sabeen, I thought, was no different from any of the others.

Our meeting didn't last very long. I learned that

Sabeen was a refugee from Iraq who'd been granted leave to remain. She was thirty-five years old, with black hair and green eyes, and a habit of gnawing the skin around her fingernails. I assumed initially that she'd come to me to apply for emergency accommodation, but what she wanted was to stay exactly where she was. The thing was, what Sabeen had presented to me was basically a dispute between a landlord and his tenant. And though I was obviously sympathetic, this just wasn't my department at all.

I tried to tell Sabeen this. She listened, and seemed to be taking in what I was saying. I gave her some numbers she could call, the names of some organizations she could speak to, but when at last I reached to offer her my hand, instead of taking it she suddenly started crying. Genuinely, I don't think I've ever seen anyone so distraught. And believe me, in my job you see people in tears on a daily basis. There was no chance either that Sabeen was faking it. I see that sort of thing often enough, too.

I didn't promise her more than I could offer. I said I'd call her landlord, that was all, and try to get to the bottom of what was happening. Such was Sabeen's gratitude, I immediately felt guilty for having got her hopes up. She left with a smile that sparkled, as though I'd given my word that I would find a way to help. Which I hadn't. I tried to remind myself later that I'd done no such thing. Not that it made any difference. When I discovered what it was that Sabeen was hiding, one way or another I found myself committed.

The landlord laughed when I told him who I was – who, notionally, I was representing – and when I asked him why Sabeen was being evicted he told me, first, to mind my own business and, then, if I was so bloody interested, to go and take a look for myself.

There were five of them. Crammed into a bedsit barely big enough for one. Amira, at seventeen, was the youngest. She was Sabeen's sister. Ali was the second-born, and you could sense immediately that he was furious with his powerlessness to improve his family's lot. But as well as being in the country illegally (they all were, other than Sabeen), Ali had lost a foot on the journey from Baghdad. He'd got it caught under the wheel of a lorry. He'd had it amputated in Germany, but had fled the hospital before the authorities could take too great an interest in him, so the injury had never had a chance to properly heal. It pained him constantly, though not as much, I've always suspected, as the sense he'd allowed himself to become a burden. His family had waited for him in Germany, had half carried him the rest of the way to England, and for Ali that wasn't how it was supposed to have been. He'd left Iraq in order to help them. His younger sister, Amira, but also his parents: Kalila, his mother, and Hakim, his father, both of whom looked older than their sixty-something years and who had their own ongoing health issues to cope with.

It was Sabeen's parents who had the greatest effect on me. I mean, once I'd convinced Sabeen to open the bedsit door and I'd seen them all huddled on the sofa, my first instinct was simply to turn around. I could tell just from the look on Sabeen's face that she'd misled me. But she pulled me inside, sort of dragged me apologetically before her family, and even though I couldn't understand what it was that she was telling them, or a word of what her parents were saying back, they were looking at me like . . . well . . . this is going to sound kind of pathetic, I know, but they were looking at me the way I've always wished my own parents would. Just, I don't know. Proud, I guess. Approving. Like even though I hadn't done a thing yet, they were just grateful to have me on their side.

What could I tell them? The truth, I suppose, is the obvious answer: that their landlord was entirely within his rights, and that they were lucky he hadn't reported them to the authorities. That technically I was the authorities, and that I should have been reporting them, too. But the thing was, I couldn't. I just . . . I couldn't. They needed me and it felt good to be needed – I won't deny that was part of it. But also, when I heard what they'd been through, when I saw what they were going through still . . . I simply didn't have the heart.

I imagine you've guessed where this is heading. In

the end I didn't just bend the rules. I broke them. It was easy enough to do: I added Sabeen's name to the appropriate list, used certain criteria to ensure it jumped to somewhere near the top, and then bypassed the usual bureaucracy to assign her the first social-housing unit that became available. It only had the one bedroom, but it was far more spacious than the bedsit, and most importantly it was almost entirely self-contained. There'd be no nosy neighbours to worry them, nor any more bothersome landlords. As I say, easy. But it was also reckless. I thought I was helping, but the way things are looking right now it would have been better for Sabeen and her family if I'd never allowed myself to get involved.

It was Ali, Sabeen's brother, whose call I missed, that day I first encountered Elsie's father. In the time since I'd been introduced to Sabeen's family, it was Ali to whom I'd become closest. He was a good six or seven years younger than me, but given everything he'd been through I looked up to him as I would an older brother. I half suspected Ali looked up to me as well – for no other reason than he thought my job was more important than it was – though what I liked best about our relationship was that neither one of us was prepared to show it. We mocked each other mercilessly, vied openly for his parents' affections – again just as though we were brothers, though without the complication of any genuine sibling rivalry.

'The pissing weather in this country.'

Ali's English was even better than his older sister's, and he had a fluency with swear words in particular that even Syd would probably have been impressed by.

'Is that why you wanted to see me, Al? To ask me to do something about the weather?'

I was smiling, but the fact is I was also apprehensive. When I'd texted Ali in response to his phone call, he'd replied requesting we meet up. Even the phone call had been unusual, something we'd agreed would only happen in an emergency, so the fact Ali had wanted to talk in person had told me it would be about something serious.

He scowled as he bracketed me with kisses, then turned one of his palms up towards the clouds. The sky was grey, the colour of used washing-up water, and the air was heavy with a precipitation too cowardly to be described as proper rain.

'Allah himself couldn't do anything to part these clouds. That's why he gave England to the heathen.'

We were outside Balham Tube and I looked for somewhere we could go that was under cover and also away from the crowd. I didn't suggest coffee, because Ali would only have ordered tap water and then insisted after we finished that he paid the bill. I pointed instead towards the nearby railway bridge and when we reached it we hunched together in the gloom.

'How's the foot?' I asked him. I'd managed to put Ali in touch with a doctor – someone Bart knew, not

exactly NHS – and he was getting by now with a pros-
thetic and a crutch.

'Still missing,' he replied. 'I keep hoping it'll turn
up in one of my socks.' He adjusted his weight so he
was standing more comfortably. 'Listen, Jack. You
said to call you if anyone ever came around asking
questions.'

The fact that he was so quick to get down to business only unnerved me all the more.

'Has someone been hassling you?' I asked him.
'Who?'

'Not hassling us exactly,' Ali replied. 'Just . . .
watching.'

My frown was a question mark.

'Sabeen mentioned it first,' Ali said. 'There was
someone following her home from the Tube. And
Amira, she thinks someone's been going through
our bin.'

'What?' I said. 'Why would anyone want to go
through your bin?'

Ali rolled his eyes at me. 'To look for evidence,' he
said. 'Obviously.'

'But . . . what kind of evidence?'

'Evidence about who we really are! Amira said it's
happened more than once. She's taken out the rubbish
and when she's opened up the bin the other bags have
all been ripped open.'

'That could be foxes, though. Couldn't it? Or, I
don't know. Birds.'

'Then why was all the rubbish still inside, the lid of the bin left closed? Foxes don't tidy up after themselves, Jack. Not even in this country.'

I opened my mouth, shut it again. I knew Ali wouldn't have come to me had he not been genuinely concerned, but I knew as well how helpless he felt and how susceptible they all must have been to paranoia. To be honest I was surprised it hadn't manifested itself sooner.

'What about this person Sabeen says followed her?' I said. 'Did they say anything? What did they look like?'

'It was too dark to see. And anyway they kept their distance. But again it's happened more than once and Sabeen, she . . . she's worried it was someone from the government. Like . . . an immigration official.'

This time my smile was genuine. 'An immigration official?'

Ali curled a corner of his mouth. 'I knew you'd laugh. That's why I wanted to talk to you in person.'

'I'm not laughing, Al, honest. It's just . . . I mean . . . it's a bit of a stretch, don't you think? Maybe it was just another commuter, walking the same route home.'

Ali drew back his shoulders. 'You know if someone's following you, Jack. And there's no way my sister would lie.' There was an edge to his tone that told me I needed to tread carefully. As much as Ali enjoyed a bit of mutual mockery, there was nothing he took more seriously than the welfare of his family.

'Talk me through it,' I said to him, appeasingly. 'Has anyone else noticed anything unusual? Have you?'

Ali, grudgingly, shook his head.

'What about your parents?'

'You know them,' said Ali, 'they barely ever go out. But I trust my sisters' instincts, Jack. They're worried, too, I know they are, no matter how much they pretend they're not.'

'What do you mean?'

Once again Ali shifted. 'They didn't want me to speak to you,' he admitted. 'No one did.'

I could imagine precisely how that argument had played out. Sabeen and Amira and their parents would have resisted sanctioning anything they would have regarded as an imposition. It was hard enough whenever I visited them to get them to accept so much as a jar of honey. Ali, though, would have considered coming to me his duty, imposition be damned. I respected that passion in him enormously: the fact he would have willingly sacrificed his other foot, if it had come down to it, for the sake of protecting his family.

'You did the right thing,' I said, which ordinarily would have sounded patronizing as hell, but at that moment was what Ali needed to hear. He visibly swelled in fact, and I could picture him recounting the line to his sisters when he reported back on our conversation later. 'So this . . . immigration official,' I said. 'How many times has Sabeen been followed?'

'Twice, she thinks. And she wouldn't have mentioned it if she wasn't certain, Jack. I'm not making this up.'

'Relax, Al. I'm not doubting you. I'll look into it, I promise. But if you want my opinion, I don't think you've got anything to worry about. Immigration officials don't tend to loiter in the shadows. And they don't get paid enough to go checking through people's bins.'

It was an attempt at a joke – a feeble one admittedly, but even so it drew a reluctant smile.

'Probably you're just being hounded by your typical south London weirdo. There used to be an asylum just up the road, you know. It got shut down in the nineties, all the patients kicked out on to the streets. There's bound to be a few still in the area, and maybe one of them happens to have a thing for pretty Middle Eastern immigrants.'

Ali gave a snort. 'And that's supposed to make me feel better?'

'I said "pretty", Al. I don't think you've got anything to worry about. It's your sisters you want to be looking out for.'

Ali laughed again, and I could tell his mind was more at ease. 'She likes you, you know,' he said to me.

'Who does?'

'Amira. She thinks you look like Doctor Who.'

Ali was grinning now, and even though I was aware he was trying to wind me up, I struggled not to let my embarrassment show. It was something he'd teased me about before: the way we'd both noticed Amira gazing at me, the habit she had of touching my arm. I was flattered, obviously, but I did my best to ignore it – which wasn't always easy when her older brother was there, grinning at me from across the room.

'Which Doctor Who?' I answered. 'The short one? Or the old one?'

'The dorky one. With the silly hair.'

I responded with a sardonic smile. 'Tell her I'm flattered,' I said, 'and that if I wasn't already spoken for – and if her brother wasn't such a dork himself – I'd be asking for her hand in marriage.'

Ali tutted. 'I said she likes you, Jack. I didn't say she wants to marry you.' He shook his head. 'You English,' he said. 'You always want to colonize everything.'

And that's how we left it: with a grin and a handshake. You might have thought, given the stakes – for Ali and his family, but also for me – that I might have taken my friend's concerns a bit more seriously. But Ali, I was convinced, was afraid about nothing. What I'd said to him was true: immigration officials didn't act like members of MI5. They behaved like bailiffs, hammering on doors and demanding ID. So, no, I wasn't worried. In fact, after what had happened with Elsie's father, all I felt at that point was relief.

Sydney

There's not a thing I remember about my sister that I can trust.

Take the stuff I told Elsie. *She even looked like you*, I said to her, which although I think is probably true, might just as easily be a lie. I have a picture of Jessica in my head but it changes, flickers, fades if I try to look at it directly. The last time I saw her I was thirteen years old, when Jessica would have been eleven, and I haven't seen so much as a photograph of her in all the time that has passed since. So those high-drawn cheekbones I mentioned, those bottomless brown eyes – I can *see* them when I picture my sister but that doesn't mean they were genuinely there.

And what I said about her being brave. Again, it's how I remember her but it's an impression based solely on one thing: the fact that she did what I couldn't bring myself to. I'm living proof that I simply never had the guts.

I have memories of us being together, of course I do, but even these feel like half-remembered dreams. So really, when it comes down to it, there are only two things about my sister I can be certain of. I know I never loved her enough. And I know it was my fault she died. Or perhaps it's misleading to separate the two when one led so directly to the other.

I say I never loved Jessica enough. The truth, actually, is that I hated her. Not just because she was my annoying baby sister but because our father treated her so differently from the way he'd always treated me. He never hit her, not once, not even on one of those rare occasions when he lost his temper. Lost *control*, rather. She was spared too from the put-downs, the denigration, the subtle criticisms he'd so expertly honed. The humiliation. The *fear*. For me there was no escaping his sadistic games, whereas Jessica was firmly a spectator. Although of course this was part of the game-playing as well. My father was manipulating me to resent my little sister to deflect some of the hatred I felt for him. Manipulating my mother too. At the time I resented her as much as I did Jessica. She could have stood up for me. She chose not to. But Jessica was at least part of the reason why. It was as though my father had a knife to my baby sister's throat. One little slip on my mother's part and my father's hand would have slipped too. He was doing what the Romans did. Was it the Romans? Dividing us, basically, so he could rule.

But whatever. It worked, is all that matters. My sister wanted to be friends, I wouldn't let us. And I think, just as an aside, that's why my memories of her are so unclear. The therapists I saw, they all said I've repressed those memories because I had to. Sort of like a defence mechanism. Not sort of. Exactly. They say those memories are all still there but to protect myself from the guilt I feel I've hidden them behind a wall. Except that wall, if you ask me, came earlier. I never paid my sister enough attention. Never *cared* enough about who she was to form any lasting memories of her in the first place. Plus the other thing is, I've tried. To remember, I mean. If those memories are all still there, how come I can't see them? I mean, for fuck's sake: I remember everything else. *Everything.* Why, if I can remember all the evil shit from my childhood, can I not remember the only thing that was good?

I killed her the day I left home. She died two months later, after an overdose of our mother's sleeping pills, but it was my leaving her – my abandoning her – that cost my sister her life.

I left on my fourteenth birthday. The night before, to be precise. Birthdays were always special to my father. The day I turned seven, he held my face down against the candles on my cake. Not for very long. Just until I began to scream. And over time his means of celebrating my birthdays (my mother's too – she didn't escape the annual ritual. Only Jessica did) became more elaborate. He began to plan for them, the way normal people plan for Christmas. For my twelfth birthday, for example, he bought me a kitten. A little grey one. At first I couldn't believe my father had been so generous. I don't mean in terms of money. My father was well off enough – and I suppose, by extension, we all were – that money itself was never an issue. What I mean is, generous in terms of his affection. Because that's what it must have been – right? For him to have bought me something I'd so desperately wanted? He must have loved me on some level after all. Maybe I'd finally done something to make him proud.

He waited two weeks. Enough time for Pipkin (what can I say? *Watership Down* was my favourite book of all time) to establish himself as the central focus of my life. To be honest a day would have been enough but I suppose he wanted to be sure I was truly in love and the anticipation, for my father, would have been half the thrill. A fortnight, then, before he killed him. What he said was that Pipkin got hit by a car. That, when I'd left for school that morning, I'd forgotten to close the front door. But I hadn't forgotten, I was *sure* I hadn't, I'd been careful to the point of paranoia for the entire fortnight. And when I saw Pipkin's body – when my father *showed* me his body, laid out on a sheet of newspaper in the middle of the kitchen table – there wasn't a mark on him. No blood, no dirt, nothing. Even through my tears I was sure of that. Plus, if it had really been my fault, my father would have been furious. Instead it was all he could do not to smile.

It was my next birthday – my thirteenth – that proved the tipping point. After Pipkin you might have thought I would have wised up a bit but part of my father's talent lay in lulling you in the build-up to his next assault. This time he promised me a celebration. I didn't have friends, so there was no sense in my even wishing for a party. I wasn't unpopular as such, just overlooked I suppose you could say, because at school I kept myself to myself. But there was this one girl, Helen Donohue, who gradually, over about a year, I'd become sort of close to. That's what I thought, anyway. Once or even twice a week, and at first more by accident really, we'd fall in next to each other on the walk home from school. And I guess my father must have seen us. I tried to deny it when he asked me about her – *she's not a friend, I don't even know her full name* – because somehow, even though it had never been explicitly stated, I knew a *friend* wasn't something I was permitted to have. But my father saw through that, obviously, saw through my *longing* to have someone, anyone, I could confide in. And he suggested that for my birthday we invited Helen over. For a birthday tea, if I wasn't too grown up for such a thing. I was sceptical, of course. Not of my father's suggestion – I'd been desperate to have a birthday tea since I'd turned four years old. Rather, that this wasn't just another of his tricks. But like the naive fucking wanna-be-loved I was, I decided to trust in what he promised. I couldn't help myself. The potential reward, compared to the risk, was just too great.

On my birthday Helen was due at five. My mother took me shopping in the afternoon: for a new dress, for a birthday banner, for something special for me and Helen to eat and drink. It was the happiest day I could remember . . . until we came home in the middle of the afternoon and found Helen already there.

My father had rearranged the time. When my mother, Jessica and I walked in, Helen was seated on the sofa. My father was in the living room as well – standing up and with his back to the window. He didn't say anything when we entered the room. He kept his eyes fixed firmly on Helen. I looked at her too and saw what I'd missed when I'd first entered. She looked afraid. Not just afraid. Terrified. The way I felt inside whenever my father threatened *me*.

'Helen? What are you doing here? What . . . what's the matter?' I turned to my father. 'Dad? What did you . . .'

Helen stood and, after a frightened glance towards my father, scurried in the direction of our front door. I trailed her into the hallway, catching my father's glint of satisfaction on my way out.

'Helen? Helen, wait. My birthday . . .'

She turned on me, showing anger rather than fear now we were alone.

'You're a *freak*,' she hissed, through tears I'm not sure she was aware she was shedding. 'You, your dad, your entire family: you're *freaks*.'

They were the last words she ever uttered that were addressed directly to me. I don't know what my father said to her that day. Nothing, obviously, Helen would ever have been able to prove. All I knew at the time was that the birthday celebration my father had promised me was another mirage, and that my friendship with Helen was over before it had even begun. Worse – and this, I came to realize, was the real point of my father allowing Helen over, other than the heartbreak he got to witness in me – whatever my father said to Helen convinced her to turn the other kids against me too. Maybe he instructed her to spread the rumours she did. Maybe he didn't have to. Either way, from being ignored I became the most hated girl at school. That's what it felt like, anyway. Not only was I a freak, I was a dyke, a bed-wetter, a slut: every cruel and vindictive label my teenage peers were able to think of somehow got tarred to me. School had been my refuge up until that point: the one place in the world I felt safe. But then, after Helen, there wasn't anywhere I didn't feel afraid.

And that's when it hit home, I suppose: the realization I'd never be able to have a relationship with *anyone* on terms that weren't dictated by my father. And even harder to bear was the sudden knowledge that my father didn't love me one bit. I'd always assumed I must have been precious to him on some level, no matter how deeply his affection was buried. But it wasn't true. He hated me, *loathed me* – and rather than let me be happy, he would do whatever he could to ensure everyone else in the world hated me too.

*

So yeah, it was that, together with the prospect of another birthday celebration, that finally prompted me to leave. In the middle of the night, with a back-pack full of peanut butter and Dairy Milk, and a rolling pin from the utensil drawer for protection. Just in case my father should think to follow me. My leaving, though: it changed everything. I wasn't supposed to go. I wasn't *allowed* to. My father wouldn't just have been angry. He would have been vengeful. Old Testament-level *pissed*. I can't imagine what he must have put Jessica through in the weeks leading up to the day she died. Or I can, actually. I can imagine it all too well. All those barriers he'd set up around her would immediately have come tumbling down, all the wickedness that had been kept at bay sent crashing in. I've had years to hone the images I carry with me, to refine the scenes that play sharpest in my sleep. Ironically, it's when I imagine my father hurting her that my memories of my sister are at their clearest. It's not her face I see, though. It's her feelings. I can see the pain that twists her fragile features and the fear that shadows her eyes. The hurt is there too. The sense of betrayal.

I only heard about Jessica's death by accident. When I left, I left for good – I became Sydney Baker, in my head, the very next morning (Sydney because I liked that it was sort of a boy's name and also that it was a place so far away. I don't remember why I chose Baker. Maybe I was standing outside a Greggs or something at the time). For the first two months, however, I didn't venture beyond the borders of my home county. My medium-term plan was to go to London but at first I didn't have the courage and flitted instead between the innumerable B&Bs that served the tourists who in the summer came to visit the coast. If I'd left right away I might never have seen the story that ran one day in the local newspaper.

Tragedy strikes prominent local businessman, the headline read, and there below the fold was a picture of my father. My first thought – my first hope – was that he was dead. Hit by a bus, crushed by a tree, struck by a divine bolt of lightning. I'd imagined so many potential scenarios over the years that there was very little I could have found written in the story that would have taken me by surprise. About the only thing that could have, I suppose, was the news I eventually read.

Even the newspaper blamed me. It was only the reasoning that they got wrong. They implied Jessica's suicide was a response to my running away, which I suppose was accurate enough. But it was grief that induced her to take those sleeping pills, they said; anguish at whatever fate she imagined had befallen me. My father was depicted as a victim. An upstanding pillar of the community who, in the space of two short months, had seen calamity intrude on his life twice. They even ran a quote, addressed to me. 'If you're out there,' he said, 'reading this, I'm begging you to please come home. For my sake. For yours. And for your mother's.' They said it was a plea. It was obvious to me it was a threat.

I considered it. Not because of my mother. Frankly, she only entered my thoughts again years later. What I wanted at that point was to punish myself and what could have been more fitting than to let my father do it for me? On the other hand I wasn't prepared to let him win. For a time after my sister's death that was the only thing that kept me going: the determination to make my father suffer to the same degree that Jessica had. *I hope he was punished*, Elsie said to me and ultimately I suppose he was. Not enough, though. Not in my book. Not anywhere close to enough.

That rolling pin wasn't the only thing I'd taken to protect me. I took paperwork too. Notes, bank statements, the contacts book my father kept in his briefcase – anything and everything I could gather from his office in the hours before I stole away. I didn't know what any of it proved but I was sure some of it would show *something*. Because on top of everything else my father was also a crook. He was a cheat, a swindler, a *liar* – and a flagrant one at that. He wasn't careful. He never even bothered to lock his briefcase. For him that was part of the game: the brazenness with which he got away with all the awful things he did. No one in their right mind would try to defy him. Unfortunately for him I wasn't in my right mind, not after what had happened to Jessica.

All it took was a postage stamp and a phone call, to the same newspaper that had lauded my father as an upstanding pillar of our community. Probably not even the documents I supplied were strictly necessary. A hint would have been enough: the suggestion of where to start digging based on the information I'd picked up eavesdropping over the years on my father's phone calls. With the interview he'd given about Jessica, you see, he'd set himself up for a fall. All I did was give him a push. And I got to watch, most importantly, where he landed. In a vat of boiling sewage would have been my choice but prison was the next best thing.

After that – after I was safe – I came undone. The booze, the drugs, the comfort fucks – the *real* self-harm, it started then. I made it to London in the end but London, in my state of mind, was the worst place in the world for me to be. Christ knows how I got a job. Christ knows how I kept it. For an entire decade my life felt like an oversight – an accounting error in my favour that someone, at some point, was inevitably going to call in.

But I thought I was through it. I thought that, thanks to Jack, I'd finally come out the other side. Apparently, though, I was kidding myself. This isn't a new episode in my life. It's part one again playing on repeat.

*

Jack says that what happened to Elsie is his fault. He was the one who made the call. He was the one who suggested involving children's services in the first place. But in the end that's all Jack's input amounted to. Suggestions. There's no wriggling out of the fact that ultimately he was following my lead.

The system, then. The people who came back to us saying there was nothing they could do. I suppose I could try blaming them instead. Except I knew the system as well as they did. I knew how carefully they would have to tread, how protracted any intervention in Elsie's situation would need to be. I'd said as much to Jack. I've written it down in these pages. *It's not that simple. It's never that simple.* What did I think, that just because I wanted things to be different this time they would be? I *know* I'm not that naive. Not any more.

I've tried blaming Elsie, whose courage failed her at the last. Again, though, I remember exactly what it was I told Jack. *Elsie's not going to say anything. Trust me.* How can I hold her responsible when her only failing – not even a failing: a feeling – was to be afraid? And blaming Elsie would anyway be like blaming the victim for the crime. *They deserved to get burgled for buying themselves a nice TV. She was asking to get raped when she chose to wear a dress that didn't cover her knees.* I know I'm not that naive either. I know I'm not that fucking stupid.

I *do* blame Elsie's father. I don't know what he did

to her after the nice man from social services finished up his cup of tea. Maybe he didn't do anything. Maybe he only promised he would. That's how it works sometimes. When people are watching, the debt you owe isn't always called in right away. You pay it eventually, though, and the interest in the interim begins to accrue. Elsie would have been as much aware of that as anyone.

But even Elsie's father can't deflect the responsibility that lies with me. I showed the same short-sightedness I'd demonstrated with Jessica. The same selfishness. Apart from anything, I was the one who gave Elsie the idea. *When you're caught inside a dungeon, even the faintest flicker in the dark is like a promise of daylight. And if it turns out not to be, if it turns out instead to be a burning staircase . . . Well, you take your chances anyway.*

Sound familiar? Yep: me again. What a fountain of wisdom I'm turning out to be.

It was me who pointed out that flicker in the dark, who ushered Elsie down the burning staircase. I told her about Jessica. I told her how *she* got out. I even praised her for it! Jesus Christ. I might as well have pushed Elsie in front of that train myself.

The thing I remember clearest was the scream. Not Elsie's. Elsie didn't make a sound, nothing I could make out over the clamour of the 8.16. It wasn't a woman's scream, either. This, it was a bloke roaring in anguish. A noise there's no way he'd ever be able to repeat.

I'd spotted her first outside the station. I'd been watching for her constantly since ... I was about to say since social services had told us they had no grounds to intervene but actually I'd been watching for her before then. I hadn't stopped watching for her virtually since the day I first met her. But I *noticed* myself watching after that. In the street. At the playground. From the spare-bedroom window. After a week had passed and I hadn't seen her I had to restrain myself from marching round the corner and hammering on Elsie's front door. And then, when I was least prepared – when I was shambling from the coffee queue towards the train queue, on my way groggily in to work – there she was. Twenty, twenty-five yards ahead of me and weaving through the crowd like a leaf again dancing on the wind.

I called out to her but she didn't hear. I started to hurry, spilled my coffee, dropped the whole thing in a passing bin. I almost caught up with her but got trapped at the ticket barrier. Fucking Oyster cards. Fucking running out of credit. By the time I was through, Elsie had disappeared into the tunnel that led towards the platforms. There were three at our local station, though only two that were ever in use in the mornings. One for trains into town, the other out.

I checked the boards at the bottom of the stairwells. There was a train in ten minutes heading into Surrey, another in two for London Victoria. My train, as it happened. I remember half wondering at that point whether Elsie hadn't come to the station looking for me. I thought about this afterwards as well – whether the timing implied Elsie was sending me some kind of message. I don't think she could have been. I don't remember ever telling her how or when I went to work.

But even so.

It took me a minute to spot her. A precious minute. The platform was as crowded as it usually is on a weekday morning and Elsie had made her way along to the far end: the point where the train, as it came into the station, would have been travelling at its fastest. In fact I could see the train approaching in the distance. The rails looped out from the station the way a running track curves towards the finishing straight and the train was rounding the final bend.

'Elsie?'

I'd called out just loud enough to turn heads in the area around me. I saw Elsie move closer to the edge of the platform. Her attention was away from me, towards the oncoming train. Once again I wondered what she was doing there, where she might have been going. Two men in suits passed between us and Elsie was obscured for a moment by a curtain of pinstripe. When I caught sight of her once more she'd again shifted where she was standing, so that one of her feet had crept beyond the yellow safety line. All along the platform people were beginning to form ranks in anticipation of the scuttle for seats but out where Elsie stood there was barely anyone else around her. She had no reason to be standing so close to the edge. No reason, except one.

'Elsie . . .'

I started to move more quickly. I collided with one of those businessmen, ignored his coffee-splattered curse. I dropped the folder I was carrying, hesitated, left it there.

'Elsie!'

She heard me then. Turned, saw me, seemed confused for a moment – then smiled at me over her shoulder. That smile. I remembered it as her hello to me, that day I'd followed her home from Mr Hirani's. I recognized it this time as her goodbye.

'Shit, Elsie, wait, stop . . .'

Maybe I said those things, maybe I just thought them. To be honest I have no idea. The train by this point was the same distance from Elsie as I was – right on top of her, in other words, whereas I was still a hundred miles away. She . . .

Fuck.

She just . . . I mean I can't even describe it. But I think . . . I mean, what they tell me is . . . she hit the side of the train and not the front of it. Or the corner or . . . I don't know. Maybe she hesitated at the last. Maybe she mistimed her leap. Except she didn't leap, I remember that too. She stepped. Just as if she were climbing aboard. Calmly. Quietly. She just . . . stepped.

I tried to force my way through to her, didn't get anywhere close. The man who screamed, I didn't see who he was. I don't remember seeing much of anything after that. Just Elsie, through the crowd – lying broken where she'd ricocheted on to the platform, that leaf-green raincoat of hers steadily blooming red.

They say she has a chance. They say, if she's a fighter, she might pull through. They actually used that phrase. But it's bullshit however they choose to say it because, firstly, I could see what they were really thinking when they told me and, secondly, because I know Elsie hasn't got any fight in her left. That's the whole entire point. When you fight it has to be for *something* and as far as Elsie's concerned there's nothing in her life that's worth the struggle. I want to tell her she's wrong. I want to *prove* it to her. But even if they were to let me see her there'd be no guarantee she'd be able to hear me – and even less, given everything, that she would listen.

So what am I doing here? Why is it I keep coming back to the hospital? It's like Jack said: I'm spending every spare minute, it feels like, sitting in the same orange plastic chair.

The truth, if you want to hear it, is that I'm afraid. I don't like admitting it, least of all to myself, but I am. I'm afraid for Elsie, I'm afraid for Jack, I'm afraid for me. I'm afraid of what's coming. I'm afraid of all the things I've already done. I'm afraid, above all, that everything I've been through – everything I've put *others* through – will count for nothing. And so I'm hiding, basically. Here, in the only place that feels safe, like the coward I only ever pretended not to be.

Jack

What happened to Elsie happened at the beginning of August. Last month – even though it feels like it happened yesterday. She's still in hospital. She still hasn't regained consciousness. The doctors still don't know if there's anything more they can do. We're in a holding pattern, basically. Nothing has changed. Which is odd when you consider that over the same period, for me and Syd, everything has.

Syd says she's hiding. I don't blame her, but hiding isn't going to make any of this go away. I'm not saying I know what will, but writing this, getting things straight, it has to help. Right? It has to. And there's so much we haven't covered yet. All the important stuff, in fact. Which, Jesus, makes it sound like I don't think what happened to Elsie is important, but that's not what I'm saying, I swear.

It's just . . . it's beginning to feel like I'm losing her. Syd, I mean. Like the longer this goes on, the closer she is to giving up. And that just isn't like Syd at all.

I'm scared too, Syd. Especially now. Because of the police, yes, but also because it's starting to dawn on me that maybe – probably – you were right. About what's been happening. About *why*. I mean, honestly?

The truth is I'm bloody terrified. But that just makes me want to get on with this all the more. To *do* something instead of just sitting here, waiting for whatever happens next. And if people are going to understand, it's up to us to try to make them. Right?

Please, Syd.

Please.

Sydney

Jack's just left. He came to the hospital to see Elsie but also I think to check up on me. I got the impression he wanted to talk, though in the end we barely exchanged a word. What *could* we say, given the circumstances? They still won't let us into Elsie's room, but you can see her if you press against the glass. Obviously I've been doing that on a regular basis and each time I retreat to my chair afterwards feeling worse than I did when I got up. Elsie looks so small in that bed she's in, she barely makes a lump in the bedcovers. There are tubes running from her nose, from her arms, from every part of her, it seems to me, to the extent it appears almost as though it's the tubes that are trapping her. She's like a butterfly caught in some malformed web and though I keep hoping she'll find the strength to break free, whenever I check on her she appears more ensnared than she did before.

But I'm not giving up, Jack. Not on Elsie, not on *us*. What I wrote before, that was just ... it was just a wobble. There's no way I'd ever leave you to face this on your own. Trust me on that. *Please*. Although I suppose that's easy enough for me to say. When it comes to judging who to trust or not, my record is about as bad as anyone's.

Timing has never been one of my mother's strong points. After what happened to Elsie, a visit from her was the very last thing I was in the mood for but when she asked less than a week after it happened I wasn't in any state to put up a fight. And actually there was a part of me that wanted to see her. Two parts, in fact, neither one of which did me any credit. There was the little girl in me who simply wanted her mummy. And there was the bitch in me who wanted someone to blame. For Elsie. For everything.

I'd never before let her see where I lived. Not since I'd left home. We wrote to each other mainly, so she knew where to find me, but since I'd first got back in touch with her – five years ago, roughly – I'd made it clear that she was never, *ever* to call on me uninvited. To be fair to her she hadn't complained. She was grateful I was even in contact with her, so anything more than that she would have regarded as a bonus. And it wasn't that she'd made a particular fuss this time. She'd mentioned how nice it would be to be able to picture where I was living, that was all. To *see* it in her mind rather than just imagine it. It was because we'd finally bought somewhere, I assumed – her perception I was approaching a happy ending.

Ha.

'Hello, Sydney.'

She was smiling broadly to cover her nerves. I saw my mother so rarely – twice a year, if that – that I was always caught off guard in some way by her appearance. Today I was surprised mainly by how old she looked. Not old. *Tired*. She was clothed and coiffed as elegantly as ever. Even though she no longer had access to my father's money, was these days practically a pauper, she endeavoured to present herself to the world as she always had. She still bleached her hair a silvery blonde once a month, spent twenty minutes each morning painting her face. The make-up this time, though, didn't offset her pallor. I knew she struggled with sleep as much as I did and I assumed she was just tired . . . until she moved inside and I noticed her hobble.

It was her hip, then. Not tiredness that was weighing on her, pain. Her hip had been broken (*had been broken*. It sounds so passive. What I mean is her hip was broken for her) the one time she'd attempted to insert herself between her eldest daughter and her husband. It happened when I was small, soon after my father's attentions began to wander from my mother towards me, and it was only as I grew older that I started to appreciate what my mother's actions that day really signified. I'd always blamed her for failing to protect me, for not just *leaving* and taking me and Jessica with her – and in many ways I still did. But that hip of hers in my mind had become her saving grace. If she hadn't tried *just that once*, my leaving home would have been the end of it. I never would have wanted to see my mother again. As it was it had taken me almost a decade to get back in touch and even longer to trust her with anything more revealing about my new life than an email address.

'It's Syd, Mum,' I reminded her. 'Only my boss calls me Sydney.'

I pressed myself to the wall to allow her to pass, careful not to let her brush against me. The first time we'd met up, I remember, she'd tried to hug me. There'd been no attempt at physical contact since.

'Oh darling, this is lovely,' she gushed. 'This is yours? All of it's yours?'

'It's ours, yes. Mine and Jack's and the bank's. The kitchen's at the back, Mum. Straight through there.'

'But it's enormous! How on earth did you afford it?'

'We saved, Mum. We worked. That's the sitting room, Mum. The kitchen's –'

'At the back. I know, dear, I heard you. But I can't resist having a nose. Look at those ceilings!'

'I'll give you the tour, Mum, but let's just . . . I don't know. Put the kettle on or something first.'

My mother continued making clucking sounds as we ambled along the hallway and I did my best not to sound irritated by her enthusiasm. Even the way Mum said my name sometimes annoyed me. Not sometimes. Always. I'm not sure she could have said it any other way – apart from by calling me *Syd*, that is, as I'd asked her to about a gazillion fucking times – but somehow she made it sound like a rebuke. A *chastisement* for having tossed aside the name she'd given me. And that limp. It was more pronounced than I'd ever seen it and I couldn't help but wonder whether she wasn't half putting it on. She never would have dared to say so but probably she was disappointed I'd allowed so much time to pass since we'd last seen each other, and playing up her suffering was her way of letting me know.

'Where is Jack?' Mum said, when we finally made it to the kitchen. 'Will he be joining us?'

I started to fill up the kettle. 'He's working today,' I lied. 'All weekend actually.'

The truth was he'd made himself scarce. Not my choice. His. Rather sweetly, Jack's always been less ready to forgive my mother than I have. Not that I've exactly forgiven my mother either but if it were up to Jack she would have been sentenced to life without the possibility of parole. He says he understands why I would want to see her (which is more than I manage, half the time) but that he can't bring himself to be part of it.

(Just as an aside, I've always found it odd that Jack doesn't apply the same standards in judging his own parents. My mother's sin was one of omission and Jack's parents' failings lie in what they've always neglected to offer their child, too. Attention, for example. Encouragement. *Love*. And yet Jack calls them – religiously – every Sunday, with such longing in his voice my heart aches just listening to him on the telephone. Although I realize that the distance between them is partly my fault because they made it clear they disapproved of me from the beginning.)

'Sit down, Mum. Just shove all that clutter to one side.' I made a start clearing the kitchen table but my mother continued towards the window.

'I'm happy standing for the time being, darling. I was sitting all morning on the train ride.'

My mother's fingers drifted towards her hip but she didn't take the opportunity to mention it, which made me wonder whether the pain was genuine after all. In the brightness of the kitchen I could see she was even paler than I'd first thought, and all at once I felt a wave of sympathy. Of shame, too, that I'd treated her thus far so coldly. My mother had suffered at my father's hand just as much as I had, and being forced to watch what was happening to me must have in itself been a form of torture. And though she'd escaped, eventually, just as I had – after Jessica; after my father went to prison – she'd hit a snake and not a ladder. She was divorced and living all alone. She had a shitty job and a shitty little flat and not even the comfort of any real friends.

That's why I saw her, I reminded myself. That was the reason I'd got back in touch. As much as I resented her, I also pitied her. As much as I hated her, I also loved her. Because, well ... she was my mum. No matter what she'd done, no matter what I blamed her for, there was nothing I could do to change that.

We drank tea. Two cups each. We didn't *chat* exactly because that's far too frivolous a word for it but we talked, cautiously – her about the price of things, mainly; me, at her prompting, about my job, which at least distracted me from thinking about Elsie – and I watched her as she nibbled at a biscuit. The hour almost passed by incident-free – until Mum, at the end of it, started crying.

She was still by the window. She'd turned away, so that without knowing it she was directly facing Elsie's house, but I caught the whimper that escaped her throat.

'Mum?'

Up until that point I'd almost been glad I'd invited her over. My mother was never going to be a shoulder for me to cry on but in a weird, complicated way I'd drawn some comfort from her presence nonetheless. And, for the most part, I'd managed to keep my inner bitch in check. Yet I felt precariously balanced and the sight of my mother sobbing only tipped me closer to irritation. Maybe that's counter-intuitive but as far as I was concerned she had no *right* to cry. Not in front of me.

'What is it, Mum? What's wrong?' I tried to keep

my tone neutral. The impatience would have been plain for her to hear.

'I'm just . . . I'm happy for you,' my mother said. 'That's all. Seeing you here. In your new home.'

I felt myself frown.

'I just think . . . I just *know* you're going to be fine. You and Jack. That it's all going to work out for you both.'

Which I suppose was meant to be reassuring but only made me think once again about Elsie. And because of that – because my mother was crying – I allowed myself to ask something I knew very well would upset her but that, in light of Elsie, had been playing disproportionately on my mind. The way I saw it, both my mother and I had made a choice: me to intervene, my mother – bluntly – to stand back and watch. The thing I was struggling with was how two contrasting answers to the same question could both end up being so wrong.

'Tell me something, Mum,' I said.

She'd been tidying her tears and she paused, as though she could sense what was coming. We'd never before spoken about our past. Not directly. Up until that day there'd never seemed much point.

'Would you do things differently?' I asked her. 'If you had the chance again. Would you . . .' I searched for the words that would help me clarify, to explain more specifically what I meant, but I ended up simply repeating the same question. 'Would you do things differently?'

Whatever answer I was expecting, I wasn't prepared for the response my mother gave me. Her neck and head sank physically towards the floor, so that in that instant she appeared six inches shorter. The tears she'd dammed welled up again and her hands came together in silent prayer. She shuffled awkwardly, as though her instinct at first was to move towards me but part of her wanted simply to run away.

'Oh Sydney,' she said. 'Darling, I . . .' She shook her head and it took a moment for me to realize that the gesture was also her answer.

I frowned again – alarmed, angry, I don't know. 'Mum?'

She was trying to speak – trying to explain – but she was struggling to find her voice. 'I just . . . I don't think I could,' she said at last. 'Even now, if you gave me the chance . . . I'm not sure I'm strong enough. I've just never, ever been strong enough.'

Her hand reached out and then fell away again. She was watching me, waiting for me to judge her, the tears dry now but the fear visible on her face. The self-loathing too.

'I'm sorry, Sydney. Really I am. For what happened to you. For everything.'

It was the first time she'd said it, even counting in all her letters. And quite honestly I wasn't sure how to react. The survivor in me wanted to sneer at her, the little girl longed to be held. I was both, neither, one and then abruptly the other: an adult on a seesaw with a child. No doubt I looked as lost to my mother as she did at that point to me.

It happened as she was leaving. I'd given in and offered my mother the tour, and we were making our way back along the landing when I sensed her come abruptly to a halt.

'Sydney?'

I turned around. She was staring at the pictures on the wall.

'Where did you get this?'

It had been a long time since I'd heard my mother speak to me that way, in a tone that implied an accusation. She looked shaken. Angry too, as though she suspected she was the victim of some trick.

I peered to try and work out what she was looking at. The pictures on the landing were spaced so densely her finger could have been directed towards one of several.

'I told you, Mum. All the pictures came with the house. We've been meaning to take them down but so far we haven't got round to it.'

'But *this* picture . . . this one right here . . .'

I drew closer and realized the one she was staring at was a portrait of a child. It was faded, though printed in colour, and it showed a brown-haired little girl with a lollipop stick poking through her grin. I'd noticed it before but only in passing. To be honest I'd always found it slightly creepy, though I'd never quite been able to pinpoint why.

'What about it?' I asked.

'You don't see it?' My mother was frowning now, first at me and then again at the picture. She seemed to want to edge closer for a better look but at the same time appeared wary of moving too near.

'See what?'

She didn't answer.

'Mum? See what?'

She drew away. 'I . . . nothing,' she said. She shook her head. 'I just . . . I made a mistake. That's all.'

I looked again at the picture. My mother in the meantime moved past me and started awkwardly down the staircase towards the hall.

'Mum, wait.' I hurried to catch up. 'Let me help you.'

But even with her hip the way it was she was moving quickly and soon enough she'd negotiated the stairs all by herself. I tried asking her again what the matter was but she just mumbled something about having to hurry to catch her train. For a moment it looked like she might cry again and I was so thrown by her behaviour that when she kissed me I didn't even flinch. From the way my mother was acting, I don't think she noticed doing it herself.

I climbed back up to the landing after she was gone. There was something about that picture that had upset her: some likeness she'd detected in the image she'd been surprised I hadn't recognized myself. But I couldn't see it. As far as I was concerned that picture had nothing to do with us: it was a memory from someone else's past. And so I left it there. I had no reason not to. Until the day I ripped her sobbing from that cage of hers, I barely gave that little girl another glance.

Jack

'Jack? Can I borrow you for a moment?'

It was Mr Yazdani, my boss. He was a long, spindly man, so devoid of both hair and body fat that you could see the exact shape of his skull through his head. I liked him a lot, in spite of his Death-like appearance, but there was something uncharacteristically formal about his tone. Behind him there were at least three other department heads I recognized, as well as Margery from HR.

'Jack? Now, if you don't mind.'

I looked over at Bart. 'Right,' I said. 'Sure. Just let me –'

'Don't touch your computer. Bring a pen, if you like, just in case you want to take notes, but the rest, just . . . just leave it alone,' Mr Yazdani finished, and I couldn't tell whether the distaste he was exhibiting was because of some new initiative our department was being lumbered with or whether it was aimed more specifically at me. Bart, when I looked this time, avoided my eye. Practically everyone else in the office was staring directly at me, however – including those three department heads. Whatever was coming, I knew it wouldn't be good.

*

Bart caught up with me afterwards. I was crossing the lobby of our building when he called out to me from the doorway to the stairwell.

'Jack! Hey, Jack, wait up.'

I heard his voice as though through a bubble. I was moving on autopilot and it took Bart calling out again to bring me to a halt.

'Jack! Hold on, will you? What happened in there? What did they say to you?'

I turned to look at him. His face seemed different somehow. Everything did. 'They found out,' I said.

'Found out? Found out about what?'

'About Sabeen. About Ali. About all of them.'

Except for the security guard there was no one around us, but Bart checked across his shoulder and pulled me into one of the lobby's dimly lit alcoves. I didn't resist.

'What do you mean?' Bart had lowered his voice to something like a whisper. 'How could they possibly have found out?'

I shook my head. All I could think about was Sabeen's mother and father, the disappointment I imagined etched on their faces.

'What did they say, though?' Bart pressed. 'Why are you leaving? Did they . . . I mean, are you . . . ?'

'I've been suspended,' I told him. I'd said it almost as a question, but voicing it made it seem real. I'd been suspended. I would probably – definitely – be fired. And that made me think about my own parents. What

175

would my mother say? My father, I knew, wouldn't say anything. He wouldn't have to.

'Fuck,' I announced suddenly. 'Just . . . fucking . . . *fuck*.'

Bart smiled at that – I suppose at the spectacle of me swearing. He was trying to be encouraging – I recognized as much even then – but nevertheless it was the wrong thing to do.

'It's not funny, Bart.'

'I'm not laughing, Jack. I'm just –'

'You are laughing. You're smiling even now.'

His face went deadpan. 'I'm sorry, mate. I honestly wasn't laughing at you. I'm just trying to get my head around it, that's all.'

Now I laughed. *Bart* was trying to get *his* head around it.

'How did they know, though?' he repeated. 'Did they tell you how they found out?'

I gave another raw little snort. 'They mentioned a concerned neighbour. They said they couldn't go into specifics. And it's bullshit anyway because the whole point is they didn't have any neighbours. That's why I put them there.'

'So . . . what? You think Mr Yazdani and the others were making that up? That they found out some other way?'

In truth, until that point, I hadn't been particularly concerned with how they'd found out. I'd been thinking more about Sabeen and her family, about what would happen to them now. And, yes, about what would happen to me. It hadn't even crossed my mind by that stage that I might be subject to criminal proceedings. Losing my job – getting fired: that was bad enough for me.

Bart was waiting for me to answer. I was about to shake my head again, to insist I had no idea, when it struck me the answer was staring me in the face. Literally.

'Why don't you tell me?' I said.

I knew for a fact I'd covered my tracks when I'd set up Sabeen and her family in their new home, so there was no way I could have been caught through something I'd left showing on the system. I briefly considered Ali's phantom immigration official, but if the Home Office really had been involved in the discovery, Mr Yazdani and his cronies would have told me. They had no reason to hide behind a lie. There was always the possibility some neighbour had stuck their oar in, precisely as Mr Yazdani had claimed, but it was like I said: Sabeen and her family didn't have many neighbours, and none that would have had any cause to complain. And besides, Sabeen and the others – they were careful. To the extent half the family rarely ventured out. If somebody from their community had dobbed them in, it would have taken someone peculiarly vindictive. And, personally, I'd always held the belief that people in general do their best to get along. It's only when they feel threatened that they lash out, and no one from Sabeen's family had the temperament, or any reason, to threaten anyone.

No, the way I saw it, the explanation was right in front of me. Bart was the only other person in the world who knew about Sabeen. I hadn't even confided in Syd. And here he was now, quizzing me on what I knew about how the department heads had found out. I mean, for Christ's sake, he was more interested in that than the fact I'd just been suspended.

He was looking at me, pretending he hadn't heard right. 'What did you say?'

I faced him fully. 'I said, why don't you tell me?'

That smile again, more pointed this time. 'You think *I* told them?'

'You're the only one who knew. You're the only one I *trusted*.'

'Seriously, Jack. I know you're pissed off right now, but think for a moment about what you're saying. What possible reason could I have for going behind your back?'

'I can think of dozens of reasons, as it happens.' There'd been talk recently of a spot opening up at the pay grade above ours and it was possible Bart was positioning himself for the promotion. But that was tenuous to say the least, and I had enough sense even at that point to recognize that for Bart any such manoeuvring would have been completely out of character. In fact, if I'm honest, there was really only one possible explanation that had come to mind.

'Maybe you were just pissed off at me,' I said. 'Jealous, even.'

'Jealous? What on earth would I be jealous of?'

'The house, for example. *Syd.*'

'Syd? What the fuck, Jack!'

Bart's outrage, in my mind, seemed only to validate my accusation. His relationship with Syd was something that had been needling me virtually since the day I introduced them. I'd never quite shaken the feeling they were sharing a joke at my expense behind my back. It was little things: glances they shared, expressions that passed between them. I'd always tried to dismiss the way I'd felt as paranoia, but it's like I said before, right? *Just because you're paranoid* . . . And quite honestly it felt good to finally voice the suspicions I'd been nurturing. To be on the attack, too, when so far I'd been wholly on the defensive.

'I'd expect you to deny it,' I said. 'But I've seen the way you look at her. I've seen the way you sidle up to her when you think no one else is watching.'

Bart was doing a good impression of being too flabbergasted to speak. '*Sidle up to her*,' he managed to echo. He glanced around him as though in search of some assistance. The security guard had taken an interest in us, but the lobby otherwise remained empty. I suppose that's one thing I can be grateful for now: that as I stood there making a tit of myself, there was nobody else around to watch.

'I came down here to see if I could help,' Bart said.

'You know, to lend a bit of moral support. I didn't expect to be fucking *accused*. Of losing you your job. Of trying to steal your girlfriend. I mean, *Jesus*, Jack!'

I think I must have realized at that point, at least on some level, that Bart's outrage was genuine. That yet again I was in the wrong. And I must have known too that if I was going to rescue our friendship, I would have to start trying right then. I couldn't *un*accuse my friend. But Bart knew what I was going through. He knew me well enough not to take what I'd said to him too seriously. Sure, even if I were to apologize he'd be pissed off at me for a while, and would probably still feel genuinely hurt, but we'd fallen out before and got past it. I had no reason to suspect that this time would prove any different – if only I could set aside for a moment what was left of my misplaced pride.

The security guard had moved out from behind his desk. At most I had another ten seconds, after which I'd be escorted from the building and Bart would disappear back upstairs. Time enough to say sorry, though. More than enough time to make my choice.

'Thanks,' I said to Bart. 'But if this is what your moral support looks like, frankly you can stick it up your arse.'

Sydney

I got the drugs from a guy I know at work. I suspect Jack will worry about me talking about this because he wouldn't want me to get myself in trouble. Plus, I suppose, there's the idea that my taking drugs makes me unreliable. Except, the way I look at it, what type of person would come across worse: someone who took drugs and owned up to it or who pretended they didn't and was later found out? And they *will* find out, I know they will. Jack's friend Karen? She's probably found out already. As for me getting in trouble, I'm fairly sure that horse has bolted too. Besides, a caution for possession: if that's as much as all of this amounts to in the end, I'll be laughing all the way to rehab.

So, yeah, I scored, when for four whole years the thought of doing so hadn't even crossed my mind. OK, OK, so it had crossed my mind but only the way a memory might. Or, actually, a worry.

Again – as with my mother's visit – it was after what happened to Elsie. In fact I'd just come from the hospital, where for several hours I'd watched Elsie lying immobile on her bed in exactly the same position as when I'd visited the day before. I was at my desk, pretending I was thinking about something else, when I noticed Howard (not his real name. *Any resemblance to persons either living or dead*, etc. etc.) loitering on his own near the coffee machine. And I just got up. And I walked over to him. And I said, hi Howard, how's it going, and before I knew it I was sixty quid poorer.

In my defence I didn't use right away. Not for almost a fortnight. It was only on the day Jack was hauled into his boss's office that I finally succumbed. Again, not because of Jack's job. The timing in that sense was purely coincidental. Or not, actually, but you know what I mean. And you see, that's why it *is* important I admit to this. That I lay my coke-encrusted credit card on the table. Because it was partly due to the drugs that I reacted the way I did when Jack got home. And it's *definitely* because I reacted the way I did that Jack, afterwards, went straight to the Evening Star. So that's on me too, is what I'm saying. I fucked up. Again. And Jack's day, which hadn't begun well, was about to get a whole lot shittier.

I got an email. That's what started it. As Jack was at his desk, unaware that his boss's hand was priming itself to settle on his shoulder, I was sitting on the lid of our toilet staring at the screen of my iPhone. The shower was running and the bathroom mirror was already dripping with mist but I still hadn't even shed my pyjamas. I think I had my toothbrush in my mouth too. I did, because I remember the toothpastey drool that hit the screen of my phone after it fell from between my parted lips.

I hadn't recognized the sender. I only opened the email at all because Jack's name had been the subject line. And the attachment had displayed automatically. There was no message, no writing of any kind. Just the picture that had sent me blindly groping for the toilet seat.

The photograph was one of Jack. Smiling. *Leering* – in a way I'd never seen him doing before. And beside him, with a look in her adoring eyes that conveyed way more than any line of text could have, there was a girl planting her lips on his cheek. A woman, I suppose you could have called her. Barely. She looked foreign. Like, Mediterranean. Middle Eastern, maybe. As well as kissing him she was clutching Jack's arm. Clasping it. And the two of them were heading through a doorway I didn't recognize. Into an apartment, it looked like. A bedsit? Which got me thinking that maybe it was one of Jack's. One of the ones he'd allocated – just as the girl was probably one of Jack's as well. Someone he'd *saved*. Someone who felt they owed him. Someone, basically, as grateful and as gullible as me.

For some time I sat there too stunned to think.

Jack. *My* Jack. Doing . . . *this*.

I stared for another moment at the photograph and then I hurled the phone – Jack's *leer* – against the towel rail. It hit a towel (surprise, surprise) and didn't break, not even when it landed on the hardwood floor. I kicked it as it rebounded towards me and it skid-spun under the washing basket and cowered against the skirting. Fucking prick. Fucking cradle-snatching, two-faced, two-timing *prick*. I spat my toothbrush into the sink and wrenched off the shower, not caring about the water that soaked my sleeve. I stood there for a while adding to the steam, glaring at the shower curtain as though it were *him*. My mind started racing through all the things I felt a sudden urge to do, all of which culminated in a vision of something breaking. The mirror behind me, my toes against the side panel of the bath, Jack's jaw. If my phone had been in my hand I would have called him, would have started by perforating his eardrums. I needed to do something that would feel that gratifying, something as pure a release as a scream.

And that's when it came to me. The memory of that little package I'd tucked away in one of my old handbags. Fuck Jack, fuck being used, fuck fucking *sobriety*. After resisting for so long, the alternative was suddenly *way* more appealing.

When Jack got home I was sitting on my yoga mat. Still in my slightly damp pyjamas. My hair a frizzy disaster probably, from all that steam. Toothpaste drool like a slug-trail down my front. My anger hadn't diminished. Instead, thanks to the half a gram or so of slightly urine-tinged coke I'd consumed (in my more discerning days I would have had words to say to Howard but I wasn't presently in any mood to be fussy) it had become more focused. Honed, like that kitchen knife we were only vaguely aware at that point had gone missing. I had no idea what the time was. Too early for Jack to be home on any normal day but as this wasn't turning out to be a normal day I wasn't all that surprised to hear him come back. I'd go as far as to say I'd been expecting him.

'Syd? Are you at home? Why's all your stuff here?' Jack's voice calling from the hallway.

I didn't answer. I didn't move.

'Syd?'

I heard him head into the kitchen. After he failed to find me there, he came back along the hallway and took the stairs two at a time. I felt a surge of revulsion as he drew near.

'Syd? Are you in there?'

After the pounding of his feet his voice, outside the door, was oddly hushed. I guessed he must have assumed that, as I wasn't at work, I must have been ill.

His smile when he saw me sitting there was half frown.

'Syd? What are you doing in here? Are you OK? Listen, I . . . something's happened. At work.' He gave me a look then. I could see the guilt but it was masked behind regret.

I tossed him my phone. Threw it at him, really. He was so surprised he only just caught it. And I think that's when he noticed the little make-up mirror beside me. The dusting of powder, the rolled-up banknote. The state of me, basically. The fire in my broad black eyes.

I stood and pushed past him. By the time Jack reacted I was already halfway down the stairs.

'Syd?' He sounded incredulous. 'Syd, what the . . .'

I heard him trailing after me. I went straight from the bottom of the staircase into the living room and couldn't resist slamming the door.

I was by the window when I heard it open again behind me.

'*Wanker*,' I spat, spinning, and Jack recoiled as though I'd slapped him. 'You lying, arrogant wanker!'

'What the hell, Syd? What have I done?'

He was still holding my phone. The screen, I noticed, was blank.

'Look at the picture, Jack. Look at the picture and then you tell me.'

'What picture?' Jack stared dumbly at my iPhone. He hit the home button, swiped the screen with his finger. 'It's locked,' he said, looking up.

'For fuck's sake.' I marched across and snatched it from him. I swiped, jabbed in my code. Got it wrong, jabbed again. Harder this time, slower. The picture appeared and I held it two inches from Jack's nose. He recoiled as though I'd meant to hit him, then gradually his eyes began to focus. His face became a portrait of confusion, so perfect it must have been practised.

'Amira?' he said.

I barked out a laugh. '*Amira*. How exotic.' I sniffed, wiped my nostrils with a knuckle.

Jack had somehow taken hold of the phone. He was studying the picture, pinching and zooming, and the movement of his fingers looked to me like a caress. I flung out a hand and knocked the phone from his grip. It hit the granite surround of the fireplace and the screen – finally – shattered.

'Jesus, Syd!' Jack was left holding thin air. He was looking at me now as though I was as cracked as my iPhone.

'Get out, Jack. Get the fuck out of this house.'

'Syd. Seriously. I don't know what you think that picture shows, but I promise you it's completely –'

'Get out! Get out or I swear to God I'll throw you out!'

Which sounded so ridiculous I'm surprised Jack managed not to laugh.

'She's just a tenant! Someone who came to me for help. Although *she* didn't, her sister did. This thing at work I was trying to tell you about, it –'

'I don't want to hear it, Jack! I don't want to hear about your little harem. Although, actually, I'm curious: was the sister not young enough for you? Is that why you ended up with *her*?' I flicked my chin towards the carcass of my phone.

'*Ended up with?* I wasn't sleeping with her, Syd! I wasn't sleeping with anyone! I was just . . .' Jack paused all of a sudden and whatever had come into his head caused it to tilt. 'Where did you get it anyway? That picture. Did you . . .' He straightened, as though sensing he had cause to be affronted. 'Have you been following me?'

'What? No, I haven't been fucking following you!'

'So where did you get it?'

'It doesn't matter how I got it. All that matters is what it shows. Don't tell me you're denying that's you.'

'Why would I deny it? It's a picture of me standing in the street!'

'It's more than that and you know it!'

Jack exhaled. 'Where did you get it, Syd?' he repeated. 'If you're going to accuse me of something, at least tell me where you're getting your evidence. Or are you too coked up right now to remember?'

'Fuck you. Someone sent it to me. OK? It was on my email when I woke up.'

'Who?'

'What?'

'Who sent it to you?'

'Just . . .' I shook my head. 'I don't know. It was just some random AOL address. Letters and numbers. No name.'

Jack stooped to pick up my phone, tried to get it working again. It bit him.

'Ow. Shit.' He sucked at his finger, bloodied by the shattered glass.

I sniffed out a smile. 'Serves you right. I hope you get fucking gangrene.'

Jack ignored me, tried again with the phone. 'It's buggered. You've completely buggered it.' He was staring at it, fiddling with the power switch. 'Not that it matters. I know exactly who sent it to you. Although I'm surprised he bothered to do it anonymously. I'd have thought he would have wanted to claim credit.'

'What are you talking about? *Who* are you talking about?'

'Bloody Bart, that's who.'

'*Bart?* Why would Bart —'

'Because he wants to get into your knickers, that's why! He wants my job, too. My promotion. He wants to screw me basically, to give himself a chance of screwing you.'

Now I laughed. I couldn't help it. 'That's ridiculous. Bart doesn't want to *screw* me. He's your friend, Jack – remember?'

'That's what I thought, too. Until he got me fired.'

'Fired? You've been fired?'

'Fired. Suspended. Same difference.'

I pressed my palms to my temples. That focus I'd been cultivating had started to dissipate. What I wanted was another line of coke. Not wanted. *Needed.*

'Anyway, I should have known you'd defend him.'

I looked up. 'What?'

'Bart. I should have known you'd defend him.'

'What the hell is that supposed to mean?'

'What do you think it means?'

I gaped. 'You're the one who's been sleeping around, Jack! Don't try and turn this around on me!'

'I'm not turning anything around. I'm stating the facts, that's all.'

'Jesus, Jack. And I thought *I* was messed up. Your parents have made you so insecure you can't even trust your best friend. Your *girlfriend*.'

Jack recoiled. He seemed to flounder briefly but then recovered himself. He met my eye. 'Yeah, well,' he said. 'It could be worse. At least I'm not a bloody drug addict.'

I don't know what it was exactly that finally tipped me over the edge. That Jack had struck so close to the mark, probably. That little raw bit deep inside that when someone touches it causes us to kick out purely as a reflex. And that's exactly what I did. I flew at him with everything flailing, so that he had no choice but to reverse into the hall. In the end he managed to catch hold of my arms but not before one of my fists cuffed his cheek.

'Bloody hell, Syd!'

I wriggled and twisted myself free. Jack held out a palm like he was trying to stop traffic. With his other hand he was dabbing at the spot beneath his eye where I'd punched him, checking for some evidence I'd drawn blood.

'You hit me!'

'Good! I was trying to!'

Jack looked again at the tips of his fingers, determined

to produce something that would show how much he was hurt.

'Get out, Jack.' I was breathing heavily, exhaling my words. 'Just fucking go.'

I think Jack briefly considered putting up a fight. He would have won if he had, because I'd expended all the energy I had left. After all that coke it was time for the comedown, which for me always feels like I've been drained by a Dementor. Usually the only thing that cures it is another big fat line but all I wanted to do this time was curl up beneath my duvet in a ball.

Jack turned and snatched up his keys. The bowl we keep them in tipped from the sideboard but he didn't pause long enough to right it. He slammed the door so hard it rebounded and as I sank to the floor I watched him storm into the street. And that was the moment it first struck me: the worry that's been gnawing at me ever since. Jack said before that it feels like he's losing me but the danger is we're losing each other. And I realize that's part of this – that it's the point of this whole sordid game – but even so I'm worried I don't know how to stop it. That's what scares me the most, Jack. That maybe now there's no way to stop it.

Jack

We're going to the police. OK, Syd? We're going to take what we've written and we're going to explain, to tell them everything we know. It's what we said we would do at the beginning, if it ever came down to it, and I don't see how we've been left with any other choice. Besides, it's clear to me now. It's obvious, the way it was obvious to you right at the start.

First, though, we have to finish what we've begun. It won't take long. We're almost there. The only part left to tell is the bit we've both been dreading. The part that makes me sound guilty and Syd, in her words, like she's going insane. Which I admit isn't all that far away from what I thought at the beginning of this, too. I figured Syd was just reacting to what had happened to Elsie. That she was putting two and two together and coming up with one: one cause, one threat, one absurd rationalization. I couldn't see how such disparate elements could fit together. I didn't want to see it. It was easier – less frightening – to view what was happening as a run of bad luck. But imagine, I don't know, that your vision gets blurry. That you're getting headaches. That sometimes when you cough, you cough up blood. Perhaps you'll be able to fool yourself that everything's fine, that none of the symptoms are related, but to an onlooker the reality will seem self-evident. That there's something darker at work. Something deadly. Something, to stop it from killing you, that sooner or later you're going to have to face.

It was barely lunchtime when I got to the Evening Star. I mentioned before that I'm not much of a drinker, but this was one of those occasions when the pub seemed about the only appropriate place for me to go. Syd and I had been to our new local once before, but only for form's sake. You know, to say we had. But quite honestly, and even though it looks OK from the outside, the Evening Star wasn't the kind of place I'd normally have been in any hurry to visit again. It wasn't rough or anything, not that I witnessed, just a bit depressing. It was your typical south London boozer, basically. The type of establishment where, if you were to ask to see the wine list, you'd be offered a choice of either red or white. There was no music, no Sky Sports, not a gourmet burger in sight. Before the smoking ban the air inside would have been more carbon monoxide than oxygen, and since then the odours that had previously been masked had taken over: urine and bleach blocks in the area closest to the toilets; soggy bar towels and stale lager everywhere else.

'Can I help you?'

The bartender, a man with tattoos on his forearms that had faded green, and whose age might have been anything between forty and sixty, was looking at me as though he suspected I'd wandered in lost. It wasn't quite *An American Werewolf in London*, but for a moment I was transported from SW17 all the way to the Yorkshire moors.

'Pint of Foster's, please,' I said. 'No, wait,' I amended. 'Jack Daniel's and Coke. A double.'

The barman hesitated slightly before picking up a glass, as though he was still weighing up whether to serve me. He pumped two shots of Bell's from the optic without checking whether I was happy with the substitution and then turned to face me once again.

'Ice?' he said, and I shook my head. He filled the glass part way using the dispenser, so that my drink was half whisky, half sugary brown water. 'There's a ten-pound minimum,' he said, when I presented my card.

'Keep it,' I answered. 'I'm going to want more than one.'

I carried my glass to a table beside the dusty, unused fireplace and settled on the least-stained chair. Other than a guy seated at the bar with his dog lying at his feet, there were only three other patrons in a room that was maybe a third of the area of our ground floor: two blokes seated together by the window, nursing the final inches of their pints, and another loner at the table nearest the door. He was doing a crossword, from the look of things. Heads had turned when I'd come in, but once I'd settled it was only that dog under the bar stool that continued to stare. I tipped my glass to it, then drained half my drink in one swallow.

What a day. I mean, seriously: what an utterly crappy day.

First work, then Syd. And, caught in between, Sabeen and her entire family. I still couldn't get my head around everything that had happened. How it had happened, when the morning had started out like any other. It was that photo that was foremost in my mind, the one showing me and Amira. Syd had only let me see it for a moment, but there was no denying that it hadn't looked good. I recalled Ali's teasing, the way I'd tried covering my embarrassment with a joke, but no one was laughing now. Least of all Syd. Although how Syd could think I would cheat on her – with a seventeen-year-old, for heaven's sake! – was beyond me. And based on a photograph, which in Syd's eyes had been enough to dispel any reasonable doubt. I'd been accused, convicted and sentenced before I'd even known I was on trial.

And Bart. My so-called friend. It was what he'd done that stunned me above all. As well as telling our boss about how I'd helped Sabeen, he'd emailed that photo to Syd. More than that: he'd spied on me, picked his moment, taken that photo and *then* made sure Syd saw it, all while hiding behind his bullshit, made-up email address and his phoney friendship with me. I couldn't believe I'd trusted him, even further with some things than I'd trusted Syd. Which made me worry, briefly, about what else he might have up his sleeve – what other secrets of mine he planned to share. But it occurred to me fairly quickly that it hardly mattered. He'd lost me my job, sabotaged my relationship with my girlfriend. Things were already about as bad as they could get.

I'd had four double whisky and Cokes by the time he walked in. Elsie's father. My favourite neighbourhood nutcase. He spotted me immediately and paused for half a step, but when he noted the bartender watching him he headed directly to the bar.

I must have been more drunk than I realized because I sniggered. Aloud.

Elsie's father dropped his chin towards his shoulder. 'Is something funny?'

Which struck me as funny in itself. I mean, how clichéd could you get? He might as well have accused me of spilling the pint the barman had just placed in front of him.

I managed this time to keep my amusement to myself. 'Just the day I'm having,' I said.

Elsie's father continued to stare, then after a second or two turned towards his drink.

I should have left then. I'd finished what was left of my whisky and Coke, and I wasn't particularly taken with the prospect of approaching the bar to order another. But as I was contemplating my next move, it occurred to me that I would need to go up to the bar anyway to settle my tab. And if I was going to do that,

I might as well get another drink. Because I didn't *want* to leave yet. And I certainly didn't want Elsie's father to believe I was only going because of him. So screw it, I thought. Screw him, screw Bart, screw everyone. If I wanted another drink, I'd bloody well order one. I'd had enough of pandering to what people thought. Of modifying my behaviour to please others, only to have them stab me in the back.

I carried my empties to the bar with me.

'Settle up?' the barman said.

I shook my head. 'Same again.'

The barman glanced at Elsie's father, then took one of my dirty glasses and reached towards the optics.

'You sure you haven't had enough?' said a voice from the bar stool beside me. 'What did you do, hit your head throwing up in the toilet?'

I'd intended to ignore Elsie's father if he opted to speak to me. 'What are you talking about?'

He swivelled on his stool. 'That mark on your face,' he said. 'Looks like you either fell over or someone came at you with a flying handbag. Now who might have done that? That pretty little lady of yours, by any chance?' He angled himself slightly towards the man seated on the bar stool beside him. 'The one who would be pretty if she didn't have a nine iron sticking halfway up her arse.'

The man beside him looked down at his pint, as though he knew what was coming and wanted no part of it. I touched my cheek where Syd had walloped me. I flinched, as much in surprise as from the pain I felt.

This time Elsie's father was the one to snigger. 'It *was* her, wasn't it? She kicked you out too, I bet. That's why you ended up here.' He laughed into his upturned pint jug. He was still grinning after he'd swallowed.

My hand fell from my cheek and I picked up my refilled glass. I was halfway back to my seat when it struck me what Elsie's father had said. What he'd failed to say, rather. Because he surely must have guessed by that point that Syd and I had been the ones to call social services. And yet in spite of what had happened to Elsie since, his daughter evidently hadn't even crossed his mind.

'Don't you care?' I said, turning.

Once again his chin touched his shoulder, his upper lip cocked halfway to a sneer.

'Your daughter's lying in hospital and you're sitting here . . . what? Celebrating, is it?'

That sneer of his faltered, and I saw his eyes dart towards the barman. He might not have cared about his daughter, but he clearly cared enough about his own skin to worry about what other people might have been thinking. The pub was by no means full, but in addition to the regulars who'd been here when I'd arrived, there was a man and a woman seated in one of the booths now, as well as another couple standing at the bar. And all eyes were focused on us.

Elsie's father rose from his bar stool. Slowly, preparing himself, he sipped his drink at me.

'I would've thought you'd've learned your lesson,' he said, carefully placing his pint jug down beside him. 'I warned you about sticking your beak in where it doesn't belong.'

The memory of our previous altercation came back to me; of the pain when his knee had struck my groin. I pressed on with my attack regardless. 'Have you even visited her?' I said. I was sure that if he had, Syd would have seen him, would at some point have mentioned it to me. 'Do you even know what hospital she's at?'

Elsie's father bared his teeth and started forward. The barman reached between the beer taps and caught his shoulder. 'Sean,' he said. 'I've warned you about kicking off in here.' He aimed his gaze then squarely at me. 'And you, you should have taken the hint and settled up. Now I suggest you leave. You can come back for your credit card tomorrow.'

There was a finality to his tone that reminded me from out of nowhere of my father. It bore no ambiguity, left no room for quarrel. It was brusque, business-like: nothing personal. What he said would simply be done. And that was why, with my father, it had always hurt so much. It was never personal with him either. He spoke to me the way he would have to a stranger on the street. Politely, when called for, but never affectionately. Curtly, more often, and never with any suggestion he cared.

I dropped my eyes, sensed them skitter around the room. I slid my drink on to the nearest table and turned to snatch up my coat. I got as far as the door.

'Poor little lamb,' called Elsie's father. 'Now he's got nowhere left to go. Why not do everyone a favour and put yourself out of your misery?' He sniggered then, and it was that snigger – gleeful, vindictive, *triumphant* – that caused me to turn.

'What?' I said.

Elsie's father shrugged himself free of the barman's grip. 'I said, put yourself out of your misery. Go take a bath in the Thames.' Another snigger, a satisfied little glance at the other regulars closest to the bar. He wasn't just laughing, I realized. He was gloating.

And that's when it struck me. Because who else had motive the way he did? Syd and I had interfered in his life, now he was interfering in ours. And all at once it made sense why he hadn't tried confronting me sooner: the man had already taken his revenge.

'You?' I said. 'You did this?'

I thought of Bart, then. Of what I'd accused him of. My best friend. My only really close friend, actually, apart from Syd. But I'd been wrong. Hideously, hopelessly wrong. Syd's reaction had said it all. *He's your friend, Jack – remember?* And I did, finally – but too late.

Elsie's father didn't say anything. But given the look on his face, he didn't have to.

'You, what? You followed me? And Ali ... Sabeen ... that was you?' I started towards him from my spot beside the door. 'You . . . you cost me my job. My best friend. My *girlfriend*.'

I said before, when the policewoman asked, that I don't get angry. And I don't. Genuinely, I'm not that type of person. But everyone has a limit, and in terms of what I was willing to put up with (as well as what I'd drunk), I was already well beyond mine. And it wasn't just about me. It was about Sabeen and Ali and all the rest of them. It was about Elsie. About Syd, in my mind, more than anyone.

It wasn't much of a fight. Perhaps if I'd managed to get in one good swing that would have been enough for me. But the barman was out quickly from behind the counter and he had hold of me before I'd even realized he was there. Someone was holding Elsie's father back too, I think, although if I'm honest it's all kind of a blur. I recall trying to hit the bloke and failing, and then getting driven back towards the door. Like in rugby, when one of the skinnier blokes gets lifted off his feet by a forward. Before I knew it I was out on the street, on my arse basically, the barman on top of me, and screaming the first thing that came to mind.

So I'm not saying I didn't say it. I did: I admit it. But the point is, I didn't mean it. I swear to God I didn't. I said other stuff as well, stuff I don't even remember. And that's part of the point, too: I was out of my mind. All those people can say what they want, can tell the police whatever they like, but there's no way they can say for certain what I was thinking. I mean, you hear it practically every day. Don't you?

I'll kill you. I'll fucking kill you.

It's just, you know. An expression. Just because someone says it, doesn't mean they actually plan to do it.

Sydney

Jack left me messages. Long, rambling explanations that basically explained nothing at all. It was all a mistake, he said. A misunderstanding. He mentioned a fight at the pub, some altercation – another one – between him and Elsie's father. He said that Elsie's father had engineered it all. The photo, our argument, *everything*. He said he'd set him up at work, that him getting suspended was Elsie's father's fault too. Which to me sounded almost delusional, like Jack's innate insecurity had morphed into crazed paranoia. And anyway it entirely missed the point. It wasn't Elsie's father who'd come between us. It was *Jack*. His lies. His *infidelity*.

I called Bart, told him to tell Jack to stop ringing me. I assumed because I hadn't let him back into the house that Jack must have been staying with him but Bart hadn't let Jack in either. Jack had come to him, tried to make some half-arsed apology but screw him, Bart had said to me. If what Jack had accused him of was really what he thought of him, Bart said, then frankly it was good riddance to bad rubbish. Which is pretty much how I'd felt as well at first but even so I was surprised to hear it from Bart. He and Jack must have had more of a falling out than I'd realized. I knew how fond Jack was of Bart and all at once I found myself feeling sorry for him. To the extent, actually, that I wondered if I hadn't been too hard on him. That photo had been pretty fucking compelling but I recognized too that I hadn't exactly been in the most secure frame of mind when I'd received it. Maybe, somehow, I'd misinterpreted it.

I made a start on looking through Jack's stuff. I'm not proud of it. It's not the type of thing I'd ever thought I would have found myself doing. It made me feel fucking crazy if I'm honest and resentful too that circumstances had brought me to this point where I was behaving like a schizophrenic housewife. But anyway, that's how I found it. I was rifling through the pile of shoeboxes at the bottom of Jack's wardrobe, looking for, I don't know, love letters? More photographs? Fucking *panties*? Anything, basically, that would prove or disprove that Jack had been having an affair . . . and there it was, buried beneath a stack of Jack's trainers.

He let himself in. I was sitting waiting for him in the kitchen.

'What the fuck is this, Jack?'

Jack checked his watch. He was early and he must have assumed I was having a go at him for that. He didn't appear to have noticed the shoebox, which I'd placed on the kitchen table.

'I'm sorry, Syd. I thought . . . I mean, I didn't think . . .' He looked at his watch again and I shook my head at him dismissively.

'I don't mean the time, Jack. I mean *this*. This . . . whatever this is.' I shoved the box so that it slid across the surface towards him.

Still Jack didn't comprehend. He saw the box now but showed no sign of having recognized it.

'Listen, Syd . . . whatever's inside that, I swear to you I haven't done anything wrong.'

I started to speak but Jack talked over me.

'It's Elsie's father. Sean "Begbie" fucking Payne. He's a nutcase. A mentalist. Everything that's been happening is because of him. Like that photo,' he pressed before I could interrupt. '*He* took that. The same way he told work about Sabeen. He's mad at me. At us. Because of Elsie. Not because of what happened to her – I mean, he doesn't give a shit about that – but because we interfered.'

Jack had moved closer as he'd been speaking and was now gripping the back of one of the dining chairs with both of his hands. He looked a mess, I realized. The way he had the day I'd first met him, when he'd blown weather-battered through the doors of that hotel lobby. From the look of him he hadn't shaved since the day I'd thrown him out and I was fairly sure he was still wearing the same clothes. I wondered where he'd been sleeping. There's no way he would have gone to his parents' place, not in such humiliating circumstances, and seeing as Bart had refused to put him up he'd most likely been staying in some cheap hotel.

'Jack –'

'I'm begging you, Syd, please.' Jack's knuckles, around the chair back, were bulging white. 'You have to believe me. Elsie's father, he practically admitted it.'

'Jack –'

'I mean, for Christ's sake, Syd – he even broke into our house!'

I'd been pressing my fingertips to my temples but at that my hands fell away. I looked up.

'He did what?'

Jack was pacing now, two steps one way, two steps back, traversing the width of our kitchen.

'I can't prove it was him, but someone was definitely in here. More than once, I'm thinking now. This one time I heard a noise and I went downstairs and when I didn't find anything I came back into the bedroom. And you, you said . . .' Jack stopped then, looked at me. 'I mean . . . I just . . . I had this feeling, that's all,' he went on and his eyes skidded away from me. 'And I've been thinking about it, is the point, and I reckon he must have got in through the kitchen, through one of the windows maybe, or even the back door if we left it unlocked. And then, when I came back upstairs, when I went to the toilet I expect, all he would have needed to do was sneak past me and let himself out the same way.' He looked at me urgently. 'You see?'

What I saw was that Jack was even more of a mess than I'd realized. I'd already gathered from the messages he'd left me that he was convinced Elsie's father was out to get him. That he'd hatched some elaborate plot and was intent on sabotaging Jack's life. *Elsie's father.* The same man who, when he'd had a problem with Jack before, had opted to simply knee him in the bollocks. Clandestine surveillance, to my mind, didn't exactly seem the man's style.

'Jack, listen to me –'

'I'm telling you, Syd,' Jack persisted, 'he's a lunatic. At the pub he –'

'JACK!'

He'd been pacing again and he stopped short, midway between the back door and the oven.

'It doesn't matter,' I said. 'Don't you get it? All this . . . *paranoia*, it doesn't change anything. It doesn't alter what you *did*!'

'But that's the point! I didn't *do* anything! I mean, yes, the work stuff I'll admit to, but in the circumstances you would have done exactly the same thing. They were destitute, Syd. About to be kicked out on to the street!'

I turned away then and Jack must have realized that he was losing me. That once again what he was saying was beside the point.

He raised a hand, shook it frantically.

'The photo,' he said. 'I get it, Syd. I do. What it looks like. What you must be thinking. But I swear to God:

it's completely innocent. Amira, she's just a kid. And that photo: I remember now when it was taken. Amira's brother, he was standing right beside us. It's just been cropped to make sure he's out of shot. I told you, it . . .'

This time I was the one to hold up a hand. I'd heard enough. About Elsie's father, about Jack's precious Amira. Just *enough*.

'All I want to know,' I said, enunciating, 'is where you got that box. What it was doing hidden away at the bottom of your wardrobe.'

For the first time since he'd entered the room Jack looked properly at the shoebox on the kitchen table. He'd barely glanced at it before but now when he looked at it he saw it fully. And he recognized it, I could tell. He knew exactly what I would have found when I'd looked inside.

'Syd . . .' He started forward, his hands spread to try and contain yet another lie. 'Syd, that's . . . it's just . . . it's nothing. It's something I found, that's all.'

I scraped my chair back from the table. I stood, picked up the box and tipped it so that its contents spilled on to the surface. I held out the lid so Jack could see it. So he could read what was written on its underside.

'Syd, I know. I know what it says. That's why I didn't –'

'*Jessica*,' I read. 'My sister's name, Jack. Written in felt-tip. Like, the way a kid would write it. Is this . . . I mean . . . all this stuff . . . is it . . .'

Is it real? I wanted to ask but all I could do was shake my head. Because I knew. Even though I didn't recognize the things inside – the postcards, the shells, that fucking Care Bear – somehow, the moment I'd found it, I knew the box and everything in it was real. It *felt* real. Like . . . I don't know. Like books. Like the way when you pick up a book that's been read you can always tell whether it's also been loved. And I say I didn't recognize the things inside. Maybe I didn't – but somehow I felt like I should have.

'Where did you get it, Jack? Why were you hiding it?'

'Syd, please . . .' Jack tried to touch me then and I pulled away.

'Just tell me! Just for once give me a straight answer!'

'I did tell you!' Jack said. 'I found it! Up in the attic. At the same time I found that dead cat. It was tucked behind the –'

I'd been looking again at the things on the table. My gaze snapped up.

'What cat?'

Jack closed his eyes, pinched them tight.

'Jack? What fucking *cat*?'

It all came out then. All the things Jack had kept hidden. Beginning with the box, how he'd found it, how he'd concealed it from me. The cat too, which as it turned out he'd buried in our overgrown garden. His worries about the house, about how they'd led him back to Evan – and about how, after that, he'd even spoken to Patrick Winters. They were small things, I suppose. Small *pieces*, as Jack says, but together they amounted to something bigger. A tableau of lies, just for starters, and the first thing I remember thinking was that I would never be able to fully trust Jack again. But something else was becoming clearer in my mind too. Something darker. It was like I was peering down into a pit, watching the shadows there slowly taking shape.

'What did I say, Jack?'

He looked at me blankly.

'You said I said something. That night you heard someone in the house. You said you came back upstairs into the bedroom and I said . . .' I left the sentence hanging, tried to stifle my dread as I waited for Jack to finish it.

He swallowed. 'You said . . . you said you'd felt a hand on your cheek.'

'But you . . . I mean, couldn't it just have been . . .'

'It wasn't me, Syd. But you were asleep. Dreaming probably. I figured . . .'

I was shaking my head again, I realized. Not just to cut off Jack's explanation but to keep at bay the one dawning on me. The house, this house we should never have owned. The box . . . Jack's work . . . that email . . .

The hand I'd felt on my cheek.

The sob built from my stomach and erupted sounding like a plea. I frisked the air blindly behind me and used the chair back to lower myself down. I'd never before had a panic attack, had never really understood what exactly the term meant. But it feels like that moment you wake from a nightmare, when the only thing you're sure is real is the terror that has its hands around your throat. Your heart is hammering against your ribcage and you're so cold your whole body starts to sweat. Even sitting I felt short of breath. I sensed Jack reach out to try and steady me but somehow I gestured him away. I didn't want him near me. I didn't want *anything* near me: the walls around me, the floor below me, the ceiling that was pressing on my head. I felt like I was being smothered, like all at once the air was some noxious gas.

It was my mother who hauled me to my feet. The memory of her, of the time I'd let her in the house. My forearm swept the table as I stood and my sister's treasures clattered to the floor.

'Syd?' Jack's voice, more distant than his proximity to me made possible. 'Syd, wait. Are you OK? Where are you going?'

I stumbled past him, into the hallway. I climbed the stairs, tripped, scrabbled higher. I was dimly aware of Jack's presence close behind me, but my focus was on what lay ahead. On those pictures. Winters's pictures. All, that is, except one.

I spotted her instantly. This time, for the first time, she shone out. My arm, though, felt heavy – clumsy with adrenaline – and I knocked several frames to the floor as I reached forward. With the picture in my hand I scrabbled at the backing, then I turned and collided with Jack. He stepped aside or I pushed him, I can't remember. I was aiming for the newel post, the picture now tight in my grip. I swung it, glass first. It shattered immediately but I swung it again. A third time, a fourth. When I flipped it over I was already bleeding but all I cared about was freeing the photograph from its frame. My grip was slick, sticky, and the glass chewed hungrily at my fingers. I was numb to it, though. All at once, in a way I hadn't experienced since my childhood, I was numb.

Coming home. In films, in poetry, in cheesy Christmas songs, it's become a concept so laden with sentiment it's almost impossible now to view it as something bad. Yet *home*, for me, is like a darkened corner. A foul place, somewhere sullied, which for most of my life I've been focused on trying to escape. I thought our new house would become my home, at one stage. As things turned out it never had a chance. Perhaps nowhere does. Perhaps the place you call home is something, once it's been chosen for you, you don't ever get to alter.

The journey took less than two hours but somehow, simultaneously, it took both more and less than that. A blink, in one sense. In another, a lifetime. As I sat rocking to the movements of the empty train, I clutched the photograph from the landing in my shredded fingertips. The picture itself – that little girl's face – was obscured by blood but on the back the writing I'd discovered was still visible. Just a date, a name. The same name I'd found written on the lid of that shoebox. This time, though, I recognized the handwriting, just as my mother had recognized the picture itself. She would have taken it, after all, and the annotation was hers as well. She made a note on all the photographs of me and Jessica that she took. I could see myself watching her doing it.

It was typical of my mother that she'd failed to move away. Typical of her weakness. Of her cowardice. After my father went to prison she'd had a chance to build her life anew but she'd settled after the house had been repossessed for renting a flat on the edge of the same neighbourhood. The *very* edge. The grubby fringe. Not really the same neighbourhood at all, in fact, but it was like the way she still dressed, the time she continued to spend applying make-up. If she walked the same streets, shopped at the same shops, she could fool herself that life was a continuum, that the mistakes she'd made – and what mistakes she'd made! What a howler, above all, marrying my father – weren't forks in the road but bumps, potholes, little things she could glide over as she continued on her journey. It was another act of denial, for all the good it did her. Because although I didn't understand everything yet, that much, at least, was clear: it was the things my mother had clung to – her habitat, her *routines* – that in the end had given us both away.

As I walked I felt the anger in me beginning to build. When I'd stepped off that train I'd expected it to melt away, to turn instead into something like fear. But I barely noticed the landmarks that in my mind had become so loathsome to me, didn't even flinch when I caught sight of our old house from across the street. When I reached the block containing my mother's flat I used the tradesmen's bell to let myself inside. I took the stairs, two at a time, and once I'd located the door I was looking for I beat at it with the fleshy part of my fist.

'How could you?'

My mother's startled eyes peering through the gap. She had the chain in place, otherwise I would have forced my way inside.

'Do you even know what you've done?'

I glared at her and hit the door again, with both hands this time, both palms, so that even though the chain held firm, my mother's instinct was to recoil.

'Sydney, please,' she hissed. 'You shouldn't be here. You –'

'Open the door! Open the fucking door or I swear to God I'll break it down!'

I hit the door again and didn't turn when I heard another door opening just behind me.

'What's going on out here?' came an old woman's voice.

'Let me in, Mother,' I said without looking round.

'Sydney, please . . .' she replied, her eyes darting between mine and her busybody neighbour's.

'Open. The fucking. *Door.*'

I heard tutting from across my shoulder as my mother retreated inside. As soon as the chain was off I shoved my way into my mother's hall. She spread her arms wide and continued to try and barricade my path.

'Listen to me, Sydney. Please. You need to leave. You need to *go.*' Even though the door to the flat was closed now she didn't raise her voice above a whisper.

'What did I say to you?' I said, ignoring her. 'What was the single thing I asked?' It didn't escape me that I was the one speaking like a parent. My mother, before me, was cringing like a frightened child.

'I'm sorry,' she said – pleaded, even – and I could tell she was just about to cry. 'But Sydney, please. Let's . . . let's go outside. OK? Let's talk about this outside.'

'I'm not going fucking anywhere until you give me an explanation!'

Which is when it struck me that she already had. That day she'd come to see me. *I'm not strong enough,* she'd said. *I've just never, ever been strong enough.* And what else, really, was there to add?

My mother shrivelled on her side of the hallway. Her resistance had crumbled: against my onslaught, to her tears. But that wasn't all. She appeared to be waiting for something, resigned to it. As though my onslaught, her tears, weren't the only things she'd been trying to hold off.

I glared at her, still furious, but all of a sudden that fury felt closer to fear. It was the way I'd expected to feel when I'd stepped off that train.

'Mum?'

The voice I heard was no longer my own. Or it was, just not Sydney Baker's. It belonged to the old me. To the girl I thought I'd left behind. I'd always worried whether the woman I'd become was just a front – whether, rather than armour, *Sydney Baker* was in reality nothing more than brittle shell. And there, standing in my mother's dismal hallway, I realized I was at last about to find out.

'Oh Mum. What have you done?'

I found myself backing away towards the apartment's front door. My mother was watching me pityingly.

'He's here, isn't he? He's actually *here*.'

I smelled him then, even before I heard him. The scent – the *stink* – was of nothing, individually, that would have been unpleasant and maybe it carried on a memory rather than physically through the air. But I smelled his aftershave, something like oranges. The coffee he drank. The gunk he slathered in his hair. Collectively it was worse than sewage and I might have gagged had a figure not at that point stepped into the hall. Like he was home. Like he'd never been away.

He smiled at me. The man who'd taunted me, tricked me, beaten me, broken me. He was here, now, right in front of me, *smiling*.

And then he spoke.

'Hello, Maggie,' my father said.

II

Jack

'And that's when we started writing.'

'When?'

'After Syd saw her father. After, three days later, they found Sean Payne in the alleyway behind our house.'

Inspector Leigh raises her head. 'His body, you mean,' she says. 'After they found Sean Payne's *body*. With a total of seventeen stab wounds in his neck, chest and stomach.'

She's studying me and I do my best not to look away. I feel guilty, of course I do, but wouldn't anyone? *Seventeen stab wounds.* It's just . . . it's brutal. There's no other word to describe it. And I can tell she's thrown the fact at us deliberately. She hasn't mentioned it before. No one has, not even the papers.

Seventeen.

I look at Syd and I can see she's thinking about the same thing I am. The morning the body was discovered we were looking out of our spare-bedroom window, and even through all the police officers we could see it. The blood. Sean Payne's blood. It was everywhere. Syd, for one, almost vomited. It's linked to her sister, I guess, this thing she has about death, but in the end the sight of all that blood is what got her to agree to my suggestion that we start writing things down. For her it was never about trying to understand, not the way it was for me, because Syd was clear about what was happening from the start. She recognized this was something her father had been building up to, and she realized what Sean Payne's murder, for us, really meant. But all that blood ... it made her recognize how important it was that we get our story straight. That we get it on record, in preparation for the point we're at now.

Detective Inspector Karen Leigh links her hands together and lets them rest on the stack of pages in front of her.

'Why?'

Syd and I exchange another glance.

'Excuse me?' Syd says.

'Your father's been on parole for barely six months,' says Inspector Leigh. 'He's only just begun to rebuild his life. And yet on a whim he takes it upon himself to murder a complete stranger. To butcher him, in fact.' She pauses, just long enough to check my reaction. 'That's your theory, if I'm not mistaken. So what I'm asking you, Ms Baker, is *why*?'

There is a flash in Syd's eyes that anyone who knows her would recognize as a warning sign. 'Didn't you read it?'

I shift slightly in my seat. We're in an interview room, bare apart from the grey plastic furniture.

There's just the three of us: Inspector Leigh on one side of the table, Syd next to me on the other.

The inspector's hands are still resting on the print-out. She doesn't bother to move them when she glances down. 'I read it, Ms Baker. Twice after you brought it to me yesterday. Once again just this morning.'

'So what the fuck kind of question is that?'

'Syd . . .'

'No, I'm sorry, Jack, I'm serious. "*Why?*"' she mocks. 'I thought you were a fucking detective. So fucking *detect*, why don't you.'

'Syd, please!'

Inspector Leigh, to be fair, doesn't even flinch. She just tips her head slightly, as though re-evaluating whatever judgement of Syd she first made.

'It's a game,' Syd says, exasperated. 'OK? Payback, revenge, whatever you want to call it, but mainly, for my father, it's a game. "*Rebuild his life*",' she quotes, shaking her head. 'This is his life. This . . . *toying* with people. It's what my father lives *for*.'

There's a silence then, before Syd adds: 'Oh, and for the record: my father never so much as chose what suit to wear on a given morning based *on a whim*.'

Inspector Leigh smiles at that, the same little half-smile she wore practically the whole of the last time I saw her. So far it's not been much in evidence. Somehow her demeanour this time is different, as though she can tell the role she played with me isn't going to cut it in front of Syd. She's as good at reading people, I think, as I gave her credit for. It strikes me I should probably be reassured by that, but instead it only makes me more worried.

'So in this game,' the inspector says, with a slight emphasis on the final word that conveys her scepticism. 'This is how your father wins?' There's a barely perceptible nod in my direction then, the first time Inspector Leigh has even tacitly admitted that I'm a suspect. Not just a suspect. *The* suspect. In a murder case where the victim was stabbed *seventeen times*. It's not like it comes as a surprise – why else, otherwise, would we even be here? – but still that little nod hits me like a fist.

'Honestly?' Syd answers. 'I don't know what my father counts as winning.'

'You think you're in danger?' the inspector asks her, and I watch Syd closely for her reply.

'No.' She shifts. 'I don't know.'

'Of course she's in danger,' I put in.

The inspector turns her gaze on me.

'I mean, it's obvious she is. Isn't it?'

Syd interrupts before the inspector can respond. 'Whether I'm in danger or not isn't the point. This isn't about what my father might do. It's about what he's done already.'

Inspector Leigh stares for a moment, considering, then looks down again at the manuscript. Six days Syd and I have spent writing it – virtually every spare hour since the night of Sean Payne's murder. And, OK, so it's not like I've had a job to go to, and Syd's hardly been prioritizing hers, but even so I'm beginning to wonder whether it was worth the effort. In one sense we've achieved what we set out to, in that Syd and I are at least now on the same page. But the idea as well was to convince other people.

'It's elaborate,' says Inspector Leigh, 'I'll give you that. Unique, too. I don't think I've ever heard of a . . .' She hesitates here, glances once again in my direction. '. . . of a *witness*,' she settles on, 'presenting a written statement before they've actually been asked. Certainly not one of such depth.' She fans the pages.

'But?' Syd prompts, and the inspector meets her steely eyes.

'But there are aspects to your story I still find confusing,' she says. 'The house, for example. Your father bought it for you, is what you're saying. But without your knowledge. He . . .'

Syd is shaking her head and Inspector Leigh gives her a chance to interject. Obtuse: that's the inspector's tactic with Syd. And it's working. Syd's riled, which is what Inspector Leigh wants. She likes her interviewees flustered, I've come to realize, I suppose because she thinks it's more likely they'll reveal something they hadn't meant to. This business about the house, for example. We've been over it. In the manuscript, in our discussions. But the inspector is raising the subject again because she's seen Syd is getting more irritated every time she's required to repeat herself.

'He didn't *buy* it,' Syd says. 'He saw we were interested, then *bribed* the estate agent to make sure it ended up coming to us. Probably pretended he was just a concerned parent, insisted to Evan that he wasn't to let on. I bet he even paid extra for a spare set of keys.'

She says it with conviction, when this is the one part of our story that's mainly conjecture. It makes sense, though. Evan Cohen was operating from a grimy little office two left turns away from the footfall on the local high street. He had no employees, no new properties up for sale (judging by the cards that were on display in his office window), nor even a proper website. He was the estate-agency equivalent of a shyster, who'd probably only got Patrick Winters's business because Winters had felt sorry for him (and, most likely, because he'd felt more at home in Evan's offices than he had in the poncey-wine-bar interior of the local Foxtons). On top of which, there was that annotated copy of the *Racing Post* I noticed when I went to see him, meaning Evan at the very least enjoyed a flutter. A failing business, then; potential gambling debts: it all adds up. And he's gone. That for Syd and I remains the clincher. I went back not long after my first visit – after my conversation with Patrick Winters, in fact – and Evan's office even at that point was boarded up. When Syd and I went together the other day it was in the process of being converted into a coffee shop. Moving premises, my arse. It's like I said: Syd had him pegged right from the start.

'He bribed the estate agent,' Inspector Leigh echoes. 'Again, I have to ask: *why?* I mean, effectively he would have been helping you. Right?'

'He wasn't *helping* us,' Syd counters. 'He was controlling us. Controlling *me*, demonstrating to me he still can. For my father, *control* is all any of it has ever been about.'

'By "any of it", you mean . . .'

'I mean everything! Every single thing he's ever done to me! Like with the house – it was his way of putting us exactly where he wanted us, somewhere he could get to us any time he liked.'

'And the money?'

'What money?'

Again the inspector unleashes her little smile. 'That's exactly my point. Your father's assets were seized when he was convicted. Maybe he put in some extra stints in the prison laundry while he was inside, but what would you estimate your average estate agent goes for these days?'

'My father wouldn't have left himself broke,' Syd responds. 'Not ever. He was brazen but he wasn't stupid. Whatever assets you think you seized there would have been double that amount hidden away under someone else's mattress. And he's never been interested in money just for the sake of it. It's always been about what he can *do* with it. About who and what money can buy. That's why he was in prison in the first place – remember?'

I've always been a little vague on how Syd's father ended up in prison, mainly because Syd has always been fairly vague about it herself. But I'm up to speed now. Syd's told me about the scams her father used to run: about how he arranged kickbacks for certain prominent members of the local council to facilitate his company's property deals. And, after that, how he used to blackmail those same council members to get them to pay back what he'd given them, plus interest.

Inspector Leigh must know about this, too. She makes a face, half doubtful, half impressed that Syd is so convinced by her own story – and so able to come up with the appropriate answers. And the horrible thing is, I can see my own doubts reflected back at me in the inspector's reactions. The back and forth I'm witnessing now, it's a reprise of the toing and froing I had at the start of all this with Syd. Because I couldn't accept it at first either: that everything that had been happening to us was part of one cohesive plan. In my head, when we'd started writing, Elsie's father was still to blame for the majority of what had happened, and the rest – the shoebox, Syd's sister's name, maybe even the house – was down to . . . I didn't know. Coincidence, I guessed. Happenstance. As for Sean Payne's murder, I figured he must have had another argument or something in the pub. I mean, the bloke's a headcase. Was a headcase. It stands to reason he had other enemies apart from me and Syd.

And there was something else, as well. What I said to Syd was, I just couldn't believe that someone would go to such lengths purely out of hatred. That it was possible to harbour a grudge for so long. Which was the only time I can remember when Syd has looked at me with open contempt. If I didn't understand that, she said, I didn't understand anything.

'And anyway,' Syd is saying to the inspector, 'the house was just a starting point. A stage. A good one, for my father's needs, but if Evan had turned him down, say, or if Jack and I had walked away – it wouldn't have mattered. Wherever we'd ended up, my father would have been there too.'

Inspector Leigh is somewhere close to where I was, I think. She's not rejecting our story out of hand, but she knows there's one crucial thing we're missing.

'Evidence,' she says. 'That's what's lacking, Ms Baker. And this, I'm afraid, doesn't count.' She opens her hand to indicate the objects spread across the surface in the space between us: the shoebox and the things it had inside, the (now bloodstained) photograph from the landing, printouts of the email Syd received and the picture of me getting kissed. There's other stuff, too – things we found when, after we realized what was happening, we finally emptied out the house. A book that Syd claimed was her sister's favourite. A necklace that had once belonged to Jessica, too.

More of her father's little taunts; more clues as to what we had coming. Like that cat, for instance. Even that cat, Syd told me, was part of this. It was a signpost, first of all – a pointer to lead us to that box. And it was also a message in itself. Remember that kitten Syd's father bought her for her twelfth birthday? She claimed it was linked to that, and when I recalled what state I'd found the cat in I had to wonder whether she wasn't right. I mean, how else could it have got into our attic if someone hadn't physically put it there?

'What about all the things my father's destroyed?' Syd says. 'Jack's career, for example. His friend-ships. His . . . relationships.' Us, she means, and I remind myself she's only saying it for effect. 'Doesn't all that count as evidence too? This stuff we brought with us – these *things* – they were just props. *Remind-ers*. It's the damage my father's done that should convince you.'

Inspector Leigh reclines slightly in her chair. 'That's another thing I'm finding confusing, Ms Baker. All this damage you mention. All the things you say your father has done. It seems to me they've mostly involved Jack. Based on what you've been telling me, I would have expected them to be aimed mainly at you.'

Anger flares visibly in Syd's eyes. 'They *were* aimed at me! It all is! He's using Jack, that's all. What he wants is Jack –' She pauses, cuts off whatever thought she's about to express. 'What he wants is to hurt Jack because he knows by hurting Jack he's hurting me. I told you, it's a game to him. And the more players there are, the greater the fun.'

Inspector Leigh tips her head. 'What made you interrupt yourself?'

Syd tucks her chin towards her collarbone. 'Excuse me?'

'"What he wants is Jack . . ." Out of the way? Is that what you were about to say? What made you interrupt yourself?'

Syd shakes her head in frustration. 'Look, I . . . I just don't want anyone to worry, that's all.' She glances my way, and I realize by 'anyone' she means me.

The inspector notices it, too. 'So you *do* think you're in danger?'

'What? No. I didn't say that.' Again, another glance towards me.

I'm frowning now, I can feel it. Is Syd more afraid than she's letting on? And if so, why didn't she tell me? On the one hand I'm worried now on her behalf – more worried even than I was already – but also I'm annoyed at the thought she's keeping her true feelings from me. No more secrets, that's what we said when we started writing, and yet here Syd is doing precisely what we both agreed we wouldn't.

'You said you spoke to him,' says Inspector Leigh, changing tack. 'Your father. When you went to confront your mother.'

'I didn't *speak* to him. I *saw* him.'

'And did he say anything to you?'

231

'He said hello. And he used my old name.'

'Right.' Inspector Leigh consults her notes. 'Margaret Anabelle Robinson.' She lifts her gaze without raising her head. 'You don't look like a Margaret,' she judges.

Syd doesn't even blink. 'That's because I'm not.'

A little parenthesis appears at one corner of Inspector Leigh's lips. She closes the cover of her notebook.

'So that's it. This . . . statement, these objects, and one possible sighting of your father. That's essentially all you have to support your story.'

'There was nothing *possible* about it. It was him, OK? It was fucking him. Standing in my mother's hallway as though he owned the place.'

'Yes, but even so. To have engineered everything you claim he has, your father would've had to have been watching you for months. One sighting, in my book, doesn't –'

'I've seen him, too.'

It's the first time I've spoken in quite some time. My voice, compared to the others', sounds thin and unconvincing, but even so both women turn to look.

I clear my throat.

'At the open day,' I say. 'The day we first saw the house. He was there, I think. Watching us.' That older bloke I saw staring at me from across the living room: I'd thought at the time he was just some rich kid's snooty parent, turning up his nose at my scruffy jeans and battered trainers. But he fitted the description

Syd's given us of her father and as well as watching us he was lurking near the door, in the perfect spot to slip outside should Syd show any sign of looking his way.

Syd is visibly shocked. I catch the bulge that gets snagged in her throat. 'You didn't tell me that,' she says, her voice a frightened whisper.

I could explain, I suppose. Reassure her that until now I wasn't one hundred per cent certain. But to be honest I'm not feeling much of a need to explain anything right now, not when Syd is so obviously holding back, too. The more I think about it, the more unfair of her it seems. Because it's like the inspector said: I'm the one who's lost his job, who's borne the brunt of whatever game Syd's father is playing. Who's sitting here waiting to be accused of murder, basically. What gives Syd the right to keep things from me when it's my arse at the moment that's on the line?

'You . . .' Syd recovers herself quickly, addresses Inspector Leigh. 'You could talk to the family Jack helped. Sabeen. Amira. They saw him too. Right, Jack?' There's a question mark in her voice when she says my name that has nothing to do with what she's asked me.

'They saw someone,' I agree, not quite meeting her eye. Because that's another thing. Amira. Syd's still not apologized properly for accusing me of being unfaithful. I'm not even sure she's fully convinced yet that there was genuinely nothing going on. That would explain that comment she made about our relationship, for example. I mean, maybe she did only say it for effect, but a little show of solidarity wouldn't go amiss, even if it's just a hand beneath the table on my knee.

'Unfortunately we don't know where Sabeen and her family are,' says Inspector Leigh. 'They've disappeared.' She catches the concern in my expression when I raise my head. 'Under their own steam,' she reassures me. 'The Home Office would like to speak to them as much as we would.'

I feel myself relax slightly into my chair. That's something at least. As much as it pains me to have lost so many of my friends, at least they haven't been deported. And the likelihood is they'll be better off without me.

'My father then,' Syd says. 'You know where he is. Why not question him at least rather than wasting more time interrogating us?'

'You're the ones who came to me, Ms Baker. This conversation is taking place at your request.'

'Exactly!' Syd snaps. 'Precisely! And yet the fact that we came to you willingly clearly counts for nothing. Talk to my father. Question him. Ask him what he was doing on the night of the murder.'

Inspector Leigh watches Syd patiently, then drops the bombshell we should have seen coming.

'We already have,' she says.

Which stuns Syd momentarily into silence. We share

a look, the awkwardness that has been growing between us temporarily forgotten. But it's like I say: Inspector Leigh has had our manuscript for almost twenty-four hours. If she's already looked into my story about Sabeen, it stands to reason she would also have followed up on our claims about Syd's father.

'And?' I say.

Inspector Leigh sighs with what I read as genuine irritation. Because she believes our story and is as frustrated as we are? Or because she's angry that we're continuing to waste so much of her time? 'And he reacted exactly the way you would expect him to,' she says. 'With surprise, initially. Indignation.' Syd's boiling to interrupt and the inspector holds her off with an upraised finger. 'And he has an alibi. For the night of Sean Payne's murder.'

Syd is rigid in her seat. 'Let me guess. My mother.'

The inspector offers part of a nod. 'She says your father was with her the whole night through. She says she hasn't been sleeping well recently – something about the pain in her hip – and that she can't have closed her eyes that night for more than half an hour. She says your father was asleep beside her the entire time.'

Which is not dissimilar to my alibi, it strikes me. It's better, in a way. More convincing. My story, such as it is, is that I was in bed with Syd and at no point during the night did she hear me leave.

'Of course she's going to say that!' Syd bursts. 'She's

terrified of him. She'll do whatever he asks her to. Like tell him how to find me in the first place, for example!'

Inspector Leigh looks back at her like maybe that's so, but it doesn't change the fact there's nothing she can do. *This is over*, her expression says. *This interview, the investigation. It's over.*

'You think Jack did this,' Syd says, her voice quieter now but sounding no more controlled. 'You haven't said it yet, you haven't fucking dared, but you do, it's obvious you do.'

What the hell, Syd? I feel like blurting – as though she's the one, by giving voice to it, who's making it real.

'So why haven't you arrested him?' she blusters on. 'If you're so certain, why don't you go ahead and lock him up?'

I'm staring at Syd in outright panic now, powerless as she pokes the tiger that's got us trapped inside its cage. At the same time, though, I can't help wondering how the inspector will react. Because what Syd's saying has occurred to me as well. Of course it has. All this time that's passed since the murder, all these days the police have spent watching. I've been hoping it's a question of evidence, that they need more than they can find. Hoping, but not quite believing.

Inspector Leigh smiles her little smile. She's still for a moment, then makes a start on tidying up her things. 'May I keep this?' she asks, splaying her hand on the top sheet of our manuscript.

Syd's expression is one part disbelief, two parts disgust. Her chair screams as she slides it backwards from the table. 'Knock yourself out,' she says, and when she stands her chair clatters to the floor. She moves past it towards the doorway, clearly expecting me to follow.

When I linger the inspector stops what she's doing and turns to face me. Syd is stranded by the door.

'Can I give you some advice, Jack?' says Inspector Leigh. Ms Baker for Syd, I notice, Jack for me, as though we're old friends. Tactics again and yet I find myself being drawn in. Please. Yes. Advice. *Anything*.

'Use what time you have to find yourself a good solicitor,' she says, and then she too is heading for the door.

Sydney

Jack barely speaks on our way back to the house. We get a cab and his knee jiggles throughout the twenty-minute journey. He makes little snapping noises with his teeth, too, a habit he has when he's tense that I'm not sure he's aware of when he's doing it. I offer him a stick of gum from my bag but he shakes his head and goes back to staring out of the window.

'I've got it,' he says as we pull up and he thrusts a twenty at the cabbie through the slot in the partition. He's out before the driver can give him change but a twenty is way too much so I sit and wait for our six pounds fifty.

When I get inside Jack is drawing curtains.

'Jack?'

We're in the living room and he moves past me to close the curtain on the other side.

'It's broad daylight, Jack. What are you doing?'

He ignores me and moves off into the hall. The second curtain he's pulled has snagged and out of habit I jiggle it straight. When I catch up with him he's closing the blinds in the kitchen. He pauses first though, peers towards Elsie's house through the slats, then straightens and twists the blind shut.

'Jack, please. You're scaring me.'

He stops then and looks at me, darkly. He's about to say something – something I get the impression he thinks he might regret – but whatever he's on the brink of voicing he pulls himself back.

'I'm thinking about what the inspector said,' he tells me. 'That's all.'

His eyes dart around the room. There's another window near the table. It only overlooks the side return but Jack moves across to close the blind there anyway.

'Which part of what she said?'

Again, it's like Jack has to compose himself before he'll even speak to me.

'About how we need more evidence.'

He goes back to the window by the sink and prises the slats apart so he can see out again across the garden.

'But . . . what's that got to do with closing all the blinds?'

A sigh this time: irritated, impatient – as though it's obvious. 'Your father's been watching us. Right?'

'Right,' I agree, tentatively.

'So what I'm wondering about is where from.' Once again he peers out across the garden. 'Like from a car parked on the street? From the alleyway? But if that was the case, how come neither of us noticed him?'

'I don't know. I mean . . . maybe we did. Maybe we just didn't realize it was him.'

Jack frowns at that. 'But you would have realized. Wouldn't you? If you'd seen him.'

I don't like this. The way Jack's talking to me. The way he's looking at me. 'Not necessarily,' I reply. 'Why would either of us, unless we were watching out for him?' I suppress a shudder. It's dark with the blinds closed and I turn to switch on the light. Jack gives a start, seems about to snap at me. But then he's moving again, dragging a chair from beneath the kitchen table towards the middle of the room.

'Jack? What are you doing now?'

He climbs up on to the chair and angles his head beneath the smoke alarm. He fiddles for a minute before he answers. 'You can get cameras these days. Can't you? Tiny ones that go basically anywhere.'

Cameras. I hadn't thought of that. But it sounds too crazy, like something out of a John le Carré novel.

Jack's struggling to remove the cover. It comes off eventually with a *crack* that suggests it's unlikely to go back on. I peer up, in spite of myself, but the only component I can tell apart from any other is the battery.

'Jack, I don't think –'

'What's that?'

'What?'

'That. There.'

I can't tell what it is he's pointing at. 'I don't know. It just looks like . . .'

All of a sudden he's got both hands around the

casing and he's pulling, trying to wrench the entire unit from the ceiling. If it comes away abruptly, or the chair slips from under him, he's going to fall and hit his head. 'Jesus, Jack. Be careful.' Ordinarily I would move across to hold his hips but I'm not sure how he'd react right now to me touching him.

He's grunting, tutting. 'Pass me the screwdriver, would you?'

I scan the empty space around me. 'What screwdriver?'

'In the drawer over there. The bottom one.'

It takes me a moment to find it. When I do I'm reluctant to pass it to him but he wiggles his hand impatiently and I give in.

Half the ceiling comes down when finally Jack prises the smoke alarm free. OK so maybe not half the ceiling but some of the plasterwork anyway and I'm coughing and blinking against the dust. 'Jack . . .'

'Look.'

I try but I can't see *anything*. I cough and fan my hand to clear the cloud of plaster.

'Look here. What's that?'

I peer up to where his fingertip is pointing. 'It's just . . . a wire.'

Jack lifts the casing right up close to his eyes. He rips out the offending article and studies it. 'Yeah,' he agrees, thwarted, and finally climbs down from the chair. The front of his T-shirt is dusted white. He starts looking around the room again, the gutted smoke alarm dangling in his grip. He tosses it on to the kitchen table.

'What's that up there? In the corner?' He uses the screwdriver to direct my gaze and once again I look as a reflex. He's pointing at the burglar-alarm sensor, I think. The alarm itself was broken when we moved in and the sensor is covered in dust. Clearly no one's touched the thing in years.

'Jack, stop. Please.'

He turns and looks at me sharply. 'What?' he says. 'Why?'

'I just think . . . I think you're wasting your time. That's all.'

'He had a key, Syd. He was in the house. It stands to reason he might have put up some kind of camera or something somewhere. Or a microphone maybe.' The mention of a microphone gets him looking in different directions, at crannies in the kitchen he hasn't so far considered. 'I mean, maybe that's how he found out all the things he did,' he goes on, talking as much to himself now. 'It would have been easier than following us around. He could simply have been listening in. Watching us.' He looks again at that dusty alarm sensor. 'Who's to say he isn't watching us right now?'

I shiver, shake it off.

'I still think you're wasting your time.'

Jack rounds on me. 'Wasting my time?' He laughs and for the first time ever it's a sound that frightens me. 'I tell you what was a waste of my time. Writing that fucking manuscript, that's what.'

He's waiting for me to say *I told you so*, I know he is. He wants me to, so he can launch into me the way he's obviously longing to. I don't, though. I wouldn't anyway because I don't agree, regardless of what I might have said when Jack first suggested it. I still think it will help, in the end.

'You saw her reaction, you were there,' Jack goes on, turning his frustration on Inspector Leigh now. 'Fucking *elaborate*,' he mimics. 'Fucking *unique*. Fucking smug fucking bitch.'

This isn't Jack. Hearing him swear like this, sounding so vicious. This: it's like listening to me.

I want to reassure him but I don't know how. And he senses that, I think. I felt it when we were talking to the policewoman: the distance that's opening up between us. And I know it's my fault. I know it's inevitable, *necessary* even – but it breaks my heart even so.

I roll my lips and look down at the floor. Jack sets off towards the alarm sensor, dragging the chair with him as he goes.

'How did you know?'

We're on the landing. There are still ghosts of those pictures that until last week we'd left hanging on the wall, little blanks of wallpaper a slightly deeper shade of cerise than the space around them. I'm sitting on the floor, the balustrade needling my back. The discomfort is like a penance and I don't shift. Jack's slumped forward on the dining chair, heedless of the plaster dust that coats it now as well as him. There's a hole above him where he's ripped out the last of our smoke alarms and a pair of wires that until recently were hidden beneath the light fitting. There's no evidence anywhere of any cameras.

'How did you know?' he says again. 'How could you be so sure we wouldn't find anything?'

I've been thinking about how to answer this question, obviously.

'Because it's not the type of thing my father would do,' I say. 'He'd view it as . . . cheating, somehow.'

'Cheating?' Jack looks at me in disgust. As though they're my rules.

I nod, shrug. I've been following Jack around like a gormless puppy, watching him drag that chair from room to room and jab holes in all our fixtures and fittings. I thought that was painful to watch but this, the way he is now, it's worse. He'd clearly managed to convince himself he was on to something – one shattered smoke alarm away from finding the evidence the inspector said we needed. But now he's floundering, I guess. Desperate. Which, given the circumstances, is hardly surprising. I'd be floundering if I was in his position too. I'm floundering in mine.

'So bribing an estate agent with a wedge of cash is OK,' Jack is saying, 'but installing a camera that costs – what? A hundred quid? – isn't allowed?'

I sigh. Not at Jack. At the ridiculous logic of it. 'Bribing Evan was all right because it's . . .' I hesitate to use the word, use it anyway. 'Clever,' I say. 'It's sly, part of setting his trap. But cameras . . .' I shrug again. 'Cameras are easy. Cheap. And I'm not talking about how much they cost.'

Jack sits straighter and some plaster dust sprinkles from his shoulders.

'What about that photo he took of me and Amira?' he says. 'I mean, he must have hired someone to follow me. Don't you think? Ali said they saw someone but we don't know for sure they saw your father. So wouldn't hiring a private detective or whatever count as cheating, too?'

'Probably,' I say.

Jack frowns like I'm the one not playing fairly. 'Meaning what? That you don't think he did hire anyone? That he followed me and took that photograph himself?'

'If he could have he would have, yes. My father was never exactly one to delegate. He always did like to get his hands dirty.' I shiver again. It's not the temperature. What I mean is, if it were hotter, I'd still be shaking. 'Besides,' I go on, 'it's like with the cameras: hiring someone would have meant leaving a trail and he's smart enough not to do that.'

Jack's angry again because that's another path to securing evidence gone. And I think that, in spite of everything, he's still struggling to comprehend it: the effort to which my father would have had to go.

'What about hacking my email?' he says, after a pause. 'Could he have done that, maybe somehow left a trace? I mean, it's possible that's how he found out about Sabeen. Except . . .' His shoulders drop and he's slumping once again in his chair. 'We never communicated by email,' he says. 'It was always by phone or by text.' He ponders for a moment, then drops his gaze. 'I suppose he could have checked my phone if he saw it lying around when he was in the house. Like, on my bedside table.'

He looks towards our bedroom and this time Jack is the one to shiver. It's catching, like yawns.

I get up then. I start to head back downstairs, to get on with . . . what? With waiting, I guess. Which makes me wonder whether Jack didn't have the right idea after all. Punching holes in all the plasterwork with a blunt screwdriver. It wasn't efficient. It wasn't productive. But at least it was something.

'*Shit*,' Jack spits suddenly from behind me. As I turn he tosses the screwdriver and it gouges out another small piece of wall. 'We can't just bloody sit here, Syd. We can't just sit back and let him win!'

It's an echo of what the inspector said. *This is how he wins.* I want to offer Jack some reassurance but there's not a thing I can say. If there was I would have said it already.

'We could . . . find Evan,' Jack goes on. 'Couldn't we? Because he has to have seen your father. He must have, if only to collect his money.'

I've been wondering about Evan myself. It's occurred to me that the police, if it's true they've spoken to my father, might already have found the estate agent too. But if they had they would have *done* something. Surely. And I don't doubt that whatever bribe my father offered Evan, it would have come with some inducement to disappear.

'How much do you think your father paid him? Like . . . thousands, right? Five grand, would you say? Ten?'

'I doubt it was that much. If there's one thing I learned from watching my father, it's that people generally cost less than you might think.'

It makes no difference either way now what Evan's conscience was worth but my response only seems to dishearten Jack further. 'But we could find him,' he insists. 'Don't you think? And the police could get him to talk. Couldn't they?'

I try to nod but it comes out sideways. 'We could try.'

'Jesus, Syd!' All of a sudden Jack is on his feet. 'Why are you so . . .' He rattles his head. 'So bloody *calm*? At the police station you were about ready to throw a chair!'

And you've gone the other way, I don't point out.

'I'm not calm, Jack. I'm just . . .' I close my eyes and it's a struggle to open them again. 'I'm tired. That's all. Just . . . tired.'

It's an understatement. Jack's right: at the police station I was a mass of furious energy but it's taken it out

247

of me. The morning we've had. The fucking *year*. And I know I'm going to have to recover my strength quickly but right now I can't see how that's going to happen. I imagine this is how footballers feel when they trudge off the field three goals down at half-time. Or actors, spent after the opening scenes and resting themselves in the intermission before the grand finale.

Jack's got that look again, the one I noticed before. Suspicious, resentful: like he's on the brink of saying something hurtful and isn't even trying this time to haul himself back.

'There's something you're not telling me.'

'What are you talking about?' I say. But that's done it. So much for feeling tired. The accusation is like a shot of adrenaline.

'When we were talking to Inspector Leigh. There was something you were holding back.'

'You said it yourself, Jack. I wasn't holding back at all. If anything I was doing the opposite.'

'That's not what I mean. What I mean is you were hiding something. You *know* this isn't over. What happens next, Syd? What's your father planning from here?'

'How should I know what my father's planning? Jesus, Jack.'

'This doesn't end with me, Syd. It can't. There's something else your father wants. You know there is.'

'It doesn't matter what he wants,' I say. 'He can't get it. Not now.'

'Why not? Nothing's changed. The police aren't going to stop him. You didn't even ask them for help.'

'Weren't you listening, Jack? That's basically all I was doing!'

'For protection, is what I mean! You're in danger, Syd. Why won't you just admit it? Why won't you even admit it to *me*?'

'Because I genuinely don't think I am!' I say and even to my ear I sound half convincing.

Jack responds with a disgusted little snort. 'Fine,' he says. 'Have it your way.'

'What's that supposed to mean?'

'It means you don't trust me. Clearly.'

'I do, Jack! I trust you more than anyone I've ever known!'

'The way you trusted me about Amira?'

I stall, my mouth dangling uselessly. It is: this, what's been happening to us, it's becoming real. It's what I was afraid would happen, the thing I was terrified we wouldn't be able to stop.

'I do trust you, Jack,' I say again. 'What I need is for *you* to trust *me*.'

I think for a moment I'm getting through to him. But then Jack scoffs, evades my eye. 'Yeah, well,' he says. 'I'm finding it pretty bloody hard to trust anyone right now.'

I take a step towards him. 'Jack, please . . .'

He shakes me off when I try to touch him. 'And

that's the other thing,' he says. 'How could you not know your father was out on parole?'

I recoil from the non sequitur. 'What?'

'Didn't you think to check?'

For a second or two I'm standing open-mouthed. 'No, I didn't bloody check. I left my father, Jack. I *ran away*. I didn't give a shit where my father was after that, just so long as he was nowhere near me.'

It's an opening and Jack can't resist. 'And look how that's turned out for you.'

I feel a searing beneath my skin. *You fucking prick*, I want to say. Even now, in spite of everything. It takes every ounce of my self-control to hold it in.

Jack, to his credit, flushes with shame. Less creditable, he tries to hide it.

'I'm thinking of calling my parents,' he announces. He says it like he's daring me to object. I would of course, ordinarily. Jack's relationship with his parents is a source of tension between us we do our best to pretend isn't there. He thinks I think he should treat them with the same indifference with which they treat him; that he should disown them, effectively; detach himself. I don't. I just want him to *care* less what they think of him. To not see every slight and subtle put-down they inflict on him as something he's brought upon himself.

Jack's watching for my reaction. 'That's a good idea,' I answer. 'I think you should.'

'What?'

'I think you should. You heard the inspector. We can't afford a solicitor, Jack. Not a good one.'

The implication is unmistakable. It's as close as either one of us has got to stating openly that Jack is likely to go to jail.

Jack is too stunned for an instant to respond. Again, I want to hold him. Again, I know I can't.

'Maybe . . . maybe it would be better if you went and saw them,' I say. 'Sit down and talk to them properly. Tell them it's my fault, obviously.' I try a smile.

Jack, instead of smiling back, opts to take affront. 'Go to Dorset, you mean? *Now?*'

'Better that than asking them up.' What I mean is they'll respond better if Jack is the one to make the pilgrimage. They don't like coming to London at the best of times. And now Jack and I have moved in together, they've turned not visiting into a point of principle.

'No way, Syd. There's no way I'm leaving you alone.'

It's what I knew he'd say. It's the old Jack – *my* Jack – shining through, at a time each of us needs him to the least.

'Jack, listen.' This time I forcibly take his hands. 'This isn't about me any more. This, what happens next: it's all about *you*. And you need to protect yourself. Your parents can *help*, Jack. In a way I can't.'

He's frowning again. Thinking, *churning*. He frees his hands from mine.

'It sounds like you're trying to get rid of me,' he says.

I shut my eyes again, open my mouth to respond. But I don't speak.

'Syd? Did you hear me? I mean, forget about your father. It's like *you* don't want me here. Like you want me out of the way.'

'I heard you, Jack. I . . .'

But it's all I can say. Partly it's that tiredness creeping back. At the pretending, I realize. The misdirection. Also, I've lied to Jack so much already. I can't bring myself to lie to him again.

Sydney

In the end it doesn't matter anyway. They come for Jack that very evening.

'Jack Laurence Walsh? I'm arresting you on suspicion of murdering Sean Payne. You don't have to say anything, but it may harm your defence if you do not mention when questioned something you later rely on in court. Anything you do say may be given in evidence.'

It's like in those TV dramas, word for word. Inspector Leigh delivers the little speech in a monotone, not sounding her usual self at all. This should be her moment of triumph but instead she looks like someone beaten. I suspect she likes Jack and that because of that this has become one of those cases that do nothing to boost her professional pride.

'Syd?' Jack says as they put him in handcuffs. Just that, just my name. It's not a plea, though, not to my ears. To me it sounds like an accusation.

I reach for him but I don't get to touch him before they're leading him from our doorway and out on to the street. I'm crying, I realize. I can't help it. With my sleeve drawn over my palm I cover my mouth. Neither Inspector Leigh nor her colleague – a man roughly the size of a wardrobe – makes eye contact with me. They behave as though I'm not there. I follow them out anyway, barefooted, and it feels like I'm wading against a current.

'Jack? Oh Jack, I'm so sorry.'

I don't think he hears me. Inspector Leigh has her hand on Jack's crown and she's manoeuvring him into the back seat of the police car. The glass is tinted and when the door slams Jack is stolen from my view.

And that's when, for the first time, I look around.

It's still light outside so I can see the neighbours who are watching. One or two outside on their steps, even more peering out from behind glass. But it's not the neighbours who catch my attention. It's the man across the street, seated on the bonnet of his car. He wears a suit. His shoes are buffed. And though his face is partly in shadow I can tell his lips caress a smile. But my father also has an odd little tell, one he's never been very good at hiding. It's just a gesture: his index finger on his right hand rubbing circles around the tip of his thumb. It means he wants something. That he's growing impatient. And I know when I see it that he's angry, and that this game of ours is coming to a head.

Sydney

I'm four. Maybe slightly older. It's not the start of it but it's the start of me remembering. I'm lying in bed, my feet pointing towards the door. It's dark in my bedroom or it would be but for the light reaching in from the landing. I've had a nightmare and I've been crying, shouting out for my mother. She's there, at the threshold, but standing in front of her – blocking her entrance – is my father. He's in his pyjamas, my mother beside him in her nightie, and it's clear I've roused them both from sleep.

My mother has her hand on my father's forearm. It slides up, down, like she's comforting him, like the way sometimes she comforts me when I'm feeling ill. From his forearm it moves over to his chest and here it rests for a moment, presses itself flat. All the time my mother's whispering in my father's ear, her eyes darting occasionally – anxiously – towards me. One of her knees is bent, her foot poised like a ballerina's. She looks so pretty and I can't understand why my father, instead of looking at her, is staring so intently at me. In his hands he's holding one of his belts. It's black, made of leather, and the buckle winks at me when it catches the light.

My mother's hand begins to walk its way down, her fingers working like tiny little legs. Incy wincy spider, I'm thinking between snivels, which when my mother does it on me never fails to make me giggle. My father isn't giggling, though. He's looking at me the way he does when I'm eating and I know I'm making too much mess.

My mother starts working at the buttons of my father's pyjama top. She seems to be struggling with them and I'm thinking that maybe they're stuck and that's why she's helping him in the first place. She helps me too, if one of my dresses is inside out or I'm having trouble with the foot end of my tights. Except my father doesn't seem to want my mother's help. He wriggles a shoulder and when that doesn't work he turns and hits her. Not angrily. The same way he'd swat a mosquito. My mother yelps. She doesn't fall down but she staggers and her face when she takes her hand away is all wet and blotchy. My father doesn't appear to notice. He's looking at me again. He takes a step into my room and without switching on the light he shuts my mother outside on the landing.

I don't call out after that when I have nightmares. After that it's not the nightmares I'm most afraid of.

I'm seven. I should be happy. I did a dance at school and everyone loved it but halfway through my father got up and walked out. He isn't waiting outside for the rest of us. When we get there the car is missing from the place we parked it and my mum and sister and I have no choice except to walk. It's raining so by the time we get home we're soaked. Also my sister is crying because normally if we were going that far my mother would have pushed her in the buggy.

He's sitting on the sofa in the lounge. When my mother sees his face she starts to say something but with a hand-flick he dismisses her from the room. He tells me to come inside and shut the door.

'I hope you're proud of yourself,' he says to me.

'Daddy, I . . .'

'You looked proud. Up on that stage. *Prancing* the way you were. *Preening.*'

I don't know what preening means. And prancing, I thought, was something horses did.

'Fetch your things.'

'What?'

'Don't say *what*. Fetch your things.'

'But . . . what things? I mean . . . which things? Daddy I don't under—'

'Fetch. Your. Things.'

He must mean my ballet things. My changing bag. I set it down in the hallway when we came in.

'Open it,' he tells me when I get back. 'Your dress, your shoes, take them out.'

I don't have a dress. What I have is a leotard and a skirt but I don't tell him in case the truth makes him angrier.

'Where should I . . .'

I glance around for somewhere to put them and that's when I notice the scissors. They live in the kitchen usually. Now they're lying on the coffee table.

'Use those.'

I frown. At the scissors, at my ballet costume, at my father.

'What?'

My father slams a fist on the coffee table and I'm so startled I drop everything I'm holding.

'Don't. Say. What! The scissors. Use them. Start with the ribbons.'

There are ribbons instead of elastic on my ballet shoes. When my mother first gave them to me they were the part I was thrilled about the most. My father knows this. He was there when I took them from the bag.

'But . . .'

His fist impacts once again on the coffee table. The boom this time jostles out my tears.

'One more word, young lady. If one more word comes out of your mouth before you start cutting, I'm going to use those scissors on you.'

I should be happy. That's what I'm thinking as I pick up the scissors. My mother, my teachers, they all promised me that dancing would make me happy. And your father, they said: he'll be so proud. When I remember that I cut willingly. It's a struggle in the end to make myself stop.

*

I'm nine. My jaw is swollen and my father is beside me feeding me soup. It's Heinz tomato, my favourite, and the taste of it is making me want to hurl.

'You're spilling it, Maggie,' my father says. The soup is down my front and on the table and has probably dripped on to the floor.

'Maggie? You're spilling it.'

He keeps saying it and he keeps spooning. There's no point telling him I can't open my mouth wide enough or that the spoon – a tablespoon – is too big. He knows about the spoon because he chose it and he knows about my jaw because he was the one who threw the punch. And anyway I think he thinks it's funny. He'll keep forcing me to try to eat even when it gets to the point I start to splutter and I have soup bleeding through my nose.

'Open wide,' he says. I feel the metal of the spoon scraping against the enamel of my teeth.

My mother, with her back turned, is very slowly washing up saucepans.

My sister is seated just across from me. She has a bowl of soup too. She's allowed to feed herself, though, and the tablecloth where she is seated is spotless. She isn't looking at me but I can tell she's watching.

I'm twelve, maybe eleven. My father looks up from behind his desk and sees me staring at him from the doorway of his office. I'd turn and hurry away except my father holds up a finger. I only paused in the first place because I was so astonished to see him counting so much money.

'Daddy . . .'

The finger again. Quicker, sharper.

The money is in stacks. I can't tell what notes they are but even if they're only fivers you could probably buy a car with the amount my father has in front of him. Two cars, and two chauffeurs to drive them.

'Daddy, I'm sorry, the door was open, I . . .'

I'm not helping myself. It's like a reflex, though. There must be something I can say to him, I've often thought. Some magical combination of words that, uttered at the right moment, will work like a spell. They'll stop him in his tracks. His grimace will fade and his fist will fall and whatever evil enchantment it is that has a hold of him will give way to a light that comes on behind his eyes. Yet all I can ever come up with is some lame-arsed version of *I'm sorry*. I'm sorry, however you say it, is no abracadabra. You'd think by now I would have learned.

He stacks the stacks and carries the pile to his little safe. He keys the code (six digits, my birthday, which must be like a joke), slots the money inside, then pulls out a battered metal box. Shutting the safe before he turns, he carries the metal box back to his desk.

'Come inside. Close the door.'

I hesitate then do as he says. I don't want to but disobeying, I know, will only make things worse.

'Daddy, I . . .'

'Sit down.'

There is a chair on the door side of the desk – a chair for visitors – and I park myself cautiously on the edge of the seat.

'Were you spying, Maggie?'

I'm shaking my head before he's even finished formulating the question. 'No, Daddy, I swear! I just . . . I didn't . . .'

That finger again. Instantly it renders me mute.

'Do you know what they used to do to spies in this country?'

Silently, slowly, I shake my head. It's a trap, I can feel it, but I'm powerless to escape.

My father moves the box so it is squarely in front of him. It is a rusty, pitted thing, like something dug up from the bottom of the garden. My father, though, treats it as though it is something precious – something that requires as much care in its handling as my mother would afford her finest china.

'During the war,' he says, 'if someone was convicted of spying, they would be executed.' He peers across at me. 'They would be shot, Maggie.'

He raises the lid of the rusty box. It hinges towards me, blocking my view. My father reaches in and when he shows me what is inside I hear myself gasp.

'This was my grandfather's. He used to claim he'd used it to kill six Germans.' My father smiles slightly – in mockery or admiration, I can't tell. 'It's an Enfield,' he tells me. 'Number two, mark one, star. Single action to allow the bearer to fire quickly.'

He turns the revolver over in his hands, treating it with even more reverence than he did its metal case. I watch it weaving in his grip, then blink and see he's offering me the handle.

'Take it.'

Involuntarily my head starts to shake. 'No, I . . . I don't want to.'

'Take it,' he repeats. 'Hold it.'

Once again he leaves no space for argument. I reach out and take the gun with both hands and still they sink floor-ward as my father relinquishes the weapon's weight.

'Point it,' my father says.

I'm staring at the gun in my hands. It's cold, black and deadly heavy.

'Point it,' my father repeats. 'Not that way,' he says, when I raise the shaking barrel towards the window. 'Turn it around. Point the gun towards yourself.'

'What? But . . .'

'Don't make me tell you again, Maggie. You know I don't like to repeat myself.'

I obey his instructions – what choice do I have? – and my father watches me, satisfied.

'Now put the barrel in your mouth.'

I shake my head now and I realize I'm crying. He can't mean it. Surely he can't possibly mean it. I was only passing. I didn't even mean to look in!

'Put. The barrel in. Your mouth.'

'Daddy, I'm sorry, I really am, I won't ever spy on

262

you again, I promise, I mean I wasn't even, I didn't mean to, I just . . .'

He says nothing. He just waits. And still crying, my nose running, I learn the taste of cold steel.

'Now pull the trigger.'

I'm so afraid I feel about to pass out. I'm sobbing now, as quietly as I can, but still I can hear myself snivel. My vision blurs as my eyes fill with tears. The gun barrel only rests on my front teeth but even so it seems somehow to fill my throat and it's all I can do to stop myself gagging.

'Don't worry, Maggie. It isn't loaded. At least . . . I don't think it is.'

I feel saliva flee down my chin. I want to beg, to plead with him, but I know nothing I say will alter what happens next. And all of a sudden I feel a sense of relief, a warmness that builds from my belly. This could be over. One way or another. All I need to do is what I've been told to and everything – the pain, the fear, the humiliation: *everything* – it could all be over before my next heartbeat.

I have to squeeze with both thumbs, with both eyes, to get the trigger to shift. I feel resistance before it starts to move, until gradually there's a sense of momentum: movement it's too late to stop. The hammer cocks, the barrel rotates . . . and the pistol emits an empty click.

The gun is whisked from my hand before I can drop it. I'm sobbing openly now, almost wailing, whether in relief or disappointment I don't know. I'm aware I've wet myself. I can feel warmth in rivulets down my ankle and dampness building in my sock. And my father's voice, coming to me an inch from my ear and simultaneously from a thousand miles away.

'Clean yourself up,' he says. 'Then scrub the carpet. And next time keep those busy little eyes of yours out of my office.'

I'm thirteen. For weeks now, months, I've been telling myself to go. But what if he catches me before I can get away? What if he's waiting? Watching? What if he follows? What if I tell someone but they don't believe me or I run but there's nowhere to hide? What if it's safer if I stay where I am? What if, instead of running, I change? What if my father does? What if all I need to do is give him the chance? Or what if this is just the way it is, everywhere, and there *is* nowhere to go, nowhere safe, or any safer than the bed I'm lying in now?

What if what if what if . . .

I'm fifteen, just turned, and I think I'm free. I'm at a party, with people I mistakenly believe are my friends.

I've tried cocaine tonight and I liked it and now someone's given me acid. I like this less. Not at all, in fact. There's something on me and I'm trying to get it off but it's as fixed and unshakeable as a shadow.

'Someone?' I say and I hear laughing.

'Seriously,' I say and they laugh some more.

It's a lot of voices at first, but then it's one and I don't know anyone who laughs like that. And something's definitely on me, gripping me around the fleshy part of my arm.

That laughter. It's *his* laughter. His hand that's gripping my arm.

'Guys?' I say. 'Get him off me!'

Please, I want to add but now I'm swaying and there are groans as something bubbles from my mouth.

'Gross,' someone answers, finally, and then the laughter is back, further away.

'Just leave her,' someone says and I guess they do because I wake up alone a thousand hours later, my mouth stuck open in a silent scream and my hair glued to the carpet by my own puke.

I'm nineteen and I'm fucking some guy. I only know his first name and I don't even know if that's real. He told me his name is Charlie but to me he looks more like a Chris. An arsehole basically. I've never met a Chris who wasn't an absolute dick.

This one, though – he's pretty. Literally, like a girl. And I'm not into girls (I know I'm not because I've tried) but blokes who *look like* girls, they're a different matter. Make of that what you will.

Charlie/Chris, he's not being rough exactly but he's too eager. When he kisses me it's more like he's sucking and his hands are greedy like a child's. They pinch like a child's would too, bruising me, and he's deaf to what I'm trying to tell him with mine. I can't get away because he's lying on me, pinning me, his hips pursuing me as I try to pull back. There's no rhythm to what's he's doing. If sex at its best is like music, Charlie's the brass section falling down the stairs.

'Stop.'

My hands are on his chest now, pushing. And I don't know if I imagine it but he makes this noise then, his lips fat and wet near my ear. *Shhh*. A comforting sound, or one that's supposed to be.

I push harder.

'*Stop*,' I insist. '*Don't*.'

But I'm weak. Powerless. Charlie keeps thrusting, more urgently now, and it hurts, it physically hurts, and I want to shout out but I can't find the breath, can't keep hold of it long enough against Charlie's shoving to turn it into words.

I'm weeping as he comes. Silently, each tear a little acid drip of shame. As soon as he withdraws I press him backwards and I roll until I'm sitting, my legs over the side of the couch and my hair a curtain around my face.

'What the fuck is wrong with you?' Charlie says. I can see him from the corner of my eye and he's sweating as he snarls. He doesn't look so pretty any more. I can't believe I ever thought he did.

'That wasn't rape,' he says. 'Don't you dare try and claim that was fucking rape.'

I shake my head, as much a shudder. 'Just go,' I say. Quietly but I know he hears.

'You wanted it. You were practically begging for it. No way was that ever fucking rape!'

'Just go!' I scream, spinning, and in the end it doesn't take him long because his shoes are still on and his jeans are down around his ankles. *Slag*, he spits as a thank-you-for-having-me and only doesn't slam the door, I suspect, because he's thinking ahead now, about what it will sound like, about what the neighbours will say if anyone asks and they have the impression he left in a hurry.

And I'm alone again. As alone as I'll ever be. My father laughing across my shoulder. Still winning.

I'm twenty-four and I'm together with Jack. Finally, committed, *together*. And that place I worried I'd never find? A safe place? This is it. My father can't get to me here. He's trapped outside now, on the periphery. And I can keep him there. So long as I'm with Jack there's nothing my father can do to hurt me.

It's what I tell myself.

It's what I come to believe.

And now Jack's gone.

I'm twenty-eight and I'm four, seven, nine, twelve and all those other ages all over again. I'm lost. Alone.

Weak. Beaten. I'm all the things my father made me. I'm what you get when you add minus numbers, a figure less than the sum of her parts.

And I'm not ready. I thought I could be. I thought I *would* be. But without Jack . . . I just don't think I can handle this on my own. I forgot how strong Jack made me, what I was like before. But it's all coming back to me. I've come full circle, back to how I was at the beginning. It's like the lights have gone out and all I can do now is sit and wait, as my father draws closer through the dark.

Jack

'How could you not tell us?'

This from my mother. So far my father has barely said a word. He's still taking it all in, I think. Trying to. His expression is as inscrutable to me as ever, and it's always been a thing for my old man never to appear ruffled, but I'm fairly sure if something's going to break him, this will. At the moment, though, he's sitting rigid in his fixed-to-the-floor plastic chair, as though he were part of the furnishings, too. We've pretty much got the room to ourselves, but it's like he's trying to avoid attracting attention. He's always claimed he doesn't give a toot what other people think of him (he uses that exact phrase as well: *give a toot*), but I've always sort of known that was bullshit. I admired it anyway, adopted it as a mantra for myself, but as with so many of my father's standards, it's one I've failed to live up to.

'This has been coming . . . how long did you say? How is it you never thought to tell us?'

My mother is dressed as though she is due to appear in court herself. My father looks smart enough, I suppose, but he looks the way he always does: like a reluctant model for the casuals section of the Marks & Spencer catalogue. My mother, on the other hand, is wearing some kind of dark beige business suit, with gold and black leather accessories that in combination scream respectable. Maybe she's hoping some of it will rub off on me – that the guards and the other prisoners will treat me better if they realize my family is, wait for it: *middle class*. If that's the case she needs to be strapped to a chair and forced to watch the entire DVD box set of *Oz*.

She *tsks* when I don't answer, for about the seventeenth time since she arrived, and takes another opportunity to survey the room. The visiting area isn't all that dissimilar to an airport waiting lounge. The furniture is fixed and there are guards wandering between the rows – although they aren't armed the way the security staff at airports are and the chairs here are clustered around tables. A school canteen, then, rather than a departure lounge. Think *Scum* meets *Ferris Bueller's Day Off*. My mother is doing her best not to touch any of the surfaces. She keeps her hands neatly bundled in her lap.

'What have you been eating?' she asks me. 'Will you answer me that at least?'

'Just . . . food, Mum.'

'Are you getting enough? It doesn't look to me like they've been feeding you enough.'

'I get what they give me.' Which is slop and sliced bread, mainly. Probably it's not so bad, if you're hungry. I've barely eaten a thing since I was remanded in custody.

'You should speak to someone if you're going to bed hungry,' my mother tells me. 'Explain that you're a growing boy, that whoever's in charge of portion size needs to take that into account.'

I want to laugh at that. At my mother's hopelessly flawed perception of me, but also the idea that somewhere within these walls there's a Head of Portion Size.

My father answers before I do. 'He's twenty-eight, Penelope. He's not a boy.' He doesn't look at either one of us when he speaks, though I get the sense from his tone, and from my mother's nod of weary acceptance, that this is something else they've both opted to hold against me: the fact that I grew up. If I'd never had the temerity to turn eighteen, none of us would be in this mess, I imagine they're thinking. Because that's how they view it: like we're all in this. Just not together.

'Well,' says my mother. 'Even so. You should talk to Henry if no one else can help.'

'Who's Henry?' I ask her.

'Henry Graves. The governor here. Don't tell me you haven't met him yet?'

'Of course he hasn't met him, Penelope. He's a *prisoner.*' I look for my father's eyes, but they skip away. That word, though, lingers, together with the disgust my father attached to it.

'Well, in my judgement he's a very reasonable man. I'm sure he'd help if you asked him nicely enough.'

'You know the governor?'

My mother's circle of friends extends to book-group buddies and ladies who lunch, with perhaps, at its wildest reaches, the odd organic farmer. How she can possibly have an acquaintanceship with the governor of a south London prison, I can't begin to make a guess.

'We met him,' she explains. 'On our way in.'

I should have realized. My mother has a way of ingratiating herself with people in authority. In any commercial encounter, for example, she is rarely more than two sentences away from demanding to talk to the Person in Charge – whereupon her tone will switch immediately to one of polite and reasonable deference. Still, we're in a high-security prison, not the Dorchester branch of Specsavers. Even for her, given the time she would have had in which to operate, securing an audience with the governor was no mean feat.

'Your mother caused a scene,' my father offers by way of explanation. He's still not looking at me, but the fact that he's addressed me has to count as progress of a kind.

'And it's a good job I did,' my mother puts in. She's about to say something else, I think, when my father finally looks at me directly.

'You know why this is happening, don't you?' he says. His shoulders are drawn back, but he's leaning in slightly, speaking to me under his breath. *You don't have to whisper, Dad*, I want to say. No one here gives a toot who you are or where you're from. But I hold my tongue.

'Jack? Did you hear me? I said you know why this is happening. Don't you?'

I've told him – I've told them both – the outline of what's gone on, how basically I'm being screwed by Syd's lunatic old man. I didn't put it quite as succinctly as that, of course, and maybe I wasn't as forthright as I was in the account we presented to Inspector Leigh (in fact I left out a few choice details: that I lost my job, for example, ridiculous as that sounds; that I stabbed my supposed victim no less than seventeen times), but I get the feeling anyway that the precise sequence of events isn't what my father is referring to.

'That . . . *girlfriend* of yours,' he clarifies, making it sound like a swear word. 'She's the reason we're all sitting where we are. It's because of her that your mother had to get up at 4 a.m. so that she could come and visit her only son in prison!'

People are looking. My father's hissing probably carries further than his more regular bass-heavy mumble.

'It's not Syd's fault, Dad,' I say. 'I explained to you about her father. It's him who's doing this.'

My father's head gives a furious little quiver, like if I don't understand now I never will. 'We all get the family we deserve, Jack. Most of us,' he adds, showing me his razor-raw cheek.

'She's not right for you, Jack,' my mother chips in.

273

'She never was. She's . . .' There are all sorts of words my mother would like to use here, but she's self-aware enough – just – to recognize they'll betray her social bigotry. So she'll save them up and use them when she and my father are alone.

'Your mother and I told you when you first brought her home,' my father says. Brought her home: like a cat dragging in something rotten. 'We told you then that you'd regret it.'

'I've heard her swearing, Jack,' my mother confides. 'And I've seen those scars up and down her arms.' She shudders, a theatrical little tremor that almost prompts me to speak up in Syd's defence. There are two things that stop me. I've heard it all before, is one of them. This, my parents' lecturing – I was expecting it. It's almost comforting, in fact. A little reminder of being at home. It's like if I ever needed money when I was a teenager. My parents would put me through the same ordeal, except then the subject of the sermon would be responsibility, commitment, my failure to demonstrate first one and then the other. Listening to them outline their disappointment in me: it's the price they've always attached to offering me their support.

The other thing – the real reason I'm sitting here and remaining so quiet – is that I don't know if I'm starting to agree with them. There's a voice inside my head, loudest after my cell door slams shut for the night, that tells me this *is* Syd's fault. That I would never have got in this kind of trouble if it wasn't for her. It's not as though my parents haven't been proved right about other things. About me, for example. Their disappointment in me. Syd's always tried to boost my self-confidence, encouraged me to forget what other people think and concentrate instead on the things I think are important, and I've done my best to follow her advice. But look at me. Look at what I'm wearing, where I'm sitting. Clearly something went wrong somewhere, just as my parents always said it would.

The other thing is, she hasn't even been to visit. Syd hasn't. At first I was terrified it was because something had happened to her – something to do with her father – but I know she's OK because Bart's told me he's spoken to her on the phone. (Unlike Syd, Bart's been to see me. We patched things up, which I suppose is something, though the fact that he was so ready to forgive me only makes me feel worse about how I treated him in the first place.) And I know it's only been four days, and that Syd and I didn't exactly part on the best of terms, but if our positions were reversed I would have set up camp outside the gates on the very first night. I keep thinking about what I accused her of – of wanting me out of the way – and I can't help but wonder whether I wasn't right; whether she isn't glad, on that level at least, about how things have turned out.

'And what's all this about your driver's licence?' my father asks me.

It takes me a moment to adjust to the switch of subjects. But when I do I experience that same lurch of despair I felt when I learned about the driver's licence myself.

'They found it at the scene,' I say, suddenly uncomfortable in my seat. 'In the alleyway. Near the . . .' *Body*, I stop myself saying. 'Near where it happened.'

Aside from what transpired at the Evening Star, that's why the police were so interested in me from the beginning. It's something I only found out about after I'd been arrested, however. It was DC Granger who led the interrogation when I was under caution, and in the middle of the session, that's when he slapped it on the table like a trump card. It was in an evidence bag, the photo of me clearly visible beneath the splatters of what I was informed was Sean Payne's blood. At first I didn't know what to say. Apart from anything it set me wondering again about why, if they'd had such a damning piece of evidence all along, they hadn't arrested me sooner. When I explained to DC Granger that Syd's father must have left it in the alleyway for the police to find – that he must have swiped it one of the times he was in the house – the detective constable just started laughing. Even my solicitor – a man they'd brought in who'd been on call – struggled to mask his reaction. He's been looking at me differently ever since.

'Honestly, Jack. How could you have been so careless?'

'I didn't drop it, Mum! I wasn't even there, remember?'

'Yes, but to lose it in the first place. Haven't we always taught you to look after your belongings?'

For several seconds I'm lost for words. 'Syd's father *stole* it from me, Mum. He broke into our house and he found my wallet and he took my driving licence *from* me. I didn't *lose* anything.'

I catch my mother slip a glance towards my father.

'You do know I'm innocent, right?' I say, my eyes flitting between each of my parents and the desperation audible in my tone. 'You do *believe* that, don't you?'

This time my mother checks the room again, as though worried I'm about to make a scene. 'Of course we do, Jack,' she answers, the level of her voice an instruction to lower mine. 'We wouldn't be here if we didn't. Would we?'

Once again I'm not sure how to respond. I think I should be reassured. On the other hand, wouldn't most parents stand by their son or daughter irrespective of what crime they believed they'd committed?

'It doesn't matter what your mother and I think,' my father declares, sidestepping that little conundrum nicely. 'You're where you are and the situation is what it is.'

My mother nods at this sage summation. She glances again at my father, whose silence at this point seems to be a cue.

'Your father has a proposition for you,' my mother

announces. She glances again to check she's got the timing right.

My father clears his throat. 'We'll help you,' he announces.

With paying for a decent solicitor, I assume he means. Which obviously I'm grateful for, and relieved about. I'm also slightly alarmed, though, that the matter was evidently in doubt.

'That's great,' I say, 'thank you. The duty solicitor, I don't think he –'

'On one condition.'

I'm surprised I'm surprised. What, really, did I expect?

'That girlfriend of yours,' my father goes on.

'Syd? What about her?'

'She's no good for you, Jack. She –'

My father cuts off my mother's interruption with an upraised hand.

'Dad? What about Syd?'

'You need to grow up, Jack. You need to move on.'

'Move on? What do you mean?'

'I mean *move on*. Move past your silly infatuation.'

I glance at my mother. 'I don't understand,' I say. Except I do. They're both too cowardly to spell it out, but what they're saying couldn't be clearer. 'You want me to split up with Syd, is that what you're saying? That's the condition of your offer of help?'

'Voice, Jack,' my mother hisses. 'Please.'

My father just sits there saying nothing.

I shake my head. 'No,' I say. 'Sorry, but no. Syd and I, we're . . .' A couple, I mean to tell them. We're happy. But like a whisper in my ear I hear the *ish* Syd attached to that description before.

And she hasn't visited. Not once in four days has she come to visit.

I shake my head again.

'Your father knows someone through Rotary,' my mother says, attempting to sound appeasing. 'A solicitor. Garrie . . .' She looks to my father.

'Garrie Dalton,' my father proclaims, like a doorman announcing the guest of honour at some affair of state. Probably he has to restrain himself from adding the letters the esteemed Mr Dalton no doubt has trailing from his name.

'He's very good, Jack. Very expensive. Your father and I will have to forgo Provence next year, but it will be worth it, I promise you.'

A son cleared of murder; an ill-favoured prospective daughter-in-law scrubbed from the family portrait – all for the price of an Easter break in the south of France. Worth it? It's a small price to pay, surely.

'Forget it,' I say. 'There's no way I'm leaving Syd. Not for you. Not for anyone.'

I feel brave, like a grown-up – until my father leans in again and speaks to me in the same tone of voice I remember him using when I was five.

'For pity's sake,' he hisses at me. 'For once in your life will you please start thinking of other people. This isn't easy for us, you know. Coming here, seeing you here. It isn't easy for your mother.'

My mother dutifully bows her head.

'And I assure you it wasn't easy for me to convince Mr Dalton to consider representing you,' my father goes on. 'Can you imagine what that was like for me? How *demeaning* to have to ask a friend of mine for help? The easiest thing, I assure you, would have been for me to refuse to get involved. Unfortunately, however, you're my son. And unlike some people, I feel a certain sense of responsibility.'

That, right there: that's the closest my father has ever come to telling me that he loves me.

'So you have a choice, Jack. You either do as I ask or you deal with this on your own terms. With your own money. And personally I'd like to see how far that gets you.'

My father isn't a big man. He's slim for his age and only a few inches taller than my mother. I outgrew him when I reached seventeen, but I've never had a conversation with him where it didn't still feel like he was looking down on me. Even now: I could climb up on to the table, instruct my father to sit cross-legged on the floor, and even then it would feel like he had the higher ground.

'But Dad, I –'

'Where is she?' my father cuts in. 'Will you tell me that? This girl you're so madly in love with. Where is *she* now you're stuck behind bars?'

'She hasn't visited you, Jack. We know she hasn't. Henry, the governor, he –'

'She doesn't *care* about you,' my father ploughs on, in no mood for one of my mother's digressions. 'If she did she'd be sitting in one of these chairs. Wouldn't she? And you said it yourself. She's the reason you're in this mess in the first place.'

This is the thing about my father. He has a talent for pinpointing my insecurities. It's frustrating, and disconcerting, but it also makes me wonder whether he doesn't know me better than I give him credit for. Whether he doesn't know what's better for me, too.

My parents are waiting for my response. When I fail to say anything my father rises from his chair.

'Come on, Penelope. It looks to me as though he's made his decision.'

And it's that, I think – the act of them getting to their feet; the knowledge they're about to turn their backs on me – that makes me panic. I just . . . I don't think I can take it. Without them . . . without Syd . . . I don't think I can face being entirely on my own.

'Wait. Dad, please. Just . . . just wait a minute.'

My father has moved out from behind his chair. He turns, but not fully.

'Couldn't I . . . I mean, if I promised that –'

'This isn't a negotiation, Jack. Do you want our help or don't you?'

'I do. Of course I do. It's just –'

'Come on, Penelope,' my father says, taking my mother by the elbow.

'OK! Dad? Dad, please, wait! I said OK!'

'I want your word, Jack. I want your word that if you accept our help you'll put an end to this foolish association. That after this is all over, your mother and I won't have to see or hear from Sydney Baker ever again.'

For a moment I manage to hold his eye. But it's a blink, a final flash of wilful defiance, and eventually my head bobs as I let it drop.

Jack

I never imagined that in prison it would be so silent. Not so much during the day perhaps, but at night it's even quieter here than it is at home. There's no traffic noise, for one thing. No neighbours with their televisions blaring or teenagers playing music through the walls. And the biggest difference, I suppose, is that you're alone. I am, I mean. And maybe actually that's all it takes. Maybe the silence isn't as complete as I'm imagining, and instead the thing I'm adjusting to is that I'm lying here trying to sleep without Syd.

Tomorrow I meet my new solicitor. It's a good thing. I keep telling myself it's a good thing. If anyone will be able to help me he will, because I don't doubt he's as competent as my parents say. Except . . . when we spoke on the phone he was already talking about my options. About the potential benefits, as he put it, of pleading guilty. That's the phrase he used. The *potential benefits*. He wasn't advocating it necessarily, he said. It was just something for us all to bear in mind.

The other thing he said to me was that I should have faith, and that's the part, actually, that's been bothering me most. Faith in what, I keep asking myself? Not God. I don't think he meant God, and if he did that's not much help to me at all. In my parents, then? In him? Maybe – but again it's hard advice to follow given that this man my parents have imposed on me has already countenanced amending my plea. Plus, however good a solicitor Mr Garrie Dalton is, there's no escaping the fact he's part of the system. And if the system functioned as it's supposed to, there's no way I'd be sitting where I am.

Which just leaves Syd.

I've given up on expecting her to visit. What I'm still struggling to come to terms with, though, is how things between us have got to the point they have. It can't simply be to do with what's been happening. Or if it is, there's something obvious I'm failing to understand. Or . . . I don't know. Something I'm missing. Except the worst part is I don't think there is. I've been going over and over everything that's happened, and all I'm left with is this sense I've been betrayed. Syd didn't want me by her side: I'm as sure of that as I'm sure of anything. She didn't want me there and she doesn't care that I'm here, that's basically what it boils down to. And though there's still a part of me that insists that can't be true, all the evidence tells me that it is.

So faith in what? I keep coming back to the same question. And as much as I try, I can't come up with an answer. All I can do is lie here in the silence, trying to work out how it all went so wrong.

Sydney

We're six floors up. I can barely distinguish one figure down below us from any other but I scan them all nonetheless. Doctors and nurses smoking cigarettes, patients admitting themselves or being released. One or two people who only seem to loiter, and it's these I study closest. My fingers are prising apart the blind slats and it feels like I'm opening up my suit of armour: presenting an opening to my enemy through which he might fire his arrow.

'Syd? Is that you?'

I spin at the unexpected voice but when I see Elsie lying there with her eyes open that rush of fear ebbs rapidly away.

'You're awake,' I say. 'I can't believe you're really awake.' I step from the window towards Elsie's bed and try to take in the sight of her. 'How are you feeling?'

She smiles at me thinly. 'Pretty numb, I guess.'

I can't tell if she means physically, mentally or both.

'Do you want some water?' I ask her. There's a jug on her tray table. While she was sleeping I made sure it was fresh.

'Uh-uh.' She struggles to sit straighter but she can't, shouldn't.

'Stay there, Elsie. I'll get a nurse if you want to sit up.'

She shakes her head and sinks, defeated, into her pillow. 'It doesn't matter how I lie anyway. The only time I'm not uncomfortable is when I'm asleep.'

'Rest then,' I tell her. 'You need to anyway. And I won't go anywhere, I promise.'

She shakes her head again. She swallows and it looks from her expression like she's swallowing glass.

'Are you sure you don't want some water?'

This time she allows me to hold the cup up to her lips. The gratitude in her expression afterwards makes me want to cry.

'Where have you been?' she asks me, her voice less fractured now when she talks. 'I wasn't sure you were ever going to come.'

It's been three days since Elsie woke up and I can still hardly believe she has. The doctors had been saying she was improving but I didn't allow myself to accept that it was true. Although I must have. Mustn't I? At the very least I must have had *hope*.

There's a visitor's chair by the window and I drag it closer to Elsie's bed. I sit down then stand up again, and adjust the chair so I can still see the door. *We're six floors up*, I remind myself. With all the security doors and nurses' stations that are between us and the hospital's entrance, we're as safe here as we would be practically anywhere.

'I know, Elsie. I'm so sorry. I would have come sooner but this week it's . . . it's just been mad.'

As excuses go it's worse than pitiful. What can I tell her, though? *I couldn't come and see you because I didn't want to put you in danger. Because my father's back and he wants to hurt me and if he sees how much I care about you, there's a chance he'll try to hurt you.* Probably if Elsie knew the truth she wouldn't want me visiting at all. And in fact that would have been safer. I *should* have stayed away, at least until this is all over. But I couldn't. I tried but in the end I simply couldn't. With Jack it's been easier. Not easier – I miss him so badly the ache is a physical pain. But at least I've already told Jack everything he needs to know, even if he doesn't understand it yet. With Elsie, there's still so much I need to explain.

The problem is, now that I'm here I don't think I can. Which makes it doubly foolish that I've come. Doubly reckless.

'I've missed you,' Elsie announces – and this time I do cry. I can't help it. And actually? So fucking what. I think I've earned a few tears. Before I would have considered them an indulgence, a show of weakness. And maybe they are . . . but it's not like I've got any vestiges of self-respect left.

'I've missed you too,' I tell Elsie and I take her hand. I try to smile and the effort of doing so makes me sob.

'Syd?' Elsie's expression shifts from one of surprise to alarm. 'Are you OK?'

This little girl who's suffered so much she felt she had no option but to throw herself in front of a train: she's lying in a hospital bed asking *me* if I'm OK. Now those tears do feel self-indulgent. As for self-respect, apparently it's a bit like love. The opposite of it. With love there's no upper limit, no brim past which you can't fill. With self-respect it turns out there's no bottom. You think you're empty, then something happens and you leak just a little bit more.

I don't say anything. For a moment I can't. I just look at Elsie and try to bask in the change in her. Her injuries, I know, are beneath the bedcovers. The most serious deep beneath her skin. But she's out of danger now and from the parts of her I can see you wouldn't be able to tell she'd been hurt. In many ways she looks better than at any point since I first saw her, that day I trailed her through the breeze to Mr Hirani's. She's tired, no doubt, but she looks rested. The skin on her arms, her face, is free from bruises. She still looks fragile to me, small in her oversized bed, but I realize this is an illusion. If events have proved anything, it's that whoever made her made this girl tough.

'Nothing's the matter, Elsie. Nothing you need to worry about.'

I smile again, manage it. I was starting to regret coming here but seeing Elsie the way she is now – maybe it was worth it. Maybe it was *all* worth it, I allow myself to think. But that just reminds me again of Jack, who's probably more scared now than I've ever been.

Elsie is watching me closely.

'They told me about my father,' she says, her voice testing the silence.

I allow my head to nod. 'I know.' I spoke to the staff before I came in. 'Elsie, I'm . . .' *Sorry*, I want to say but somehow it doesn't feel appropriate.

'I'm glad,' Elsie declares, and I see that steeliness in her I've come to recognize shining out from behind her eyes. But then that shine becomes a shimmer and I realize Elsie is about to cry too. 'I am,' she says again. 'I *am*.'

'Oh Elsie.'

I want to hold her but the bed makes it impossible so I grip her hand, tighter now, and I stroke her cheek, her forehead, her tears – only occasionally breaking off to wipe away mine.

'Oh God, Elsie. Look at us. What a pair.'

Which makes her smile, which in turn only makes her cry more.

'I hated him, Syd,' she tells me. 'I did. I really did. But . . .'

We're both doing our best to get a grip on ourselves.

' . . . but I didn't want to,' Elsie says. 'You know? I only hated him because he hated me first.'

She says it like it's something she's ashamed of. Like it's her fault – *all* of it. And I can't have that.

'Elsie, listen to me.'

She looks up.

'You did nothing wrong,' I tell her. '*Nothing*. Do you hear me?' I wait for her to nod. 'The hard part for you,

Elsie: it starts now. I'm not belittling what you've been through. I'm the last person who would ever do that. But it's what comes next that will be the real test. Do you understand what it is I'm trying to say?'

She doesn't answer. But I can tell from the fear I see that she understands perfectly. Better than I ever did anyway.

'You're free now, Elsie. You're safe. But it might not . . . it might not always feel like you are. There are ways you can still let him win. It's important to remember that. He's gone but he's still playing. This game, once it starts . . .' I swallow. 'It never stops.'

God, I hate myself. I hate who I am, who I've had to become. Maggie Robinson, Sydney Baker. They're the same and I hate them both.

'You'll help me, though,' says Elsie, 'won't you? You're not going anywhere, are you?'

'Elsie, I . . .'

'Please, Syd.' She's gripping my hand so tightly I can feel the sharp ends of her fingernails. Before her accident they were always bitten to the quick.

'I'll help you if I can, Elsie, of course I will.'

'Because I don't want to feel the way I used to. I don't want to do . . . what I did.'

'You won't,' I tell her. 'If you remember what I told you, you won't.'

'How do you know?'

I look at her. I wait until I'm sure she's looking properly at me.

'Because I know you, Elsie. I've seen how strong you are. How brave.'

'Like your sister,' Elsie says. 'Like Jessica.'

I shake my head at that. 'Jessica was . . . trapped. It was brave, what she did. I mean . . . I always thought it was. But only because I could never do it myself.' I'm looking at my hands, I realize, and I raise my head. 'The thing is, Elsie, you're braver than both of us. And carrying on, being the person you want to be: I think that's the bravest thing of all.'

'Like you, then,' Elsie says. 'Isn't that what you've done?'

I smile at her sadly. 'It's maybe what I tried to do,' I say. 'What I thought I was doing. But I don't think that's quite the same thing.'

I'm talking in riddles now. Not helping at all.

I reach towards the floor and into my handbag. 'I almost forgot,' I say. 'I brought you these.' I hand Elsie the packet of Fruit Pastilles I picked up from the little Sainsbury's on my way in.

Elsie laughs. 'For a moment I thought you were going to give me cigarettes.'

I laugh too. 'I'd probably get arrested if I tried.'

My laughter withers.

'Listen, Elsie . . . when they told you about what happened to your father,' I say. 'Did they . . . I mean . . . what did they . . .'

Elsie's fingers interlock with mine. 'I know what you're going to say, Syd.'

If she does she's doing better than I am.

'You're going to tell me it wasn't Jack. Right?'

I barely hesitate. 'Right,' I say.

Elsie looks at her bedcovers. 'I thought at first that's why you were staying away,' she says at last. 'You know. When they told me who they'd arrested.'

Did she speak to Inspector Leigh, I wonder? I hope so. I liked her, even if I gave the impression I didn't. And I know she would have been kind.

'But then . . . I don't know. I kept thinking about when the woman . . . the policewoman . . . about when she was talking to me. It was like she didn't believe what she was saying. Like . . . like she had to tell me what she was telling me but she didn't want to. Does that even make sense?'

It does and it gives me hope. Precious, dangerous hope.

'I swear to you, Elsie: Jack would never hurt anyone. Whatever happens, whatever people say, please don't ever think that it was him.'

All the reassurance I've offered Elsie, assuming I've actually offered any, it comes undone. 'What do you mean? What's going to happen?'

I open my mouth to respond but all of a sudden there's movement in the room and I spin, startled. I've let my guard down. I can't think when I even last checked the door.

But it's just a nurse. She slips into the room with a tight, *don't mind me* little smile and makes herself busy with the equipment that surrounds Elsie's bed.

'I should go,' I say. I stand and kiss Elsie on the forehead. Her skin is warm, *alive*, and that kiss has power like you'd read about in a fairy tale.

'Syd? What's going to happen?'

I glance at the nurse, who has her back turned. I adjust Elsie's cover, so that the Fruit Pastilles I brought her are tucked out of sight.

'I'll see you soon, Elsie,' I say. 'OK? I'll be back soon.' And with that kiss still lingering on my lips, the power I've drawn from Elsie's skin, for an instant I almost believe it.

When I walk out of the hospital I walk out openly. There's no more hiding. No turning back. I'm not sure I'm ready because I'll never be ready but I'm as prepared as I'm ever going to be. And I'm tired of waiting. My father's been more patient than I gave him credit for but I don't doubt he's had enough too.

So let's just finish this, shall we?

For Elsie's sake, for Jack's: let him come.

Sydney

I'm lying in bed when I hear the house begin to shift. I'm attuned by now to every creak and there are so many in this old building of ours that I've come to understand how Jack, back at the start of this, must have felt when he thought he heard someone walking around. The feeling, it's almost electric: the same sensation you get when you're being watched.

The noises I hear are coming from the staircase. I almost panic then but I still have time and actually, anyway, the adrenaline helps. I was worried that when it came to it I would freeze. That's what used to happen when I was young. At the sound of my father's footsteps, his voice calling me if I'd done something he'd perceived as being wrong, my muscles would seize, tense up, so abruptly and so hard that my entire body would permanently ache.

I place my phone face up on the bedside table and slip quietly from beneath the bedcovers. Deliberately I position myself in a corner, trapping myself in case I feel the urge to run. I'm in my pyjamas, as I would be, but also the hoodie I wear sometimes when I'm ill. The black one, with the deep, double-width pockets.

When the door begins to open I edge away from it.

I can't stop myself. It's how I've been programmed, like a pet that flinches whenever its owner raises a hand.

The light enters the room as my father does.

'Sydney Baker, I presume.'

Up close I see he looks almost exactly the way he did when I was young. A little greyer, perhaps, but trimmer and if his hair is thinning it isn't doing so from his temples. He's a handspan taller than me, two shoulders broader and, as ever, he wears a suit.

And that voice. As before it hits me like a spell, paralysing me for an instant the way I thought the fear would. I forget to breathe.

My father steps warily into the room. This is new: my father being cautious. Before he always behaved like he had no need, that more important than being careful was being clever. Perhaps he's both now. Perhaps that's something he's learned in prison. Should I be worried? Has this old dog acquired new tricks?

'It's a little gloomy in here,' he says. 'I can't even get a proper look at you.'

He's beside the light switch but he doesn't flick it on. The window is on my side of the room and I've deliberately left the curtains open. Given the hour there's unlikely to be anyone in the street but even my father in his more brazen days wouldn't have taken the risk. The dark suits him as much as it does me.

I edge into the light even so – mainly, ridiculously, because I don't want my father thinking I'm afraid.

I catch the outline of his smile, feel his eyes crawl greedily over me. He steps forward and I feel my heels touch the skirting.

'It was kind of you to leave the back door open for me,' he says. 'I was half expecting to have to knock. I presume by now you've changed the locks?'

We have. We got someone in the day we emptied out the house. It was a case of horses, stable doors, but there was no way Jack would have let us stay here until it was done.

With a gloved hand my father pulls out a set of keys from his jacket's inside pocket. The set of keys, I assume, he got from Evan. 'I suppose technically these belong to you.' He tosses them and I let them hit me, let them fall.

So much for my father being cautious. This time when he steps I catch that circular movement of his thumb and index finger and I realize that, for all his outward calm, the truth is he's struggling to control himself. Like the way he looked at me when I stepped into the light: there was hunger plain to see in his gaze. It's hardly surprising. Fourteen years he's been waiting. I cost him his family, his fortune, his freedom. Regardless of what he might have had planned before he came here, what he most wants to do probably is beat me bloody.

He moves again, more abruptly this time – and that's when I pull out the knife.

And this part: this is something I didn't expect. I feel the way I imagine he does. With the knife in my hand, all I want to do is start slashing. Because if his anger's been festering, so has mine. I've been picturing this moment since I was nine years old, preparing for it one way or another since the day I was born. I thought I'd exorcized this feeling, *banished* it, but it turns out it's stronger now than ever.

And he sees it, I can tell. He appears encouraged by it. Invigorated, almost. Watching me struggle to control my hatred helps him somehow to contain his.

He pauses, and I realize that whatever advantage I might have held, I've managed to pass it back to him.

His fingers tap a rhythm against his leg. 'So that's why I'm here,' he says. 'I did wonder.'

This time when he moves, he moves sideways. He reaches a hand towards the surface of my dressing table and selects one of the numerous little pots. My face cream, I think. After that he picks up my hairbrush, raises the bristles to his nose. His eyes lock on mine as he breathes in.

'So talk me through it,' he says, setting the brush down again in exactly the spot it was before. 'You stab me,' he says, 'obviously. Kill me, I'm assuming is your plan. Then – what? Claim self-defence?'

He's daring me to answer but I stay silent, watching him as he checks around the room. He notices my phone on the bedside table. It's just a throwaway, not even a smartphone – a cheap replacement for my broken iPhone. Without breaking eye contact with me, my father moves to pick it up.

'There's no one listening in, if that's what you're wondering,' I tell him.

My father raises the phone level with his chin, so that as he checks the call list he can keep watching me. 'Maybe not,' he says and I can tell he's found what he was looking for. 'But it seems we won't have quite as long to get reacquainted as I'd hoped.'

The knife wavers in my hand. I've got the cuffs of my sweatshirt pulled down over my palms and I adjust my grip on the handle.

The movement catches my father's eye.

'Is that a kitchen knife?' he asks me, smiling now. He puts the phone back down on the bedside table and moves back to where he was standing before. 'It doesn't look very sharp, Maggie. Are you sure it's up to the job?'

I glance at the blade. Before it felt as substantial as a broadsword. Now, with my father's looming form right in front of me, it feels about as threatening as a toothpick.

'I'm surprised you don't recognize it,' I say, attempting to ape my father's tone. 'It's the same knife you used to murder Sean Payne. Apparently it was sharp enough for him.'

My father looks more closely at the blade. His smile broadens. 'Of course it is. Now how on earth, I wonder, did you manage to get hold of that?'

The knife quivers again and I bite down to try and stop myself shaking.

My father's fiddling with my hairbrush again. He's growing restless once more, his fingers itching beneath those gloves.

'By the way,' he says, 'it was an interesting theory you presented to the police. It's just a shame they didn't believe you. That they arrested your boyfriend instead. It's Jack, isn't it?'

I could: I could stab him now, and there's no reason it wouldn't work out the way he said it would.

'That must have been hard on you,' my father goes on. 'Although I suppose it's not that surprising. That you should find yourself attracted to violent men. Unless . . .' He looks up. 'Oh Maggie. Oh I see.' He laughs, genuinely delighted. 'Oh my goodness, what have I done to you?' He says it like a boast. As though he's as pleased with himself as he is with me.

'So this way,' he says, working it out, 'it's murder *and* attempted murder they convict me of. Posthumously, obviously.' He nods his head. 'Very smart,' he judges. 'Very *poetic.*'

He gives me barely a moment to try and work out what he means. He sets aside the hairbrush and reaches once again into his inside pocket. When he withdraws his hand this time he's holding a white plastic bottle. He sets it down on my dressing table and turns it so the label is towards me. I can't read it from where I'm standing but the bottle looks familiar to me from just its shape and colour.

'What exactly am I supposed to do with those?'

My father slides the bottle of sleeping pills across the dressing table towards me, like a chess player positioning his rook.

'You think I'm going to swallow a load of sleeping pills just because you tell me to?'

'Not because I tell you to,' my father replies. 'Because you're . . . depressed, let's say. Because you're twenty-eight years old and the only man you've ever loved is probably going to spend the rest of his life in prison.'

I flinch at that. I can't help it.

'Plus,' my father adds, 'you always have been a little disturbed. It's not as though it would be entirely out of character.'

A car passes in the street outside, its headlights sweeping like a search beam across the room. For a moment I see my father more clearly and what strikes me is that he looks so *normal*. It's the thing I've always struggled most to comprehend. How on the outside he could look the way he does but on the inside he could be so hideously disfigured.

'Of course, you'll have to cancel that 999 call you made before I got here. Or at least wait until the police have made themselves scarce.'

Enough, I tell myself. What are you waiting for? If you're going to do this, *do* it.

'It's a shame really,' my father says. 'I was so hoping to stay and watch.'

My hand tightens around the knife. I try and

estimate how much time has passed since I heard my father on the stairs and put in the call to the police. There are no sirens yet but perhaps there won't be. Although that makes me wonder whether the police are coming at all.

I start towards my father but stop again when he holds up a finger.

'Before you do anything rash,' he says, 'think for a moment about Jack. I can get to him, Maggie. I've got friends who can, thanks to you.'

My father sees something in my expression that he enjoys.

'What?' he says. 'Did you think that by staying away from him you could fool me into thinking you didn't care about him? Or that you'd stop me from finding out where he was? I know about him, about little Elsie.'

Again he watches my reaction. Again I fail to conceal it.

My father looks ostentatiously at his watch. 'We're running out of time, Maggie. And you've got a choice to make. It's you or the people you claim to care about.'

And there it is: my father's endgame. I always knew he would want to use what I loved against me. I just wasn't sure until now exactly how.

I shake my head. 'You're forgetting,' I say. 'Jack's not *staying* in prison. And you can't get to anyone if you're dead.' Because at that moment that's the way this is heading. That rage inside me I thought I had tethered? It's coming loose.

My father shows how afraid he is by stepping towards me. He's grown. Has he grown? Or is it merely that in his presence I've become smaller? I don't want to but I find myself retreating. The only place for me to go is the narrow space between the wall and the bed.

'You know, your sister was never this obstinate,' my father says. He stops an outstretched arm's length away from me. Stabbing distance, *just*. 'Jessica never defied me the way you're doing. When she found herself presented with the choice you have, she made her decision in an instant.'

The knife is suddenly heavy in my hand. 'What did you say?'

My father tips his head. 'You didn't know,' he says, 'did you? I always wondered whether I'd got through to you.'

There's a sense of something churning behind my eyes, like that rush you get when you stand up too quickly. Blood, oxygen, *understanding*: a swirling cocktail that has me reaching for the wall.

'The pills she took. Jessica. You *made* her take them?'

All at once I can picture it: my little sister cowering before my father in precisely the way I'm cowering now. Being offered the same choice I'm being offered. And Jessica, sweet Jessica, making it.

'But . . . why? She was never a threat to you. She was *eleven*.'

For the first time I see a flash of my father's

disfigurement. 'Because you ran,' he says. 'Because you left and no one was *allowed* to leave.'

I can feel my breath becoming jagged, the pressure that's building in my lungs.

'What did you say to her? Who was it you threatened? Not Mum. She would have known it was too late to do anything to stop you hurting Mum.'

'Who do you think?' My father gives me time to catch up. *Me.* He threatened *me.* He told Jessica he'd come after me and that when he found me he'd be sure to make me pay.

My hand tightens on the knife handle. I can feel the ache building in my knuckles.

'She cared about you, Maggie. In a way you never cared about her.'

I lunge before I even know I'm doing it. I'm being reckless, risking everything. But at the moment all I want to do is draw blood. I drive the knife forward like a lance, aiming squarely for my father's sternum. But I'd settle for anywhere: his throat, his gut, his groin. I'll slice him up piece by piece if I have to.

But I'm too slow. As I move my father sidesteps and his fist hammers into my stomach. My legs give way as though they've been punctured and the kitchen knife spills from my hand. It clatters off somewhere I can't see it, into the void beneath the bed.

My father, standing over me, is flexing his knuckles. 'I'm not going to lie to you. I'm glad you did that. It's just a shame we have to stop there. Although . . .'

His hand closes around my windpipe and slowly, steadily, he begins to squeeze. '. . . I am tempted, you know. So. Very. Tempted.' He grips a little harder on each word – but then releases me before I begin to bruise. 'But we wouldn't want you damaged when the police arrive.'

He lets me drop, leaving me coughing on all fours. The pain is blooming in my stomach and there's water building in my eyes. I can see the knife now – it's within my reach – but my father is already beside the door.

In the distance, finally, comes the sound of sirens.

'That's my cue, I fear,' my father says. He shrugs his suit jacket straighter. 'It seems I've got a few phone calls to make and you . . . Well. You need to catch up on your sleep.'

'Wait.' The tears are softening my vision and my fingers are flailing for the knife.

'Sorry, Maggie. Got to run. Remember though that I can always come back – assuming you decide to stick around. And next time, I promise you, I'll make sure we get to spend more time together.'

'*Wait!*'

I sense rather than see my father halt. My left hand closes on what it's groping for and with my right I wipe the water from my eyes. The sirens are distant but closing.

My father catches sight of what I'm holding. I'm watching his expression as I move, waiting for understanding to finally dawn. Because he was right to be so confident before: in a fight I never had a chance. That's why stabbing him – killing *him* – wasn't ever what I intended.

'Oh Maggie,' he says. 'Oh Maggie you clever girl, what have you done?'

When my hand slips from the knife, my first thought is that using it wasn't as difficult as I assumed it would be. I feel elated, initially, until I notice the blood. It flows quickly, determinedly. It stains my sweatshirt, my trousers, even the floor, and that's when my elation turns to fear. It's gone wrong, I realize. This thing I've planned for so carefully: it has all gone drastically, horribly wrong.

Jack

I'm in a room I've never seen before. Not a cell, not someone's office. It's nothing fancy – painted walls, nylon carpet tiles, a wooden table and some chairs with padded seats – but it's the kind of room I imagine they take visitors to usually, not prisoners. And maybe I'm reading too much into it, but there's no way my being here can be a good sign.

Forty-five minutes I've been waiting. One day, nine hours and forty-five minutes, actually, if you count from the moment I was first informed. I say *informed*. The truth is that they've barely told me anything. Syd's been hurt is all I know. Badly. So badly that when I spoke to the governor (you see, Mum? Turns out I got to meet the governor after all) he couldn't even tell me whether she was going to be OK. She's in hospital, and the staff there are doing all they can. And in the meantime the only thing I can do is fixate on what little I've been told.

Forty-nine minutes.

I've been staring at the clock on the wall so much I know the second hand gives a little jerk each time it passes the number seven. It's like the walls in my cell. I could recite every piece of graffiti, pinpoint every boot mark, paint drip and scrape. It's funny how the little things are all your brain is able to process when you're stuck waiting for news about something big.

Fifty-two min—

The door opens and I spin. I'm expecting . . . I don't know. The governor again, maybe. The guard who brought me here, perhaps. Anyone really, other than the person who walks in.

'Hello, Jack. I'm sorry to have kept you.'

If it were anyone else I would already be asking for news about Syd. At the sight of Inspector Leigh, however, my limbs, my tongue, my brain: every part of me locks.

'How are you, Jack?' she asks me.

I blink and I find myself freed. 'What are *you* doing here?'

The inspector closes the door behind her. She crosses the room and stops four carpet tiles away from me. 'Shall we sit?' she says, gesturing to the table.

'Is Syd OK?' I respond without moving. 'Is there any news?'

'Jack, please. I really think it would be better if you sit down.'

Oh God, I'm thinking. Oh please God no.

'Just tell me! Can't you?'

'I will, Jack. I promise: I'll tell you everything you want to know.' The inspector takes a chair on the window side and gestures again to the seat across from her.

I move reluctantly and lower myself into it. I perch on the edge, my palms clammy against my thighs.

Inspector Leigh exhales deeply before she speaks again.

'They told you Syd was hurt,' she says. 'Did they tell you how?'

Frantically I shake my head. 'They said there'd been an "incident", that's all. That everyone was still trying to get to the bottom of what had happened. Literally, that's all I know.'

The inspector nods, as though rather than information that's worse than useless this is actually a reasonable summary.

'Syd was attacked, Jack. Stabbed. That's the way it's looking right now.'

'*Stabbed?* Jesus Christ!' All at once I've got so many questions there's a blockage and none can get out. 'But is she . . . I mean, will she . . .'

'I'm not going to lie to you,' the inspector says, and I feel a vacuum begin to form in my stomach. 'She's been very badly hurt. She lost a lot of blood and . . . well, for a while it was touch and go.'

'For a while?' I echo. 'You mean . . .'

'I mean she's stable,' the inspector says. 'The doctors tell me that she's stable.'

'Oh thank Christ.' I let my head come down on to the table. It barely touches before I'm lifting it up again. 'So she's . . . I mean, stable's good. Right? Stable means she's getting better?'

'She's not out of danger,' says Inspector Leigh. 'All it really means is that she's not getting any worse. But the doctors I spoke to . . . they're optimistic.'

I cover my open mouth with my hand. I want to smile, but I'm scared to.

'I need to see her,' I say. 'When can I see her?'

'Soon enough,' the inspector answers.

'What? Really? When?'

'Today, hopefully. Just as soon as your release paperwork has been processed.'

The inspector's watching for my reaction.

'I'm being released? As in . . .'

'As in all charges dropped,' says Inspector Leigh.

'But that's . . .' I shake my head. That's impossible. Isn't it? Genuinely, I'm in shock – to the extent I don't actually believe it. 'Is this a trick?'

'No trick, Jack. It seems your story wasn't quite as far-fetched as I first assumed.'

'You mean . . . Syd's father. He was the one who attacked her?'

'So it would seem.'

'And have you caught him? Has he been arrested?'

'He has.'

Shit, I'm thinking. Just . . . *shit*. It's as close as I can get to putting what I'm feeling into words. 'Where is he? I mean . . . what happened? I mean . . . you've told me what happened. What I mean is, *how*?'

'Ms Baker . . . Syd. She reported a break-in, told the operator she'd heard someone in the house. When the response team reached the address in question – your address, Jack – they apprehended a man trying to flee the scene. They found your girlfriend upstairs in one of the bedrooms. Wounded. Fatally, they tell me they thought at first.'

'*Fatally?*'

'I told you, Jack. Syd was very seriously hurt.'

'But you said she's OK? Right? You said before she's going to be OK?'

'I said she was stable. Right now that's the best I can offer you. But even for me to be able to say that means Syd's been incredibly lucky. In fact, if you had to choose where to get a knife wound in your abdomen, you'd struggle to pinpoint a safer spot.'

I expel a breath: shocked, relieved, I don't know. I only vaguely register the inspector's tone, the fact she's watching me now more closely than ever.

'So Syd's father . . . he confessed? Is that why I'm being released?'

The inspector repositions herself so she's leaning against her chair back. 'At the moment he's not saying anything. Mainly, I think, because there's not a lot he *can* say. But the CPS are all over him. No one over there seems to be in any doubt. The knife he used on Syd tallies with the wounds inflicted on Sean Payne. And forensics did a sweep at the place Syd's father was staying. Her mother's flat. They found blood traces on the sole of one of his shoes that on initial examination correspond with Mr Payne's. We're still waiting to confirm the DNA results, but no one's expecting any surprises. Also, his ex-wife retracted the alibi she gave him. Said she'd only offered it in the first place because she'd been coerced.'

It takes a moment for it all to sink in. 'So that's . . . I mean, that's everything. Right? You've basically got him, regardless of whatever story he eventually comes up with.'

'Basically. Yeah. We've got him.'

I puff my cheeks, focus on breathing. After a second or two I get to my feet.

'So what are we waiting for?' I say. 'Let's go. Can we? To the hospital, I mean.'

'Slow down, Jack. I told you: we need to wait for the paperwork to come through.'

And I don't know if it's just the way she's looking at me when she says it, or the echo of some of the phrases she used before, but all of a sudden I get a whiff of bullshit. I mean, *we just need to wait for the paperwork to come through*. I've used that very line myself, when I was being badgered by a particularly impatient client, or harassed by an overzealous landlord. It's a stalling tactic, basically. Not even a particularly veiled one.

'This "paperwork",' I say, pronouncing the quotation marks. 'How long is it going to take?'

'We're just waiting for a final signature.'

'One signature? So why don't you just . . .' I stop myself. 'Whose signature?'

'Well. Mine.'

It's all I can do when she answers to stand and stare.

The inspector links her hands together in her lap. 'Please, Jack. Sit back down. I just want to have a little chat with you, that's all. Give me . . . half an hour. Maximum. By that time your solicitor should have arrived and we can get you on your way to visit Syd.'

There's no way I can sit. 'My solicitor knows what's going on? He knows I'm supposed to be released?'

'I believe someone's telephoned him, yes.'

Translation: my solicitor's being stalled as well. Even in the circumstances, I have to laugh.

'We can wait for him, of course. If you prefer. It's your right to refuse to speak to me at all. But personally, I was hoping we could take this time to talk. Off the record – which means anything we discuss will remain strictly between us.'

Somehow I doubt that. But the message she's giving me is clear: the sooner I agree to what she's asking, the sooner I'll get to see Syd.

'The charges against me. They're being dropped no matter what?'

'No matter what,' Inspector Leigh repeats. 'You have my word. Nothing we talk about here will alter that.'

'And you'll take me to see Syd? Today. That's for definite?'

The inspector gives a single nod.

I don't know why I'm even contemplating trusting her. But two days Syd's been lying in that hospital bed.

And the fact that I haven't been to see her . . . I mean, I realize the circumstances are somewhat different, but she must feel the way I did after she failed to come and visit me.

'Thirty minutes. To talk about what?'

'To talk about the truth, Jack. About what you and I think really happened.'

At first I don't offer a response. I'm thinking again about the phrases the inspector used earlier. *So it would seem*, she said. *That's the way it's looking right now*. As though even as she was recounting her version of events to me, Inspector Leigh didn't actually believe a word.

'You know what happened,' I say. 'You're the one who's just been telling me.'

Inspector Leigh studies me for a moment, then appears to come to a decision.

'Before we get into this, Jack, I just want to make clear: I never believed you murdered Sean Payne. And I don't believe you've been involved in anything else that's been going on either.'

'*Anything else that's been going on?* What are you talking about? And if you didn't think I was guilty, why the bloody hell did you arrest me in the first place?'

'I didn't. Remember? For a long time I didn't, even though we found your driver's licence at the scene. Because of that, actually. It was as you said: it just seemed too obviously like a plant. But you wouldn't believe the grief I got for fighting your corner.'

'Is this the point I'm supposed to say thank you?'

'Of course not. I'm just trying to explain, that's all. Even if I hadn't witnessed your reaction when I came in here – when I told you what happened to Syd – I would never have believed you were part of this. That's all I'm trying to make clear.'

'But part of *what*?'

Inspector Leigh leans forward in her seat. The only time she takes her eyes off me is when she blinks.

'Part of Syd's plan, Jack. Part of her scheme to frame her father for Sean Payne's murder.'

I don't respond. And then, for a second time, I splutter out a laugh. Neither reaction appears to take the inspector by surprise.

'Let's go back to what you told me,' she says, reclining. 'You and Syd. The events you recounted in your . . . statement, let's call it. Everything you told us: it checks out. We even found that cat you buried in your back garden.'

'You dug up the cat? When? *Why?*'

'And we found Evan Cohen, too. The estate agent? And you were right. He was up to his eyeballs in debt, some of which he managed to pay off recently with a large chunk of cash. Turns out he's built up another juicy pile of debit slips in the time since then, but that's a whole different story. The point is, he confessed to all the things you accused him of. He accepted money from Syd's father. He engineered it so you and Syd got the house.'

'So we told you the truth. Right? That's what you seem to be saying.'

'That's not what I'm saying, Jack. I said your story – everything in your statement, that is – checks out. But it's from the point your statement ends that the evidence becomes thinner.'

'*Thinner?*'

To Inspector Leigh it must appear as though she's losing me. 'Let me spell it out for you, Jack. I believe Syd's father was trying to hurt you both in the way you claimed. The house, what happened to you at work, all the things that came between you and Syd. I believe he was responsible and for what it's worth I think the man's a scumbag who should never have been released on parole.'

'But?' I prompt.

'But,' the inspector concedes, 'I *don't* believe he murdered Sean Payne. That scene Syd described when she went to her mother's house, when she saw her father standing there in the hallway? I believe that's the point your girlfriend took over. Took *control*, if you prefer.'

There's a pause as Inspector Leigh allows me to take this in.

'You're saying . . . what are you saying? Are you saying that *Syd* . . . that she was the one who . . . that she committed *murder*, for Christ's sake?'

Inspector Leigh doesn't try to sweeten it. 'That's right, Jack. That's exactly what I'm saying. And afterwards – and after she'd acted to make sure you were well out of the way – she lured her father to the house so she could make it look like he tried to kill *her*. Using the very knife she used on Sean Payne.'

Again she watches closely for my reaction. Seventeen stab wounds, I'm thinking. So much anger. So much *hurt*.

I say: 'First off, a, that's bloody ridiculous. And b, what possible reason could you have for suspecting Syd? You just told me you believed us about everything her father's been doing, and you heard all the things he used to do to Syd when she was young. If you accept he was capable of all that, then why is it suddenly so hard to believe that he's capable of murder?'

'I didn't say he wasn't capable, Jack. What I'm saying is that Syd got there first. And that's the beauty of her plan, that it fits in so neatly with all the rest of it. Syd felt trapped. Terrified. Her father's back and he intends to hurt her, so she needs a way of turning the tables. Of entrapping *him*. And let's not forget Elsie. In Syd's mind Elsie was in as much danger as she was and this way she got to save Elsie too. Because that's how Syd would have seen it, Jack. Like as much as for her she was doing it for Elsie. It's all there in her statement. Maybe not in quite so many words, but her motive, her rationalization: it's all right there.'

'Her *motive*? Jesus Christ.' I'm shaking my head now. It's possible I might even be smiling.

'That was half the problem when Syd was younger, right? There was never enough evidence of what her father did to her. No one helped her, no one intervened. But this time the evidence was already established. All Syd had to do was come up with a way of using it.'

'But . . . where's this coming from? What is it that's got you thinking like this in the first place?'

The inspector adjusts the way she's sitting, hooks one suited leg across the other. 'The thing that convinced me, in the end, was the knife wound. The position of it, for one. Also, the doctors refusing to rule out the possibility that Syd's wound was actually self-inflicted.'

'Wait. They said it *was* self-inflicted? Or that it could have been?'

'They said they couldn't be certain either way.'

'But that's . . . I mean . . . that doesn't prove anything. Did you check it for prints? The knife handle.'

The inspector shows her amusement, presumably at the fact I'm trying to tell her how to do her job.

'There were no prints on the knife whatsoever. But she could have wiped them off, or wrapped her sleeve over the handle before she used it, and anyway, even if her prints were on the knife she could have claimed she'd grabbed it when her father came at her.'

'What about her father's prints? Did you check for those?'

'There were no prints whatsoever, Jack. Although . . .'

I frown at the inspector's hesitation. 'Although . . . what?'

'Although we found some leather gloves in the alleyway behind the house, near where Syd's father was apprehended.'

'So he tried to ditch them. Right? So there you go then! He was in the house, running away from it, and the whole time he was wearing gloves. I don't know about you, but it doesn't sound to me like he'd stopped by for a cup of coffee.'

'He was there, yes. But in my opinion only because Syd wanted him there. Because that's another thing: there was no sign of forced entry. There was a set of keys on the floor in the bedroom, but none fit any of the doors. They match another set we found in the house, so maybe they were the keys Syd's father used before you installed new locks, but this time if he wanted to come in Syd must have let him.'

'Or maybe she just forgot to lock up. Did it occur to you she might just have forgotten to lock up?'

Inspector Leigh looks at me like we both know the likelihood of that. 'Frankly, Jack, I've had my doubts about that girlfriend of yours for quite some time now. Don't get me wrong: I think she's played her role brilliantly. Like when the two of you came to see me with that statement. She was just the right amount of angry. Afraid, but not so afraid that we would offer her protection, because that would have ballsed things up for her nicely. And the tone she used in what she wrote, the fact that she wrote everything down in the first place . . .'

'But that was my idea! To write things down.'

'Maybe it was. Maybe you only think it was. But either way it doesn't matter. It suited Syd in the end either way. And besides, think about why writing things down felt so important to you. Because you didn't believe Syd's father was responsible. That's the impression I got. Was I wrong?'

'No, but . . . just because I had my doubts at first doesn't mean I have them now. And what about the fact he doesn't have an alibi? You said Syd's mother retracted her statement. Right? So that just proves it. She was lying before because Syd's father made her and now that she's safe she feels free to tell the truth.'

'I agree that's how it looks,' the inspector says. 'On the other hand, put yourself for a moment in Syd's mother's shoes. If you'd failed to protect your daughter the way she failed, wouldn't you do any-thing you could to make amends? Offer anything your daughter needed. Do anything – *everything* – she asked?'

'You're claiming Syd told her to change her story?'

'I am. Probably she wouldn't have even needed to explain why. A promise would have been enough: that afterwards her ex-husband would be out of both their lives for ever. As for the evidence we found in Syd's father's belongings, the blood traces on his shoe: Syd could have planted it without her mother even knowing.'

I open my mouth, but there's nothing I can say. I've been standing all this time and all of a sudden I've never felt so exhausted. I move the chair I was in before and drop into it.

'Jack . . .'

'Look, I . . . I don't know what you expect me to say. I don't know what it is you expect me to *do*.'

'Just what's right, Jack. That's all.'

'What do you mean, *what's right*? Nothing about what you're saying is right!'

'Listen, Jack. Syd's father: he's likely to go to prison for a very long time. He's fifty-seven now, which means it's unlikely if he's convicted that he'll ever get out. And I'm not expecting your sympathy. As I said to you, I agree the man's a scumbag. But he didn't do *this*, Jack. He didn't kill *anyone*.'

'But even if that's true – and I'm not saying it is – but even if it's true, what I'm asking is what you expect me to do about it?'

'You're the person best placed to refute Syd's story, possibly even to convince her to come clean. Maybe we can put some pressure on her mother, but even if she cooperates, I doubt very much her testimony will be enough. But you . . . you've seen it all, witnessed it all. And you've got a chance to do what's right. To *put* things right. That's what I need from you, Jack. That's why I'm here.'

Inspector Leigh gives me time to think. Time to recall all the doubts I've ever had about this person she's convinced is responsible for the death of another human being.

'She gave you up, Jack,' the inspector says. 'Syd's the one who planted your driver's licence. She's the reason you got sent to prison. And let's not forget, if things hadn't worked out the way she wanted them to, you would have been the one to take the fall. She's dangerous, Jack. And I'm sorry to be blunt, but she doesn't love you. If she did she wouldn't have put you through this.'

Again she lets that hang in the air between us. And I can see that: I can see how to Inspector Leigh it must look. In fact she isn't saying anything I haven't already told myself.

'I spoke to your parents,' she tells me, changing tack.

I look up. Until she spoke again I'd been staring at the carpet.

'Not about this,' the inspector goes on. 'Just to try and get a sense of who you are. Of your values. And I can tell your parents mean the world to you.' She allows a pause. 'I'm right, aren't I, Jack? That your parents mean the world to you?'

Slowly, like a reflex, I nod.

'So think about them. Think about what you helping me will mean to them. After this. After seeing you in here. Think about how *proud* they'd be of you for finally doing the right thing.'

It's true what I've often thought about Inspector Leigh. She can read people better than anyone I've ever met. The way she's speaking to me now, for example: there's nothing in the world she could say or offer that would be more likely to persuade me to agree.

I take a moment to check around the room. Not an interview room, I remind myself. Not a cell. And the inspector: she's sitting there across the table from me without any of her usual props. No notepad, no tape recorder, nothing. And there's no one else on her side of the table. Like me, she's in here all alone.

'You're the only one who thinks this way,' I say to her, 'aren't you?'

The inspector, at that, can only frown.

'None of your colleagues believe you. Even DC Granger. He's not on board with this either, is he? Would you get in trouble if your bosses knew you were even speaking to me?'

Inspector Leigh, for the first time since I met her, appears suddenly unsure of herself. 'I don't see –'

But she doesn't get the chance to finish her sentence. There's a commotion in the corridor and then a knock, which is cut short when the door swings wide.

'. . . an outrage,' the man who enters is saying, whether to the guard behind him or the room ahead of him it's not clear. 'I should have been informed about this hours ago, the moment it was authorized.'

The man looks at me. 'Up you get, young man. We're leaving.'

Inspector Leigh inserts herself between us. 'Who the hell are you?'

The man straightens his shoulders. Appears to anyway, because his tie is squint and his overcoat is crooked, so that it's hard to tell whether any part of him is actually level. Even so he manages to grow another inch, so that his crown reaches the height of Inspector Leigh's scowl.

'My name is Mr Marsh and the man you appear to be interrogating is my client. Jack: on your feet, lad. Let's go.'

'Your client?' The inspector turns towards me. 'But I thought Mr Dalton was your solicitor. That's what your parents said.'

'He was going to be,' I tell her. 'But I changed my mind. Mr Marsh here has been representing me from the beginning.' Carefully – apologetically – I tuck my chair beneath the table.

'Jack? What's going on here? Your father, he was adamant you . . .'

Slowly the inspector begins to smile. She drops her weight on to the edge of the table.

'You already knew,' she says, 'didn't you? You worked it out. Everything I've just been explaining.'

I know better than to answer. And anyway I'm not sure what I would say. Did I know? Not where this was heading, the lengths to which Syd in the end would go. If I did I would have put a stop to it. Somehow. There's no way I would have let her risk what she did.

But it's true I knew more than I've been pretending. Or maybe that's too strong a word. I suspected, rather. I've had a lot of time to think these past ten days, a lot of time to reflect on how I got to the position I was in. Even so, it was only really on that night when I was in my prison cell, the day before I was due to meet the man my parents had decided should represent me, that I began to realize what it was I'd missed.

Faith, Mr Dalton talked about – and there I was ready to put my faith in him in a way I'd never fully offered it to Syd. I should have known that if I was in here there'd be a good reason. I should have realized Syd would have had a plan to get me out. Because it was like Inspector Leigh said. It *was* all there in Syd's statement. I always assumed Syd was writing for the same person I was – for Inspector Leigh, ironically, or someone like her – but so much of what Syd wrote was really addressed to me. She couldn't tell me what she'd done, but she was at least able to explain why. And *trust me*, she told me, so many times I lost count. *Believe in me*, she said: *the way I always believed in you*. It took me a while to finally hear her, but I did, in the end. I do.

'Jack? You understand this makes you an accessory, don't you? If – *when* – Syd gets caught for what she's done, you'll end up in the dock right beside her.'

My solicitor puts a hand on my shoulder. 'Ignore her, Jack. You don't have to answer.'

I look at Inspector Leigh and I realize he's right. I don't have to answer, because I can see exactly what she's thinking. I can read her, finally, the way she was always able to read me. Syd isn't going to be arrested for this. Not now, not in the future. This, talking to me: just so long as Syd and I remain strong, it's as close as Inspector Leigh will ever get.

Sydney

It's late December. Christmas, almost. A time for family, so they say. I can't decide whether that's appropriate or ironic. Maybe it's neither. It feels meaningful but maybe that's just in my head. Like family itself. The concept. Maybe that doesn't have any real meaning either and is instead as open to interpretation as we allow it to be. There's so much in life that is, it strikes me. What's right, for example. What's wrong. And what's normal – that's what I've been puzzling over most of late. Are things back to normal? What does normal, for me, even look like?

What I think – what I've decided – is that it looks like *us*. That's my baseline, the foundation on which everything else is built. Me and Jack. Side by side. Together. So long as we're OK it doesn't matter what's happening all around us.

It's not been easy. For Jack in particular, none of this has been in the slightest bit easy. He says he understands why I did what I did and I hope and pray that he genuinely does. Sean Payne . . . I honestly never meant for it to happen. And everything that followed afterwards – between me and Jack, between me and my father, between Jack and the police – only did because I was so desperate to find us a way out.

I was standing in the kitchen when I heard the noise. It was late, around one in the morning, and Jack was fast asleep upstairs. I myself had barely closed my eyes since the day my father had revealed himself in my mother's hallway. Even lying in bed made me feel vulnerable, so I'd taken to pacing the house downstairs. I had no purpose. I was thinking, I suppose, but *thinking* implies concentrating on a particular subject when my mind was a mess of whirling thoughts. I was afraid but I was also angry. Furious in fact, above all that I felt so utterly exposed. I thought I'd found the perfect place to hide and yet all at once the monster I'd been fleeing had come from nowhere and torn my refuge down. And there was nothing I could do. I knew what the police would have said if I'd gone to them. Their reaction when we took them our statement proves they would only have acted when it was already too late. And of course there was Elsie. There was no solution I could think of for me and Jack that wouldn't also have meant abandoning her.

The noise, when it came, was like a hand upon my shoulder. I was standing with the lights off beside the sink and until that point it had been so quiet both in the house and in the darkness outside that I felt like I was the only person in the entire neighbourhood who wasn't in bed. But the sound proved otherwise. It was a careless sound – the knock of a gate? – followed by what I was convinced was the slip of footsteps in our back garden. I tensed and stared out into the night. Was it *him*? My father. Was he here, *now*?

My first thought was of waking Jack. But as the silence spread I began to question what I'd heard and Jack, I knew, was exhausted. When I'd risen after lying for an hour close beside him he'd been fast asleep: one hour into the maybe three- or four-hour stretch he'd been managing to get each night himself. If I woke him it might be for no good reason and anyway what was stopping me from checking out the noise on my own? I was Sydney Baker, not Maggie Robinson: not a little girl who flinches at things that go bump in the night. I was bigger than that, *better* than that, and if there was someone out there – if it *was* my father out there – I would show him . . . just as I would prove it to myself.

I checked the silence and again heard nothing, so started towards the back door. I slid the key into the lock, turned it and gently levered down the handle. Here I paused – and as an afterthought reached for one of the knives in the knife block. *Just in case*, I told myself. Even if it was my father out there, I had no intention of actually using it. It would be like a ward. Something to scare *him* with for a change.

I opened the door swiftly, as though I was ripping off a plaster, but the back garden was empty. The parts I could see, at least. I checked around me, above me, even behind me, even though I was still standing in the doorway, and then padded towards the end of the side return – the only place within the boundary of our plot that my father, or anyone, might have been hiding. But before I got there I heard another noise. It had come from the alleyway, I realized – and if anything it had sounded puzzlingly like a moan.

I checked the shadows in our garden nevertheless, then crept towards our back gate. The latch was old and the gate was loose, which explained how it might have knocked against the fence post. But the night air was thick, languid, with not the slightest breeze to disturb it, meaning that if the gate had moved something must have knocked it.

I opened the gate, peered through the gap and tentatively stepped into the alleyway. And that's when I saw him. Not my father. *Elsie's.*

He was slumped against one of the panels of our garden fence. He'd fallen, I judged from the way he was sprawled, which was presumably what had caused our gate to shift. As for the sound I'd thought I'd heard of someone moving: presumably that was Sean Payne trying – and failing – to stagger to his feet.

My first reaction, I remember clearly, was disgust. Even from several feet away I could tell he was drunk. His eyes were closed but there was a smile on his lips and quietly, beneath his breath, he seemed to be . . . singing? Trying to, anyway. It was like . . . I don't know. Like Jack said before. Like he'd been out *celebrating.* Like it was just another Friday night for him and his daughter wasn't lying alone in a hospital bed. Like *he* hadn't been the one to *put* her there.

I drifted towards him, not really thinking, and barely registering I was still carrying the knife. Even over the smell of the rubbish in the nearby bins, I could detect the alcohol fumes venting on Sean Payne's breath. Except it was around this point I noticed that the noise he'd been making had stopped, and I wondered whether he was actually breathing any more at all. Maybe he'd hit his head when he'd fallen. Maybe he'd had a heart attack or something and that moaning I'd heard, rather than singing, was a last, pitiful plea for help.

Against my better instincts I bent towards him – and that's when his eyes flicked open. I recoiled, might have stumbled, but from out of nowhere his hand closed around my leg. *You*, he said – or at least I think he did. The more I try to recall what really happened the more I wonder whether I just imagined it, just as it's possible I imagined the hatred in his eyes. I panicked, I know that. I thought . . . I don't know. That he'd tricked me, that he wanted to hurt me, to pay me back for having taken away his daughter. And it was in my desperation to get away, to free myself from his grip, that the knife somehow found its way home.

But then, after that – that's when I lost control. I lunged again, and then again and again, until it felt like I would never stop. All the fear I've ever experienced, all the *rage* that for so long had bounced around inside me – it spewed from me in a torrent. At that instant Sean Payne *was* my father and I . . . I was Sydney Maggie Jessica Elsie, all the victims I knew come together as one.

I don't know how long it went on for. Seconds maybe, though it seemed like longer. Like actually it's not a moment now that in my mind will ever stop. I remember collapsing afterwards on to the stony floor and I remember forcing myself to look at what I'd done. And I remember too that I felt . . . not glad, exactly. Never that. But I remember it wasn't what I'd *done* that I was most alarmed about. What worried me, at that point, was what it *meant*.

The plan, after that, came to me in stages. For some time I just sat there, expecting to be found. But the night remained as empty as it had seemed to me when I'd been standing in the kitchen – how long ago *that* felt – and though I waited for someone to come, no one did. Which is when it occurred to me that maybe no one would. Gradually my breathing stilled and the adrenaline left my shaking hands. And I noticed the blood. *Saw* it properly for the first time. It was black in the darkness but wet. Warm, at first, though steadily, against my skin, it turned cold.

I stripped right there in the alleyway. I felt panic rising within me as I did so and it was only once I'd torn what I'd been wearing from my body that I felt it gradually subside. And then again after that I just stood there, not knowing what was supposed to happen next. I held my clothes before me in a bundle. I had to get rid of them, obviously. My clothes, the knife: I had to get rid of *everything*.

I would throw them in the Thames. I would wrap them in a rubbish sack from one of the nearby bins and I would drop them into the river the next morning. I would shower, clean myself up and act as though none of this had really happened. Except . . . there would be evidence, wouldn't there? I couldn't possibly hope to erase it all. And it had happened right outside our house. The police wouldn't just ignore that, particularly given our history with Elsie's father. Jack in particular. He'd *fought* with Sean Payne. Shouted at him, swore he'd *kill* him in front of everyone in the local pub! The police, if they didn't blame me, would surely try to pin what had happened on Jack. They'd have to. Wouldn't they? Unless . . . unless . . .

It was like a daydream, initially. One of those *what ifs* that feel as fanciful as the prospect of flying to the moon. But then, as one thought dominoed into another, that daydream turned into something *real*. Not a *what if* any more – a *why not?* I began to understand how what I'd done could offer a way out, for Elsie, for Jack, for us all.

I can't tell you whether I believed it would really work. After . . . what had happened . . . I couldn't think straight. At least, it didn't feel like I was making decisions logically but perhaps it was some deeper instinct at that stage that took over. I knew my father, at some point, would come after me – and that if I kept the knife I could make it look like he'd used it to attack me. The knife, in turn, would tie him to Sean Payne's murder. And as for his motive . . . my father had been trying to hurt Jack from the start. Couldn't this, if I presented it correctly, be seen as another step on that road? Not only did he want Jack blamed, he wanted him out of the way, because with Jack gone he could finally get to *me*.

The hardest part was planting Jack's driving licence. Not the physical act itself. The driving licence was in Jack's wallet on the kitchen table. Once I'd taken care of the rest of the evidence, I wouldn't even need to go sneaking around upstairs. No, the difficult part was convincing myself to leave it for the police to find. It felt so *wrong*. So counter-intuitive. I had to remind myself over and over again of the reasoning, just to be sure I wasn't making a huge mistake. But after a while I felt as certain as I would ever be. The driving licence would be enough to put Jack in the frame – to make it look like my father had set him up – but it was also tenuous enough in terms of evidence that it would surely never hold up in court. Assuming it ever came to that, and the whole point was it never would. I wouldn't *let* it – because if all else failed I would turn myself in. That was the lifeline I clung to: the know-ledge that at any point I chose, I could act to bring things to a stop.

*

But Jack. There was so little I could do to reassure him, which is why it's so important to me that he understands now. And he does, I think. I really think he does. He knows now the full story about what happened between me and my father and he understands how terrified I was when I found out that he'd come back. Above all, he knows that I was only ever trying to protect him. To protect *us*. That was the other reason for leaving the driver's licence: for my plan to work, I needed Jack out of the way. I needed him *safe*. Somewhere my father couldn't get to him, because I knew that if he could he would hurt Jack to hurt me – more so, even, than he had already. So that's why Jack had to go through what he did. That's why, when it looked like Inspector Leigh wasn't going to arrest him, I tried to drive Jack away. I couldn't confide in him because if he knew what I planned to do he would have stopped me. Or, worse, he would have tried to help me and I could never have allowed him to do that.

If anything that's the part Jack was upset about most of all: that he couldn't be there for me, as he sees it, when I needed him most. But now . . . it's strange, the way things have turned out. There's a closeness between us – a *tightness* – that somehow surpasses what we had before. And in other ways, too, Jack's about the happiest I've ever seen him. I know for a fact he doesn't miss his job. There was never any real threat of criminal proceedings against him – that was just the police trying to scare him – and now that he's finally got the time, he's relishing the opportunity to try writing. He still calls his parents every Sunday but I get a sense when I hear him on the telephone that the dynamic between them has changed, that rather than a child ringing up to seek approval it's a conversation now between adults. Maybe that's not quite how Jack's parents view it yet but given time I don't doubt they'll come to see it that way too.

If Jack worries, I think it's mainly about other people. There's Bart, for one, who Jack continues to insist on apologizing to virtually every time they get together. Also, Sabeen and her family. It was Bart, it turned out, who tipped them off, who warned them Jack's secret had been discovered, the very day Jack found out himself. None of us knows where Ali and the others have ended up but that they're safe is the only thing that matters. And – to me at least – that they know that they are because of Jack.

Which just leaves me, I suppose – because it's about me I know Jack worries most of all. Sometimes I catch him looking at me and when I notice he just gives me this little smile – like he wants to say something but also like he realizes he doesn't have to and that for me that smile is enough. He's concerned, I guess, about my well-being, about how everything that's happened has affected *me*. I don't mean physically. The wound I suffered has left a scar but it's not like I'm not used to scars. I'll admit I wasn't as prepared as I thought I'd be for the pain, nor for the sight of so much of my own blood, and for a time right after it happened I was convinced I'd driven the knife too deep. But I'm fine now, basically. Physically, I'm fine.

As for the rest of me . . . I guess that's all fairly fine too. As fine as it ever was. I expect Jack wonders mainly about the guilt I'm experiencing and I admit I worry sometimes about that myself. Because . . . I don't know. It's not clear to me how I feel about that side of things either. I know guilt is something I've lived with all my life and that I feel less guilty about Elsie's father than I did – than I *do* – about what happened to my sister. Plus, there's Elsie. There's nothing anyone could say that could convince me she's not better off now than she was before.

So I do: I feel fine. Better than fine, if I'm honest, and if ever I feel guilt it's usually about that. But that's a long-term thing really, something I'm not sure I'll ever be able to reconcile: my determination on the one hand to be happy and my uncertainty on the other hand about whether I have the right. But I'm working on it. I'm working on a lot of things. My relationship with my mother, for one.

Even though my mother was more directly involved, she knows less about what happened than Jack does. Jack knows everything: there are no secrets between us any more. But my mother . . . she knows what *she* did, obviously – retracting the alibi she'd given my father, letting me in so I could plant what I needed to among his things – but I never fully explained to her what I was planning. She did what she did because I asked her to and because I told her that in the end it was the only way to keep us safe. She's aware that my father has been charged with murder of course but it's as though the fact that he's gone is the only detail she needs to know. It's just how she is, how she always was: happy to turn a blind eye. I don't blame her for being like that the way I used to. She has her way of coping, I have mine, and it's not like I can claim now that hers is any more destructive.

So, yeah, me and my mum: we're doing OK. I'm not suggesting we'll ever have a model relationship. All I'm really trying to say is that we're better than we used to be. Probably, actually, than we've ever been. And it's not that I haven't always loved her. It's just . . . I don't know. It feels *easier* to love her now, that's all. And it's safer now my father's gone too.

My father.

I have to remind myself every so often that he really is. *Gone*, I mean. Because he's going to prison, I know that, and I know he's never getting out, but even so I sometimes wonder whether it wouldn't have been better if I'd actually killed *him*. I thought I would have to, at one stage, and when I came face to face with him in our bedroom I genuinely tried. I couldn't stop myself, the way I couldn't stop the anger when I confronted Sean Payne. But whereas Elsie's father was in no state to defend himself, my father swatted me aside so easily it was blind luck I was able to finish what I started. And this way . . . what was the word my father used? *Poetic*. That's it exactly. It's poetic that he'll be found guilty of precisely the type of crimes he really committed. I try to remember that whenever I feel afraid. Whenever I wonder whether the police are still watching me, for example, or I succumb to a sudden rush of guilt. It's *right* what's happening to my father. He killed my sister. If he could have he would have killed me. And if I hadn't done what I did, nobody would have had the chance to impose on him the punishment he's always deserved.

But you know what? I don't want to think about my father. What I want to think about is what I started to, before I allowed myself to get distracted.

Jack and I, we're in a flat now. When we put the house on the market it was sold by the first weekend and now we're just waiting for the conveyancing. I'm disappointed, obviously, because had the circum-stances when we found the house been different it might genuinely have had a chance of becoming our home. Our forever house, just like on those cheesy TV shows. But it's served its purpose and frankly the apart-ment we're living in is a thousand times more practical. It's purpose-built, two bedrooms, with a little Juliet balcony and access to outside space. We're only renting for the time being but living here has made us realize that a place like this is all the three of us really need.

No, I'm not pregnant. And no, it's still not likely that I'll ever be. I mean maybe . . . one day . . . but not just yet. For the time being I want to relish this feeling I've got that this family I have around me right now is as perfect already as I ever could have wished.

Officially Elsie lives with her aunt. Her aunt's OK, sort of, certainly not as bad as her brother was. But despite Elsie growing up practically around the corner from her, she's only ever met Elsie half a dozen times. And she admits it: she only took Elsie in for the money. Her father didn't have much but there was a surprising amount of equity in their old house. And the way all the legal stuff worked out is that the cash went with Elsie to her new guardian. So Elsie's aunt, she's happy enough. All the more so given that Elsie spends most of her time these days with us.

And we are: we're like a family, and that's the point I set out to make. My real family was broken, defective right from the start. But who's to say what constitutes a family anyway? Ours, it's non-traditional, a bit like our Christmas is likely to be. We each have our roles but the best part is that none of them are fixed. Take Jack and me. We're the parents, mostly, but sometimes we're also the kids. Jack to me is like my husband but he's also my very best friend. To Elsie Jack acts like some wise old uncle but I suspect she sees him more as an overprotective brother. A good one, though, a kind one – and the knowledge that there is kindness in men is something it's important Elsie's able to believe.

As for me, I do my best to be whatever Elsie needs me to be. It's hard sometimes, given this secret that will always exist between us, and I can't help worrying that if we spend too much time together, one day she'll turn out the way I have. Although, who knows? It's just possible it will be the other way round. Because it's like I said: it's not always Jack and me who play the parents. I tend to assume that it's my role to look out for Elsie. But like an angel sent by my little sister, maybe it's really Elsie who's here to save me.

Acknowledgements

Love and thanks to my wife, Sarah, without whom this novel simply wouldn't have been written. Frankly, she deserves a co-author's credit on the front cover. Thanks as well to my mum, dad, sister, Matt, Sue, Kate and Nij: family, all. Kristina Astrom and Jane McLoughlin were two of the earliest readers of this novel, and I cannot thank them enough for their generosity and their time. A special mention, too, to Jess Lavender and all at Brighton Shotokan Karate Club for helping me work out my writerly frustrations – of which, as ever, there were a few. Finally, thank you to everyone at Berkley, Viking and Felicity Bryan Associates, Amanda Bergeron, Katy Loftus and Caroline Wood above all.

KC

He just wanted a decent book to read ...

Not too much to ask, is it? It was in 1935 when Allen Lane, Managing Director of Bodley Head Publishers, stood on a platform at Exeter railway station looking for something good to read on his journey back to London. His choice was limited to popular magazines and poor-quality paperbacks – the same choice faced every day by the vast majority of readers, few of whom could afford hardbacks. Lane's disappointment and subsequent anger at the range of books generally available led him to found a company – and change the world.

'We believed in the existence in this country of a vast reading public for intelligent books at a low price, and staked everything on it'
Sir Allen Lane, 1902–1970, founder of Penguin Books

The quality paperback had arrived – and not just in bookshops. Lane was adamant that his Penguins should appear in chain stores and tobacconists, and should cost no more than a packet of cigarettes.

Reading habits (and cigarette prices) have changed since 1935, but Penguin still believes in publishing the best books for everybody to enjoy. We still believe that good design costs no more than bad design, and we still believe that quality books published passionately and responsibly make the world a better place.

So wherever you see the little bird – whether it's on a piece of prize-winning literary fiction or a celebrity autobiography, political tour de force or historical masterpiece, a serial-killer thriller, reference book, world classic or a piece of pure escapism – you can bet that it represents the very best that the genre has to offer.

Whatever you like to read – trust Penguin.